THE TWO SHAPESHIFTERS
FACED EACH OTHER

"Escape is not possible," Odo said to the other morph.

At either end of the corridor, the forcefields were in place. Standing just beyond the forcefields were security squads. And with the squad on the right-hand side was Commander Benjamin Sisko, armed with a phaser, as were all the security men.

"Blocked into this corridor," said the shapeshifter. "It's time to move on to a real game. You and me, Odo. You and me. The main event."

Odo stepped toward him, stopping less than a foot away. "I'm giving you one last warning," he virtually snarled in the shapeshifter's face. "Start moving. Or I'll knock you out and carry you there myself."

The shapeshifter's red face—which had taken on an almost crystalline look in its hardness—smiled. "I'll tell you what, Odo. I'll tell you all about yourself. Your race. Your roots. How to discipline and improve your morphing ability. Everything you've always wanted to know. And all you have to do is one simple thing."

"I don't make bargains with murderers."

"This isn't a bargain. This is a challenge. All you have to do . . . is catch me."

Look for STAR TREK Fiction from Pocket Books

Star Trek: The Original Series

Star Trek: The Next Generation

Star Trek: Deep Space Nine

THE SIEGE

PETER DAVID

POCKET BOOKS

New York   London   Toronto   Sydney   Tokyo   Singapore

This book is a work of fiction. Names, characters, places and incidents are either products of the author's imagination or are used fictitiously. Any resemblance to actual events or locales or persons, living or dead, is entirely coincidental.

POCKET BOOKS, a division of Simon & Schuster Inc. 1230 Avenue of the Americas, New York, NY 10020

STAR TREK is a Registered Trademark of Paramount Pictures.

This book is published by Pocket Books, a division of Simon & Schuster Inc., under exclusive license from Paramount Pictures.

ISBN: 0-671-87083-1

First Pocket Books printing May 1993

10 9 8 7 6 5 4 3 2 1

POCKET and colophon are registered trademarks of Simon & Schuster Inc.

Printed in the U.S.A.

To Paullina's TV set . . .
Long may it wave

Preface

Several years ago, when Rene Auberjonois was starring on Broadway in *City of Angels,* I waited at the stage door after one performance and, when he came out, got him to sign my plush toy of Sebastian the Crab from *The Little Mermaid*—his nemesis in that film, since he had voiced the crazed French chef.

Who would have thought that my little autographed plush crab (notice I avoid saying "stuffed crab") would suddenly, with the debut of "Star Trek: Deep Space Nine" be transformed from a novelty item into a valuable Star Trek collectible.

A lot of things have been surprising about "Deep Space Nine." I'm surprised that I've been enjoying the series as much as I have, since I must admit the initial descriptions didn't sound promising. But as of this writing, five episodes have aired and I've found them to be, by and large, rather entertaining. I've certainly liked it a lot more than the *extremely* uneven first season of "Star Trek: The Next Generation."

I'm surprised that I'm writing this novel. I figured I'd get around to doing one and had even been discussing a "Mr. Scott and Lwaxana Troi Visit Deep Space" novel because my last few Trek books have featured Lwaxana, and I figured I was on a roll.

But this isn't that novel. This had its origins much the same way that *The Rift* did—namely, editor Kevin Ryan came to me and said, "How would you like to be the first writer to . . . ?" In the former case, it was "have two Trek novels out back-to-back?" In this case, it was "write the first original Deep Space Nine novel."

How could I resist such an opportunity? Being offered the chance to work on a group of characters, using five scripts and the series bible for guidance, knowing full well that by the time the book comes out the characters might very well bear little resemblance to the way they're being depicted right now? Knowing that I might have fans saying, "How come the book isn't consistent with the way Sisko was portrayed last week?"

Well . . .'cause I thought it might be fun. And besides, my car is breaking down and I need a new one. Two solid reasons as far as I'm concerned.

I wish to thank my wife, Myra, for her support as I once again put myself into one of these suicidal deadline-or-die positions. Myra, who can probably sympathize with Abigail Adams, wife of John, who proclaimed, "Think of it! To be married to the man who's always first in line to be hanged."

Likewise, the girls—Shana, age twelve; Jenny, eight; and Ariel, seventeen months—who stayed out of my way. Far out of my way.

Also, Mike Okuda of the Trek offices, who gave freely of his time to answer my many questions about DS9 in general and Odo in particular. For several days he fielded questions like "What about Odo's mass?" and "Can Odo fly?" Little things like that.

(Note to sticklers: Throughout this novel you will see Odo do lots of stuff that, chances are, you won't see him do in the series. Having covered my bases thoroughly and checked and rechecked, I will state here that the reason Odo hasn't performed many of the stunts I have him doing is not because he *can't*. Rather, we're getting down here to the realistic TV constraints of budgets. The only way that Odo could pull off on TV the stunts he does in this book is if "Deep Space Nine" had a budget of $85 million, rather than $2 million, per episode. Novelists are not limited by monetary constraints. I don't have to figure out how to make something work on screen; all I have to say is "It happened." So if you're going to be one of those people who say, "Gee, we've never *seen* Odo transform his arm into a spiked sledgehammer, so that means he *can't*," well, in the words of Robin Williams, "I'm sorry . . . I'd agree with you if you were right.")

Likewise, to my intrepid editors at the various comic book offices I work for—which, by the way, is *nothing* like what you see on Bob Newhart's new program, so stop asking, okay?—who were, once again, kind enough to cut me some slack—particularly Bobbie Chase and Joey Cavalieri. Thanks, guys.

Also many thanks to several people who influenced this book, including Agatha Christie, James Cameron, and Alan Young.

Oh . . . the tone of this book? For those people who like to be warned about such things?

Well . . . it's . . .

It gets kind of intense, actually.

There. Now you're warned.

So . . .

Let's get deep.

THE SIEGE

PROLOGUE

THE VESSEL with the killer on it moved through space.

The vessel was small and quite energy-efficient. It moved quickly and briskly through the depths of the void. Its destination lay not too much farther off.

Soon.

Soon the business would be done.

The killer stared out one of the small viewports, watching the distant stars move past. His thoughts were his own, his face inscrutable.

Soon.

Soon it would be done. . . .

But of course before it was done . . . it had to begin.

This was not going to be a problem for the killer. He was quite certain of that.

He had had a long and very successful history. He went where he wished. Did what he wished. None could anticipate his moves. None could stop him.

He would visit terror upon them and do his business, and then he would leave, when he felt like it.

And none would stop him. None could.

He turned away from the window . . . and released the shape he had assumed. His body oozed downward, reconfigured itself. . . .

And, moments later, had become a simple suitcase.

The killer went to sleep and dreamed of the killing to come. . . .

And no one would ever see him. . . .

CHAPTER
1

"Now watch carefully."

Miles O'Brien, square-jawed, curly-haired, and the most aggressively patient individual on Deep Space Nine, smiled broadly, which was the only way he was capable of smiling. He had a look in his eye that gleamed of mischief and deviltry. It was, in fact, the exact look that he had used several years previously on a certain young botanist aboard the USS *Enterprise,* when he had first spotted her lounging in Ten-Forward. And she had found that look refreshingly guileless, even playful. A pleasing mixture of a little boy's soul in a grown man's body.

That was over four years ago.

Now she just found it damned irritating.

Keiko, his wife—the irritated woman—did not look up from the lesson plans she was preparing for the next day.

At first glance, and even at second, Miles and Keiko O'Brien were mismatched. In contrast to the buoyant Irishman's open expression and "Hi, pal, gladdaseeya" air, the Asian Keiko was far more low-key, far more reserved.

3

When O'Brien's spirits were high, they couldn't be anchored with a crate of gold-pressed latinum. When they were low, a team of horses could be hitched up and whipped into a frenzy, and still not drag him out of the doldrums until he was ready to go.

Keiko, on the other hand, was far more steady. She was not quick to anger, but instead would build gradually. O'Brien sometimes teasingly called her "the slow cooker." But when she did get angry, volcanoes had nothing on her.

She was light-skinned where he was swarthy, delicate where he was coarse. Yin, as she put it, to his yang. He, on the other hand, would say that she was Abbott to his Costello—a reference that she did not begin to understand, along with most of his references to arcane and archaic Earth matters.

There was much about him that she did not understand, even after four years of marriage.

She did not understand his fondness for poker, a relatively dishonorable game where the object was to win through deceit and trickery rather than through an honest matching of skill against skill.

She did not understand why *she* was supposed to adjust to such a radical change in her life as coming to this godforsaken space station that was so isolated it wasn't even in the middle of nowhere but rather in the distant, bleak outskirts of nowhere.

She did not understand why in the world he had been dead set on naming their offspring Elvis if it had been a boy. Fortunately the issue had been dodged when a girl arrived, during one of the more tempestuous days of *Enterprise* life that she had experienced.

And most of all, she did not understand why *he* did not understand.

"Miles, please," she said, rubbing her temple—an early warning sign indicating that her beloved husband was really pushing matters. "I've really got a lot on my mind right now."

O'Brien, who rarely, if ever, picked up on the afore-mentioned early warning sign, said, "It'll just take a minute."

"Miles . . ."

I miss the Enterprise, *and I miss my life, and it's a struggle to get any children to come to my classes because they'd all much rather be out causing trouble or something, and anyway, I never intended to be a teacher —I'm a botanist. And I never intended for Molly to grow up in a snake pit like this station, and I hate that she has to, and I hate this station, and I hate feeling grungy all the time, and I hate this whole stupid situation, and I hate—*

"Something on your mind, hon?" he asked.

She looked at that hurt puppy dog expression of his, and she couldn't help but smile. "I've never been one for kicking helpless small animals," she said softly.

"What?"

"Nothing." She waved it off and put down her padd. "Go ahead."

"All right." He grinned, fully comfortable with her dismissal of anything being wrong. "Quark showed me some magic tricks, and I figured when we have Molly's birthday party, I could entertain."

"Miles . . . Molly isn't interested in magic tricks. You know what she wants for her birthday: a pony, like she's seen in her books. She wants to ride a pony around the habitat ring."

"Well, it's not bloody likely, okay? A magician will have to do. Now . . . watch carefully."

He held his hand out, palm up. There was a coin in it.

Keiko, trying to muster enthusiasm, applauded.

"I didn't do the trick yet," said O'Brien.

"Oh . . . sorry. I just thought the coin was pretty. What is it, anyway?"

"A Ferengi tri-esta. Now . . . watch carefully."

"You said that already."

"Well, *do* it," he told her, trying not to sound irritated.

Gamely he held the coin up in his left hand. Then with his right hand he reached over and scooped it up. He held his right hand up high over his head and then snapped it open.

The coin was gone.

"Taa-daaa!" he proclaimed.

She stared at him.

"Well?" he said. "What did you think of that? The coin's gone."

"It's still in your left hand," she said flatly.

His face fell. "No, it's not."

"Yes, it is." She reached over and pried his clenched left fist open. O'Brien rolled his eyes as the tri-esta glinted in the dim lighting of their quarters. "See?" Then, when he didn't say anything immediately, she added uncertainly, "Taa-daaa."

He waved his empty right hand around in irritation. "You were *supposed* to be looking at this hand. It's called misdirection."

"But that wasn't the hand the coin was in."

"Yes, but that was the point!"

"I thought," she said cautiously, "that the point was that I was supposed to watch carefully. That's what you said. Twice. I remember. I counted. If I'd watched your right hand, I'd have been looking in the wrong place."

"But that's the bloody trick!" he said in exasperation.

She sighed and rubbed her forehead again. "I'm sorry, Miles. Would you like to do it again? I promise I'll look in the right wrong place this time."

"No, forget it," he said. "Just forget it. Go back to . . . to whatever it was you were doing."

"Fine," she said. "I wouldn't have stopped if you hadn't disturbed me."

He paused a moment. "Y'know . . . I think I know what I did wrong. I wasn't fast enough. Look, let me try it again—"

At that moment his communicator beeped. He tapped it and said, "O'Brien here."

"Chief, this is Dax," came a calm female voice. "Could you come up to Ops for a moment? Something's going on that I'd like you to double-check. I know it's late, but—"

"On my way," he said. He turned to Keiko. "Sorry about this," he said apologetically. "You always complain that you hardly see me."

"No, it's all right," she said quickly. "I'll find something to do while you're gone."

"Thanks, Keiko." He squeezed her shoulder and kissed the top of her head. "You're the best."

He left their quarters, and she sat there in the blissful silence. She picked up her notepad to continue lesson plans . . .

At which point Molly, from the next room, started to cry.

Keiko sighed deeply. She seemed to sigh a lot these days.

O'Brien's quarters were in the habitat ring, as indeed were everyone else's quarters. Deep Space Nine comprised a series of ringed structures connected by crossover bridges and vertical and horizontal turbolifts. The outermost ring was the docking ring, which contained the docking ports, cargo bays, facilities for the mining operations that had been Deep Space Nine's original *raison d'être,* and six protruding docking pylons.

The next ring in was the habitat ring. In addition to the roughly three hundred individuals who were permanent residents of Deep Space Nine—including, as Keiko O'Brien would have said, some fairly reluctant residents—there were enough quarters to accommodate several times that number. This greatly facilitated Deep Space Nine's ability to service and deal with the various travelers who stopped by to conduct business, get their ships serviced, get themselves serviced, or see to whatever other needs might arise.

The habitat ring was also the location of the defensive weapon sail towers, which had been outfitted with Starfleet phasers after the original armaments had been stripped away by the departing Cardassians. There were also six runabout landing pads—platforms that could transport the great space station's runabout vehicles to and from the runabout service bay deep inside the habitat ring.

At the center of Deep Space Nine was the aptly named core section. The operations center, or Ops—Deep Space Nine's equivalent of a starship bridge—was situated at the very top of the core. It served as the nerve center for the entire station, and lately it seemed to be O'Brien's second home. Hell, the way things had been going at home, sometimes it was more his first home.

The core section was also the location for the station's shields, its fusion reactors, its communications array, and—some people would have said most importantly—the Promenade. With its shops, cafés, and such, the Promenade was the center of commerce.

To say that it served a variety of needs was to put it mildly. In one section of the Promenade, for example, was Quark's casino, run by an unscrupulous Ferengi—"Is there any other kind?" the security chief was once heard to mutter—named Quark, who provided anything, from exotic drinks in his bar to exotic sex in his holosuites.

But in another section of the three-deck Promenade, Keiko O'Brien labored daily to try to educate—or at least keep out of trouble—the young people who resided on Deep Space Nine. It was not easy, since a good education seemed to be the last thing on the minds of the kids who ran about unsupervised on the station. And while Keiko struggled to improve their academic health, Dr. Julian Bashir labored in his Cardassian-manufactured infirmary to keep their physical health up to snuff.

Deep Space Nine—a bizarre conglomeration of requirements, goals, and desires. Sometimes it seemed only a matter of time before the entire station blew apart. The only question was whether it would blow from the physical stress that the broken-down station put on its structures and operational systems or from the emotional stress of trying to keep the lid on a variety of disparate, and oftentimes contradictory, individuals.

Lieutenant Jadzia Dax stood a respectful distance away as O'Brien labored at the science station. "I appreciate you taking the time, Chief."

O'Brien didn't speak at first. To be precise, he wasn't "at" the science station so much as under it. He had the bottom panel off and was lying on the floor, his body slightly contorted, running a series of tests on the sensor arrays.

This was not regarded as an unusual sight in the operations center. Some damned thing or other was always breaking down. Quark had once commented in a snickering tone that there were prostitutes who spent less time on their backs than O'Brien did. Although O'Brien was not exactly enthusiastic about the humor at his expense, he had to admit somewhat grudgingly that Quark had a point. At Ops—indeed, at points throughout the space station—something was always going wrong. O'Brien sometimes wished he were twins, but then he would dismiss the notion as inappropriate. After all, why wish a life like this on anyone else?

Dax was infinitely serene. "Is there anything I can do to help, Chief?"

"Just stand back and give me room, Lieutenant."

Since she was already standing far enough back to accord him sufficient space, she presumed that he was speaking metaphorically. Her hair was pulled back tight, revealing the graceful arch of leopardlike spots that tapered gracefully down around her forehead. She looked, in every respect, like an attractive, confident, young woman.

Which was simply an example of the age-old lesson that one should not take what one sees as a given.

After a few more moments O'Brien sat up. "I understand your caution, Lieutenant," he said, "but it's not the instrumentation this time. I've double-checked all the arrays, and the readings you're getting are perfectly accurate. For once, the equipment isn't screwed up."

"Indeed."

Dax turned with raised eyebrows and regarded the image on screen.

At first glance, nothing appeared there except the emptiness of space.

That, too, was an example of looks being deceiving.

"Thank you, Chief," she said. And with that she headed up to the office of the station's commander, Ben Sisko, to report her findings. It was not a report that he was going to be overly pleased to hear.

O'Brien replaced the paneling and, as he watched Dax go, muttered, "The Trill is gone. And here I guess I'm just a Trill-seeker."

"What was that?"

O'Brien looked up, embarrassed that his little jokes had been overheard.

Odo stood over him, his hands behind his back.

Looking Odo directly in the eye was always a bit disconcerting, since his face—with its smooth forehead, lack of eyebrows, and "unfinished" nose—wasn't quite "right." It was not, of course, unusual to encounter an alien species who happened to have developed differently from humans.

But O'Brien was well aware that this appearance was one that Odo had assumed in an endeavor to look human. It was the attempted approximation of humanity that O'Brien found just a touch unsettling. Nothing that he couldn't get used to, of course. Just something that was going to take some time.

"Just a little joke, Constable," he said.

O'Brien remembered how Data had always looked at someone with childlike curiosity when he didn't immediately comprehend something.

Not Odo. Oh, he encountered things that he didn't understand, but when he did, he simply looked annoyed. Even impatient, as if the person who *did* understand the situation had no business being better informed than he.

He had one of those looks now.

"I always understood that humans liked to tell jokes to an audience," said Odo. "For mutual entertainment."

"Well . . . sometimes we'll make little jokes to ourselves as well, just to keep ourselves entertained, or to show ourselves how witty we are."

"And substituting 'Trill' for 'thrill' is an example of that?"

O'Brien shook out his foot, which was starting to fall asleep. "Kind of. Yes."

Odo didn't smile, because he never did. He did, however, grimace, which he did a lot.

"Hilarious," he said sarcastically.

"Thanks for the vote of support." O'Brien pulled himself to his feet, then said as an afterthought, "Hey . . . I want to show you something."

"What do you want to show me?" Odo sounded cautious.

O'Brien pulled out the coin and said in a low, conspiratorial voice, "Magic."

Odo sighed and feigned interest, about as successfully as he feigned a human nose.

Which didn't matter a whit to O'Brien. "Now . . . watch carefully. . . ."

CHAPTER
2

COMMANDER BENJAMIN SISKO looked at Dax's results on one of the video monitors behind his desk. Normally the monitors were used for keeping track of routine station data or for communications.

But they had been put to a different use now, as Dax had transferred the contents of her preliminary studies to Sisko's office.

Dax was seated in the cramped office. Standing just to her right was Major Kira Nerys. Nerys was, in fact, her first name, which was why she was usually addressed as Major Kira, Kira being the family name.

Whereas Dax had an inner peace, Kira seemed to burn with an inner fire. She demanded instant answers before people were ready to give them. As far as she was concerned, if people didn't have the answers within the period of time that she allotted, then they probably didn't understand the question.

"Are you sure about this, Dax?" she asked.

She nodded. "At first I allowed for the possibility of instrument failure," she said. "So I had Chief O'Brien check the systems. He confirms that they are working to within correct specifications."

Ben Sisko swiveled his chair around to face her. His features, as was so often the case, gave no real hint as to what was going through his mind. His eyes glittered in his dark face. "A steady, high flux of neutrino particles from the wormhole," he said. "And getting progressively higher."

"That is correct, Benjamin," said Dax. "Whenever the wormhole is in use, of course, it emits concentrations of neutrinos."

"But it's not in use at the moment," Kira said thoughtfully. "Dax, could it be that the wormhole is becoming unstable? Even . . . collapsing?" She looked to Sisko. "That would be a damned shame."

When Sisko replied, it was in that slow, measured tone that people had come to know. "No one is more aware than I am of what a damned shame it would be if the wormhole suddenly disappeared. Having the only gateway to the Gamma Quadrant has certainly not hurt the Bajoran economy . . . not with all these dignitaries and high-muckety-mucks passing through."

Kira acknowledged the accuracy of his comment with a slight dip of her head. "There's no harm in being concerned about the state of the Bajoran economy," she pointed out. "I am, after all, Bajoran."

"So is the vast majority of this station's population, Major," allowed Sisko. He drummed on the table for a moment and then said softly, "Ever since we discovered that wormhole, it's been both a blessing and a curse. Without it—frankly, and nothing personal intended— things would be pretty damned boring around here. On the other hand, it's the equivalent of staring down the barrel of a gun. Any time at all, something very large and very heavily armed could pop out of there and turn us to space dust before we could blink an eye. And they wouldn't give a damn about me, you, or the Bajoran economy."

"Are you saying that you hope the wormhole does collapse?" said Kira. "We've been so certain that it's stable . . ."

He fixed her with his piercing gaze. "How do we really know that, Major? The fact is, we don't. We have only the vaguest understanding of the beings who created that . . . anomaly. Stable? By whose definition? Ours or the wormhole's creators' or that of the universe itself? The whole of humanity has been around, in cosmic terms, for less than an eye blink. We *believe* it's stable. We hope to hell it's stable. But we don't know beyond any shadow of a doubt that it is. In fact—again, in cosmic terms—it probably isn't. Even if its life span is ten million years, sooner or later the clock will run down . . . and who knows precisely when that will be?"

"That's very eloquent, Benjamin," said Dax with a small smile.

"Thank you, old man."

Sisko's occasional offhand way of addressing Science Officer Dax still threw Kira Nerys, as did Dax's faintly amused, paternal air when talking to Sisko. Sisko and Dax had a history together, but in that history Dax had been an old man named Curzon Dax—the host body for the wormlike symbiont that was now part of Jadzia Dax. Dax had been something of a mentor to Sisko, hence his affectionate use of "old man" despite the decidedly female form that Dax now inhabited, the old man's body having worn out.

It was a situation that Sisko continually had to try to adapt to. And that was not easy.

"However," continued Dax, "your speech was of no real relevance."

"Oh?" He raised an eyebrow. "Is that a fact?"

"Yes. Because I don't believe that the wormhole is collapsing. This situation is, in fact, not unnatural."

He sighed. "Lieutenant," he said in a more formal

tone, "I hope this won't shock you, but when I was at the Academy, I didn't realize I was going to have to become Starfleet's leading authority on wormholes. I learned enough about them to know that I should not go into them. I learned enough to know how to get out of one if I did wander in. I learned enough, in short, for survival. Beyond that"—and he spread his hands wide—"I leave it to science officers to educate me." He turned to Dax. "What's happening out there?"

"Subspace compression."

"Ahh," he said. "Subspace compression."

"Do you know what that is?"

"Just a guess here," he said. "Technobabble?"

She smiled and shook her head. "Nature abhors a vacuum, Benjamin. Well, space is a vacuum. And space abhors a wormhole. It's a rip in the fabric of reality, and reality is constantly trying to stitch itself back together. That's why most wormholes are unstable. The force that's keeping this one in place is a function of the alien technology that created it . . . but that doesn't make it immune to the pressures being exerted upon it to try to eliminate it.

"To a degree, subspace compression is the wormhole equivalent of sunspots. It's fairly routine, but that doesn't make it any less dangerous. What's essentially happening is that the subspace field is—"

But she didn't get to finish the sentence. Ultimately, she didn't have to.

They were about to have fairly graphic evidence of the effects of subspace compression.

"You never took it out of your left hand."

"Dammit!"

Odo looked mildly surprised at O'Brien's reaction. "Were you unaware that the coin was still in your left hand?"

"No, but *you* were supposed to be unaware," said O'Brien in frustration. "I don't get this. When Quark did it—"

"Ah," said Odo, "well, you see, that's part of it. You're attempting a simple misdirection trick. Quark is so blasted ugly that people find themselves staring in fascination at his revolting face. They're paying only the slightest attention to what he's doing with—"

Abruptly, Lieutenant Chafin, who had stepped in to monitor the science console when Dax went into Sisko's office, called out, "Drastic neutrino acceleration! Levels are hitting the upper register! Something's coming through!"

Odo immediately turned and bolted for Sisko's office. He got there just in time to hear Dax saying something about the subspace field, but she was already halting in mid-sentence. Sisko's office overlooked Ops, and at the first sign of something happening, he was on his feet. He was halfway around his desk when Odo appeared at the door.

"Something's coming through the wormhole," said Odo without preamble. That was hardly unusual for him; Odo was not someone who wasted a lot of words.

"It won't make it," said Dax.

Sisko glanced at her. There was sadness in her eyes, but also a firm conviction based on her personal understanding of the wormhole. "It won't," Dax said again. "I'm sorry, Benjamin. There's nothing you can do."

Sisko pushed past her and down into Ops. He took his position at the operations console and didn't even have to glance over to know that Kira was right next to him.

The main viewer was already focused on the familiar coordinates of the wormhole. "Extreme magnification!" called out Sisko. There was a subtle shift in the picture, but still nothing visible. Naturally, the wormhole was not detectable until something actually went into or out of it.

Resuming her place at the science station, Dax said calmly, "Readings off the scale."

Abruptly Sisko became aware that, if the wormhole was indeed starting to go haywire, it might have rather dire consequences for anyone or anything in proximity . . . like, for example, Sisko and his crew.

There was, however, no trace of apprehension in his voice. "Shields up," he said as calmly as if it were a casual afterthought. "Go to yellow alert."

The deflector shields flared into existence around Deep Space Nine. And then, moments later, the wormhole itself flared into existence as well.

The second he saw it, Sisko knew that something was wrong.

Usually the wormhole looked like a swirling purple vortex . . . a thing of beauty, really. A cosmic miracle.

Now, though, there was nothing beautiful about it. The outer rim roiled like an ocean during a storm. Energy crackled out in all directions, greedy fingers extending to see what they could grab and hook on to.

"Pulse waves!" Kira shouted.

Sisko hit a comm link that fed his voice throughout the entire station. "All hands! Hold on!"

It was barely enough warning as the station shuddered under the buffeting.

Down at Quark's, the Ferengi screamed in fury as bottles of his finest vintage tumbled down out of their shelves. They didn't shatter; they were too sturdy for that. They did, however, ricochet off his skull and body.

Keiko had just gotten Molly back to sleep when the trembling knocked her off her feet. Molly rolled right off her bed and hit the floor, her piteous wailing filling the air. *"I hate this place!"* Keiko shrieked, forgetting that her life on the *Enterprise* had hardly been less hectic.

Up in Ops, Sisko raised his voice to make himself heard. "Damage report!"

"Shields holding!" said O'Brien.

They could see, just for a moment, into the maw of the wormhole. Instead of the funnel shape through which ships safely passed, the interior was writhing, as if some invisible force were clamping down on it. The sides met, energy rippling out of the wormhole, filling the main viewer with a display of fireworks that gave them the barest hint of what it would have been like to be present at the Big Bang.

Dax, imperturbable, was running a sensor sweep. "I'm getting a lot of subspace interference because of the heightened neutrinos," she said, "but I've got something coming out of there. At three two two mark five . . ."

"Get tractors on it," Sisko snapped. "We can still save—"

But Dax wasn't finished. ". . . at three two seven mark five . . . three five seven mark five . . ."

He turned to her, not understanding at first. But then he did. "Debris," he said tonelessly.

She nodded.

The wormhole, like a cat coughing up a hair ball, spit out the remains of the unfortunate traveler. And then it simply vanished, folding back in on itself and disappearing as if it hadn't been there at all.

". . . Three nine three mark five," she was continuing. "A *lot* of debris, Benjamin. Whatever it was, it was shaken to bits. Any crew members were probably ripped to pieces by the stress."

There was a long moment of silence.

Kira, standing near Odo, happened to look over at the security officer . . . and saw a sadness in his face

19

that cut right through her. But it was only there for a moment, and then he replaced it with his usual hard-bitten feral mien.

Then Sisko said, "Chief, stand down from yellow alert." He looked at Dax. "So that's subspace compression."

She nodded. But she wasn't looking at Sisko. Instead she was studying her readouts.

"Anything we've encountered before?" he asked.

She didn't answer Sisko immediately. Instead she ran a quick check. But then she said, "According to analysis of the remains, yes. As a matter of fact, I can even show you a recreation of what it looked like before the wormhole pulverized it."

"Put it up on the main viewer," he said.

The image of space remained there for a moment, and then it was replaced by a visual printout from Dax's science station.

An outline appeared on the screen, with a list of technical specs running next to it. But no one was looking at the specs. Instead they were focused purely on the ship delineated on the screen.

It was elegantly simple in design, and eminently recognizable.

It was a cube.

For a long moment nothing was said. It was Odo who broke the silence.

"It's a Borg ship, isn't it?" he said.

Sisko nodded. His voice sounded hollow. "Yes, Constable. That's exactly right. It was a Borg ship."

"The operative word being 'was,'" Kira said. She appeared calm, but inwardly she shivered.

Sisko likewise appeared composed. But his heart was pounding at trip-hammer speed. "Major," he told Kira, his tone as neutral as he could keep it. "Kindly contact all local systems and Starfleet. Inform them that the Bajoran wormhole is temporarily closed for repairs. We may not be able to control who is entering it from the other end, but we can certainly make sure that we don't send anyone through."

"Several groups have already filed passage plans," said Kira. "They're undoubtedly on their way."

"Anyone who intended to pass through the wormhole is cordially invited to be a guest here at DS-Nine until such time as the neutrino emissions indicate that the wormhole has managed to pull itself together. If any of them complain," he added, allowing the corners of his mouth to turn up slightly, "they can view our records of this latest incident. I suspect that will deter them."

"Yes, sir," said Kira.

He stood there a moment more and then said, "Oh . . . and, ladies and gentlemen, to avoid any possible, and ultimately pointless, alarm, let us keep to ourselves the nature of our frustrated visitor, shall we?"

There were nods from all around Ops.

CHAPTER
3

"So THE WORD IS that the wormhole trashed a Borg ship today."

Benjamin Sisko looked up from his reading. Standing in the doorway of his quarters was the individual he shared them with: his son, Jake.

Sisko saw a lot of Jake's late mother in the boy—which was interesting, considering that Jake's mother had always said she saw a lot of Benjamin in him. Now, with the teen staring at him with a look that said he wasn't going to stand for any half-truths or evasions, Sisko started to think that maybe his wife had been correct.

Sisko slowly put the reading padd down. "Now where," he said gravely, "did you hear a thing like that?"

"Nog," he said.

"Ah. Of course."

Nog was a teenage Ferengi lad, Quark's nephew and the son of Quark's brother, Rom, who was also in Quark's employ. Nog was not precisely the type of kid Sisko really wanted Jake hanging out with. On the other hand, there weren't really a lot of kids on DS9 *for* Jake to hang out with . . . and considering that Sisko had assured his son that just the opposite would be true, the situation remained something of a sore point between them.

"And where," Sisko asked, "did, um, Nog, hear it?"

"From Quark," Jake said readily. Anticipating his father's next question, he continued, "And Quark heard it from Garak. The chain gets a little fuzzy after that."

"I see." He shook his head. "You know, when I'm trying to make my way around this station, it seems immense. But when we're trying to keep something quiet, it's the smallest place I've ever seen."

"It's true, then."

"Would Garak, the Cardassian prince of fashion, lie about that?"

He tried to make it sound light, but then he saw the boy's expression and knew that tap-dancing around the problem wouldn't accomplish anything. "It's true. But it's nothing to worry about."

"Nothing to worry about?"

Jake looked as if he wanted to continue, but he bit off the words and turned away. Sisko rose and went over to him. "Jake . . ."

His son wouldn't look at him. "You must really think I'm stupid, Dad."

"Of course I don't think you're stupid."

"Those . . . those Borg things destroyed dozens of starships. They . . . they killed Mom." He turned to face his father. "How long do you think DS-Nine would last against them? Huh? Do they make small enough units of time to measure it?"

Sisko's voice hardened. Normally he took such pains to be a friend to his son that he often had to remind himself that it was just as important to be his father. Putting on his command tone, he said, "Jake, you're not thinking."

"There! You *are* saying I'm stupid."

"No. Even the brightest people in the world don't think sometimes. Look . . . the Borg coming through just now was the best thing that could have happened."

Jake stared at him. "You gotta be kidding."

"Yes. As I said: think. Either the Borg discovered the wormhole in the Gamma Quadrant and decided to explore it or they stumbled upon it accidentally and were sucked in. Either way, we know something they don't. We know that, by and large, the wormhole is stable. All they know is that one of their ships passed through it and was destroyed."

He saw that the boy was actually paying attention, and he forced himself to sound reasonable. "Now, according to all the reports I've read, the Borg have a linked mind. What one knows, they all know. And that means that as the ship was being ripped apart by subspace compression, the central mind was living through every glorious moment of it. I have no doubt that by the time the remaining chunks of the Borg ship were spit out on this end, every other Borg ship out there was being warned to steer clear of that wormhole. They have no reason to believe that sooner or later the condition will reverse itself and the wormhole will settle back to normal. Why should they? Stability is not the norm for wormholes. The Borg will just post a big Do Not Enter sign for themselves and leave it alone."

Jake took it all in, and then slowly—to Sisko's relief—he started to nod.

"So you see, Jake? Nothing to worry about."

And Jake stared at him.

"Tell me, Dad, when you became first officer on the *Saratoga,* did you tell Mom the same thing—that there was nothing to worry about? That everything was going to be okay?"

Sisko had no answer. Actually, that was not quite

true. He did have an answer, and both he and Jake knew what it was. But he didn't want to say it.

There was nothing he could say, in fact, that wouldn't sound forced, hollow . . . and easily assailable by the young man who regarded him with the same fierce gaze that Sisko usually saw when he looked in the mirror.

"G'night, Dad," Jake said after a long moment, and went off to bed.

Taking a stroll through the Promenade, Kira stopped outside the security office and peered in. To her surprise, she saw Odo seated behind his desk, staring resolutely at a series of video displays. The monitors were flashing scenes of various parts of the station as Odo scanned for trouble.

Quark's face seemed to pop up often. Obviously Odo kept checking back on him more often than anyone or anything else on the station.

Kira poked her head in. "Odo?"

He glanced at her and gestured for her to enter. She indicated the screens, where Quark was busy overseeing his gambling activities. The Ferengi was rubbing his hands together greedily as an annoyed Tellarite slammed a hairy fist down after losing his third straight pass. "I've never seen anyone who revels in making money as much as he does."

"He lives for it," said Odo. "He eats it and breathes it. You know, I don't even think he sleeps."

"What about you?" asked Kira, sitting in front of the desk. "Shouldn't you be a puddle in a bucket about now?"

He winced. "You know, I hate that."

"Sorry," she said. "I didn't mean to insult—"

"Insult?" He gave her an amused glance. "Major, if I've learned to tune out Quark's mockeries, I assure you that nothing *you* say could possibly give me offense. No,

I simply meant that I hate the limitation of my physicality. I hate having to return to my natural state once every cycle. I'm convinced that while I'm sitting there, gelatinous and relatively useless . . . that's when Quark is up to his greatest mischief."

"You can't obsess about it, Odo," she said with a smile. "You'll give yourself ulcers."

"How fortunate that my lack of internal organs makes that unlikely." He paused a moment, studying her. "Major . . . your company is always welcome. Certainly our shared contempt for authority figures has always given us common ground. But I *am* curious. Did you stop by for a reason?"

"Well . . ." She shifted in her seat. "It's just that . . . I noticed while we were in Ops during the emergency . . . you seemed rather upset."

"An unknown vessel had been pulverized by the wormhole," said Odo. "If you did not find that upsetting, Major, I think you should be concerned about yourself rather than me."

"Now, come on, Odo," she said in a don't-kid-a-kidder tone. "There's more to it than that."

He sighed and then leaned forward, interlacing his fingers. "It's nothing extraordinary, really."

She waited for him to continue.

"Look . . . Kira," he said, dropping the formality, "you know what it's been like for me. I've lived among Bajorans for half a century now, ever since I was found floating about in the Denorios Asteroid Belt with no clue as to my identity."

He rose from behind the desk, as if the additional height made him more comfortable with the situation. "They thought I was a freak . . . and they were right. They were right," he said quietly. "Even after I learned to imitate humanoid appearance, after a fashion," he said, touching his unformed nose in wry acknowledgment of his limitations, "even after I worked my

way into a position of—dare I say the word?—
authority . . ."

Kira gasped in mock horror.

"Even then," continued Odo, "even now, I still hear
the word 'freak' echoing in my head, no matter how
hard I try to tell myself that I don't. And I'm always
hoping that somehow, in some manner, I'll find some of
the answers I've been looking for."

"And you think the wormhole might provide them."

"It makes sense," he acknowledged. "The ship I was
found in might very well have passed through the
wormhole. And that means that, sooner or later . . ."

"Another one might come through as well."

"Precisely. Don't you see, Kira? Every single time
that wormhole flares into existence and the neutrino
levels kick up, every single time something starts to
come through, I can't help but think, This might be it.
This time it might be the answers I've been waiting for."

"So when you saw that ship get demolished, you
thought . . ."

"I thought, Just my luck that others of my race finally
come through, and they're destroyed. Imagine my relief
when I learned otherwise."

"Indeed." She studied him a moment. "You know,
Odo . . . not that I'm trying to get rid of you or anything, but . . ."

"But why don't I leave Deep Space Nine and go
through the wormhole? Try to find the answers myself?"
He smiled gamely. "Now, Major, this station would fall
apart without me."

"I don't know about that."

"I do," he said flatly. "Besides, there is no way on
Bajor that I would give Quark the satisfaction of
watching me leave."

"You make it sound personal."

"It is, in a way. I cannot find it in myself simply to
walk away from the unjust and let them go on about

their business. Besides, I'll outlast him. I'm not certain what my life span is, but I haven't really detected any measurable deterioration of my physical body over the past fifty years. However long I do live, I'm reasonably certain it'll be longer than Quark. Maybe when he's dust . . . Ah, but there'll probably be someone just as bad to take his place. So much injustice."

"It's not just here, Odo," she pointed out. "There's injustice throughout the universe."

"No!" he said, acting as if the notion came as a shock to him.

"Yes. And you can't eliminate all of it."

"Not all at once, certainly. But," he said, pointing at her, "I'll tell you, Major . . . I've never been the sort who would walk away from a job that's half finished. I suppose I'll just have to stay here until my job is completed. And once that happens, then I'll move on. Until that time . . ."

He stopped, his voice trailing off. He was looking at one of the monitors in surprise. "Well, now *there's* something you don't see every day."

"What?" She looked at the display he was indicating.

"There. Sisko, stopping by Quark's."

Sure enough, there was the commanding officer of Deep Space Nine. He had just sat down, and an obsequious Quark was running over to him, asking him what he could provide.

"You're right," she said. "That is rather unusual. Think we should check it out?"

"I don't see why," he replied easily. "First off, it's none of our business. And second, I can always pump Bashir for information later."

"Bashir?"

And there was Dr. Julian Bashir, walking up to the table where Sisko was seated. He was pointing at the empty chair, clearly asking whether anyone was sitting there. Sisko gestured that he was dining alone and that Bashir was welcome to join him.

"Well, Odo . . . I don't really think you have to do that. Talk to Bashir, I mean."

"No?"

"No." She smiled thinly. "I'll ask Dax to do it. He's hot for her. Short of breaching medical confidences, he'll tell her anything."

"This isn't right, you know," said Odo. "The two of us sitting here, hatching nefarious little plots so that we can keep abreast of all the gossip and stick our noses into the business of Starfleet personnel."

"Oh, absolutely. It's not right at all."

"Terrible."

"Monstrous."

"A lot of fun, though."

"Hell, yes."

Odo looked down at his hand and frowned. And now Kira saw that his hand was starting to smooth out. She knew from long association that it was going to dissolve into a puddle of goo any minute.

"Looks like I'm more tired than I thought," said Odo dryly. "Major . . . I'll have to bid you good night."

She rose from her chair. "Good night, Odo."

As she headed for the door, he called to her, "And please keep an eye on Quark, if you wouldn't mind."

"Not at all," she said. As she headed out the door, she heard a thick, slurpy splash behind her. But she was too polite to look.

"May I join you gentlemen?"

Bashir and Sisko looked up to see Dax standing just behind them.

"By all means!" said Bashir, just a bit too quickly. Immediately he stood, out of a sense of chivalry.

Sisko remained where he was, laughing inwardly

despite his glum mood. Numerous men on the station were attracted to Dax, and whenever Sisko saw one of them using the typical considerate behavior that males used toward females, all he could see in his mind's eye was them fawning over an elderly, somewhat amused man.

Bashir, of course, had only known Dax since she arrived on the station. Having no preconceived notion of her, he was reacting purely to what he saw. And what he saw, he liked.

A lot.

He slid a chair over for her. Dax, who had not been a female for over eighty years, smiled that killer smile of hers and said, "Thank you, Julian," as she sat. "So," she looked from one man to the other. "What are you two gentlemen up to?"

"We were discussing the commander's trouble with his son."

"Oh, 'trouble' is too strong a word," said Sisko.

Quark immediately drifted over, ogling Dax as he purred, "Ah! More arrivals from the command crew. We're honored by your presence. Can I get you anything? Another double-whipped I'danian spice pudding, perhaps? You devoured the one you had the other day."

"I know," Dax said ruefully, and patted her hips. "And it's still with me. For some reason, ever since I became a woman again, I feel this tremendous impulse to watch my figure."

"I share the same interest," Quark replied. By Ferengi standards, his behavior was rather suave. By human—and, for that matter, Trill—standards, he was practically slobbering.

"Thank you, Quark," Sisko said firmly. "She doesn't want anything. That will be all."

Quark frowned and muttered a Ferengi oath as he shambled away.

"What's the problem with Jake?" Dax asked, turning her attention away from the departing Ferengi. "Same as usual, Benjamin?"

"Yes," he said, sighing. "Same as usual. These things don't go away overnight."

"That's for certain," said Bashir.

"Don't be too hard on yourself, Benjamin. Teenagers have tremendous difficulty adjusting to even the best of circumstances. And this"—she gestured in a manner that took in the entire space station—"is hardly the best."

"I know, I know," said Sisko in frustration. He was nursing a glass of synthale. "And why shouldn't he miss his mother? I miss Jennifer pretty badly myself. It has been easier for me, I'll admit. When I went through the wormhole the first time, I had the opportunity to work out a lot of the frustration and anger that I was experiencing. I had a chance, in essence, to come to terms with the loss." He took an unenthusiastic sip of his drink. "Unfortunately," he continued, "Jake hasn't had that opportunity. He has a lot of anger toward the universe in general and me in particular."

"Why you?" asked Bashir.

"Who better?" said Sisko reasonably. "Jennifer would have been perfectly content to live on Earth. Hell, Jake would prefer it. If I told him we were going back, he'd be halfway there before I even finished the sentence. And he wouldn't even need a ship. He'd just run.

"But they followed *me*. It was my career that decided in what direction our lives went. I brought us out into space. If it hadn't been for me, we wouldn't have been aboard the *Saratoga*, and Jennifer wouldn't have died. We'd have been on Earth . . ."

Bashir laughed, but it wasn't a pleasant sort of laugh. "I *was* on Earth," the handsome young doctor said. "The Borg were heading our way, remember? The news was all over the internet. The entire planet was going berserk." He took a swig of his own drink as if to steel himself against the memories. "It wasn't pretty, Commander. Citizens of Earth didn't exactly take it well when the end of everything they knew was barreling at light-speed right toward them. If the *Enterprise* crew members hadn't pulled a last-minute miracle out of their hats, I might be sitting here pasty white with a gun instead of an arm, saying 'Drinks are irrelevant.'"

"He's right, Benjamin," said Dax. "The fact is, no place in this galaxy is one hundred percent safe."

"Perfect," Sisko said mirthlessly. "I'll go back to Jake and say, 'Don't feel bad, son. The fact is, there are no guarantees. No matter where you are, you could still be alive one minute and dead the next.' That will doubtless assuage his concerns."

Dax shrugged. "We're all of us alive one minute and dead the next, Commander. It's just a matter of when and how."

"Dax is right," said Bashir, who would have found a way to agree with Dax even if she'd been flat-out wrong. "All we can do is try to live the best life we can and accept the restrictions that are placed on us. One of the harsh realities of medicine is that we can't save every patient. Our primary rule is that, as people of medicine, we shall do no harm."

"Do no harm to your son, Benjamin," said Dax. "Let the rest of it play out as it will. He's a good kid. He'll come around."

"I hope you're right."

"I'm sure she is," said Bashir, and he smiled at Dax. Sisko rolled his eyes.

CHAPTER
4

"THIS IS AN OUTRAGE! I am doing the work of the holy K'olkr! How dare you interfere?"

The gentleman on the Ops main viewscreen was not happy. And he looked like someone who, when he was unhappy, went out of his way to make sure that as many people as possible were unhappy along with him.

He wore a hood pulled up, obscuring much of his face. But what they could see of his skin was solid ebony black. His deep-set eyes glowed red from within the folds of his hood.

O'Brien leaned over from the engineering station and muttered to Kira, "All he needs is a scythe."

She looked at him curiously. "Why?"

He was about to explain, but decided that it would take too long. "Never mind," he said.

From his station, Sisko tried to sound calm and reasonable. "Sir," he said, "I appreciate your situation . . ."

"Do you know who I am?" His voice became louder, and he practically thundered, "I am Mas Marko! I am one of the premier spiritual leaders of the entire Edema system! I am the voice of the spirit of K'olkr. Who are *you* to tell me that I cannot follow his will?"

Sisko was one of those people who, the angrier people got at him, the more composed he became. It was as if he fed off the hostile energy. "I," he said, "am the commander of Deep Space Nine who is endeavoring to save your life. The wormhole is, at this time, closed to all travel. We sent out warnings about it; we were very specific."

"Commander, your warnings mean nothing to one who has heard the word of the spirit of K'olkr. He has told me that I am to do his work in the Gamma Quadrant. I am to spread the message of his truth. I am," he said fervently, "charged with a sacred mission to spread his word. Compared to that most holy duty, Commander, your warnings—restricted by the concerns of mere mortal existence—are of no relevance."

"Is that a fact? Very well, Mas Marko, I make you this offer," said Sisko, unruffled by Marko's belligerent tone. "My first officer will feed through to your shipboard computers a replay of the events related to the subspace compression of the Bajoran wormhole." He didn't even have to turn in order to know that Kira was doing as he had mentioned. "I ask that you view them. Then touch base with the spirit of K'olkr and see what he has to say about it. If he still encourages you to commit suicide, I won't stand in your way."

"Are you mocking me?" Mas Marko said dangerously.

"Not at all. I'm speaking the truth. You see, Mas Marko, as your viewing of the incident in question will testify, you won't have a prayer once you enter the wormhole. So all I'm saying is that you might as well get your praying in now. Sisko out."

The screen went blank, and Sisko turned to Kira. She nodded and said, "All right . . . it's been sent through."

"You weren't serious, Benjamin," Dax said. "Were you? I mean, you wouldn't really *let* them . . ."

"If I were a cynic," Sisko said dryly, "I would say that if Mas Marko and his party are stupid enough to hurl themselves into oblivion for no reason, then the galaxy's gene pool is well rid of them. I am not, however, a cynic. Chief, bring tractor beams on line."

"Aye, sir," said O'Brien.

"The Edemian ship will be in range in . . . ?" He looked questioningly at Kira.

"Twenty-two minutes," she told him.

"Twenty-two minutes. Prepare to snag the Edemian ship before it gets within range of the wormhole."

"To be fair, sir," Kira pointed out, "you *did* say you wouldn't stop them from going in if they wanted to."

"I lied, Major."

She smiled. "Good for you, sir."

It did not, however, come down to the question of whether or not Sisko should have kept his word. Because less than two minutes later Mas Marko's dark image once again appeared on the screen.

This time, however, he sounded somewhat less aggressive than before.

"K'olkr has had a change of heart," said Mas Marko. To Sisko's great surprise, Marko even sounded amused at his own words.

"How fortunate for all of you," Sisko dead-panned.

Marko took a step closer to the screen, his eyes glowing brighter. "Commander," he said, "I am not a fanatic. I have no desire to see myself or my family become fodder for a cosmic anomaly. Obviously the work of K'olkr cannot be accomplished by his servants if his servants have had their molecules scattered across thousands of light years."

"I admit I am not familiar with K'olkr," said Sisko, "but from where I stand, he seems a rather reasonable deity."

"I may indeed have the opportunity to sway you over to his view of the universe," Mas Marko said thoughtfully. "Presuming, that is, that you can find room for me and my followers at Deep Space Nine until the wormhole is safe for passage. The trip from Edema has been a lengthy one; I have no desire to turn around and end this mission prematurely if that can be avoided."

"How many of you are there?"

"Myself, two retainers, and my wife and son."

"That will not be a hardship," said Sisko. "When you are within range, we will specify docking instructions."

"It will be a pleasure to chat with you in person," said Marko. The screen blinked off.

Sisko let out a slow breath.

"How pleasant," Kira said, "to see that we aren't dealing with a fanatic. That could just as easily have gone the other way."

"Yes. But just to make sure . . . monitor them very carefully once they get within range. Their warp-coil emissions in particular. If those accelerate, it will be the first indicator that they're going to make a run past us and try to get into the wormhole."

"But Marko said they would stay here until the wormhole is passable."

He shrugged. "I don't have a monopoly on lying, Major."

The Edemian ship, however, made no suicidal run at the wormhole. Indeed, once the course of action had been decided upon, the ship glided to the docking ring with nary a complaint or whisper of trouble. Sisko, deciding to exercise protocol, was on hand to greet them personally. He also decided to exercise caution, and for that reason he took Odo with him.

Mas Marko was the first off.

Sisko and Odo looked up.

And up.

Marko was nearly seven feet tall, it seemed. He had to bend over slightly to get through the docking bay door. But he did it so smoothly that it was clear he was quite accustomed to situations that were inconvenient for someone of his height.

What impressed Sisko most was that he didn't walk so much as glide, as if he had wheels instead of feet. For all Sisko knew, he did, for his robes trailed down to the floor and whisked about the deck.

He'd heard O'Brien's whispered wisecrack earlier and now was certain that there was indeed some merit in it. If Mas Marko had been carrying a scythe, he would indeed have been the image of the Grim Reaper.

This impression was diluted somewhat when Mas Marko pulled back his hood. His face was still a gleaming ebony, but now enough features could be discerned to give him a somewhat human aspect.

His eyes still gleamed a disconcerting red, however.

"Commander Sisko." He spoke slowly, as if giving thoughtful weight to every syllable. His voice was deep and seemed to originate from somewhere around his shoes.

"Mas Marko. An honor."

"You seem a bit surprised, Commander."

"I admit," said Sisko, "that when major dignitaries arrive, they are usually preceded by their entourage. Standard-bearers, as it were, announcing their leader's arrival."

"How egocentric," said Marko mildly. "And somewhat disingenuous in depicting their station in life. I am Mas Marko, Commander. I am my people's leader. What sort of leader would I be . . . if I merely followed?"

"As you say. This is Security Chief Odo."

"An honor." He seemed to regard Sisko with some

amusement. "Security chief? Are you anticipating difficulty, Commander?"

"I always anticipate difficulty," Sisko said easily. "Ninety percent of the time, there isn't any. But I'd rather be wrong ninety percent of the time so that I can be prepared to be right that irritating ten percent. Because those are the times when my people's welfare is on the line."

Mas Marko appeared to consider that. "A very reasonable approach," he said at last.

He turned and extended a large hand in the direction of the airlock. Several other Edemians now emerged from behind him—two males, a female, and a child. They were somewhat shorter than he, but still hovering around the six-foot range, except for the child, who was a more reasonable five feet. Then again, for all Sisko knew, the boy might be at an age where, if he were human, he'd be averaging around three feet.

They are one tall damned race, thought Sisko.

All were dressed in flowing robes, but the patterns were far brighter, less solemn, than Marko's own. Perhaps, Sisko reasoned, Marko's robes were a sign of his office. Either that or he just liked to look ominous.

The two males stepped forward first. As near as Sisko could determine, they were almost indistinguishable from each other. "This is Del," said Marko, "and this is Lobb."

"An honor, sir," said Del, bending slightly at the waist.

Lobb seemed a good deal less formal. "Handshakes, right?" he asked. His voice sounded younger than Del's although it was impossible to truly discern his age based on his face.

"Pardon?"

"Humans do handshakes. Is that correct?"

"Uh . . . yes," said Sisko. "That is correct."

Lobb pumped his hand, and Sisko endeavored not to wince at the strength of the grip. "A pleasure, sir."

"Lobb is new to missionary work," said Mas Marko. "His enthusiasm is rather contagious. It gives me fond recollections of my days as a novice."

"We're going to do K'olkr's work," said Lobb, still shaking Sisko's hand. "There is no greater honor than that."

"Yes, I'm sure." Sisko politely disengaged his hand. As he flexed his fingers to restore circulation, Marko gestured for the woman and boy to come forward. They did so, with that same remarkable glide effect.

"She who is my mate," said Mas Marko. His voice sounded slightly more formal. "Azira, daughter of Eweeun and Kragar. Out of deference to your rank, Commander, you may address her as Azira. And my son, Rasa, who supports the spirit of K'olkr and hopes to enter into the presence of his holiness pure of thought and deed."

Sisko blinked. Something about that introduction sounded just a little . . . strange.

If there was anything odd about it, Azira did not let on. She bowed her head slightly in acknowledgment of the introduction. Rasa did likewise.

Sisko stared at Rasa for a moment. There was something in the boy's eyes, something in his demeanor . . .

"Commander," said Mas Marko, sounding curious, "is there a problem?"

"No," said Sisko gamely. "No. No problem at all. Azira . . . Rasa . . . a pleasure to meet you both."

Azira smiled—an amazingly sweet smile, considering the fierce-looking face that the mouth was a part of.

Rasa did not do anything. He simply stood there.

Trying not to be distracted by the lack of vigor in the boy, Sisko said, "The constable here will guide you to your quarters. You have free access to any unrestricted area of DS-Nine, although I'd explore the Promenade cautiously if I were you. Some of the inhabitants there can be somewhat . . . rowdy."

"Rowdy." Marko's interest seemed piqued. "Without religion, one would think?"

"Depends how you define 'religion.' They worship drinking, gambling, and profits. They're as fervent about that as the holiest of men about their own respective gods. No offense intended."

"None taken," Marko said. "Indeed, we may be performing K'olkr's will, despite our original intention of passing through to the Gamma Quadrant. It is possible that he has arranged for this . . . what did you call the wormhole's condition?"

"Subspace compression."

"Yes. He might have arranged for this compression expressly so that we could spend some more time here at your station spreading his word to those who need it."

"K'olkr moves in mysterious ways his wonders to perform," said Sisko.

Mas Marko looked at him as if truly seeing him for the first time.

"That is very profound, Commander," he said. "Do you mind if I quote you on that?"

"Not at all," Sisko said, as generously as he could.

"This way, please." Odo gestured to the turbolifts.

Mas Marko and his entourage preceded them. But Sisko held Odo back just long enough to say in a low voice, "If they wander about the Promenade, keep an eye on them. We don't need Marko or his people getting roughed up if any of the Promenade inhabitants feel disinclined to convert to the ways of K'olkr."

Odo nodded his understanding and followed the Edemians. "Please be careful in the turbolifts," he called. "They can be a little bumpy."

Sisko shook his head and was about to head back to

Ops when his comm badge beeped. He tapped it. "Sisko here."

"Commander," came Kira's voice. "We have another arrival. This one's unexpected. Is Odo there?"

"He's guiding the Mas Marko party to the habitat ring."

"A suggestion, then, sir: we may want to keep our new guest in the docking ring until Odo can handle him personally. This is definitely a security matter, and considering what's involved, the constable will probably want to deal with it himself."

Sisko was confused. Kira was describing a situation that sounded as if it had the makings of being very dangerous, but the tone of her voice suggested that she was entertained rather than alarmed. Trying to get a handle on it, Sisko asked, "Is it another frustrated wormhole passenger?"

"Actually, no. He's here specifically to do business with someone on Deep Space Nine."

"Oh, really? Who?"

"Quark . . ."

The Ferengi recognized Odo's voice even before he turned around. Quark's face bore his typical expression when dealing with Odo: smugly confident, but with a bit of caution. After all, he never knew when Odo might have something on him.

He turned slowly, saying, "What can I do for—"

But the words caught in his throat.

There was a Ferengi standing next to Odo. He had a singular triangle of brown spots on his eye ridge. He grinned at Quark, exposing his sharp and fairly vicious-looking teeth to their best advantage.

"Quaaaaark," he said in a low drawl.

Quark uttered a small shriek and promptly assumed the defensive posture commonly known as the Ferengi cringe. He held one arm out as if to ward off an enemy, and the other encircled his head so that, if something hideous did happen to him, he wouldn't see it or hear it.

He backed up rapidly, knocking over a table.

The other Ferengi, standing next to Odo, looked up at the constable calmly. "I told you he'd react this way."

"Keep your distance, Glav!" Quark said shrilly. "Just . . . just keep your distance!"

"Oh, stop it, Quark," Odo said. His patience with the rodentlike Ferengi was not great to begin with, and this was pushing it far beyond its tolerance. "I'm not going to let him do anything to you."

"Oh, reaaaallly." Quark's voice was dripping with sarcasm. He had backed up against a wall—another common Ferengi maneuver; that way, no one could attack from behind. "And you would just be sooo upset if something happened to me, wouldn't you, Odo?"

"If it happened here, yes," Odo said firmly. "I put aside my personal feelings when it comes to enforcing the law. If I didn't, Quark, I can assure you that something would have happened to you a long time ago. Glav here wants to talk."

"Glav here wants to see me stripped naked and strangled with my own entrails!"

"You're confusing Glav with me," came Odo's sarcastic reply.

Glav held up his hands, looking as nonthreatening as a Ferengi could possibly look. "Sir," he said to Odo, "I believe I can clear this up."

Odo folded his arms and waited.

"Some years ago I had a major investment deal going on," Glav told him. "I had put all my personal fortune on the line to ensure that it would go through. And then Quark here came swooping in and persuaded my clients to bargain with him instead. He undercut me, offering the same material at a lower price."

"I did nothing wrong!" snarled Quark. "Everything was done in accordance with the Ferengi law of dealing!

Besides . . . I was a youngster back then. You can't hold me accountable just because—"

"Because I was driven into bankruptcy," said Glav. "I had extended my credit too far. My creditors wanted payment. I had failed to make the sale. They took practically everything. I was ruined."

"And now he's come back for revenge!" Quark reassumed the Ferengi cringe.

"No, Quark. I've come back here to tell you that it all worked out for the best—for better than the best."

This prompted Quark to peer out from under his own elbow. "What do you mean?"

"I was left with only one thing, Quark—some property on Xerxes Six that was deemed so worthless that no one took it from me. I went there to live . . . and, I admit, to nurse dark thoughts against you. But—" He paused dramatically.

Quark, curious in spite of himself, slowly lowered his arm. "But what?"

"I started doing geological surveys." Glav smiled raggedly at his own ingenuity. "The preliminary surveys when I first arrived revealed nothing of interest, but I had time on my hands, so I probed deeper. And I found a massive deposit of calvinum."

Quark gasped. "Ca . . . calvinum?"

"That's right. The stuff that the Byfrexians use to power their ship engines. The stuff is in remarkably short supply."

"The Byfrexians will pay an arm and a leg for even a gram of it!"

"Bah! Arms and legs I have no use for. Two million bars of gold-pressed latinum, however . . ."

Quark put his hand to his chest. "Tuh . . . tuh . . . tuh . . ." He gulped. "Two . . . muh . . . muh—"

"Million," said Odo peevishly. "Oh, do get on with it."

"There's not much more to get on with," said Glav. "I'm rich, Quark—'rich beyond the dreams of avarice.' If it hadn't been for you, I'd still be eking out a living wheeling and dealing, not knowing that I had a fortune right under my nose. I even made a few safe investments, and I've doubled my fortune since then."

A crafty look crossed Quark's face. "This is a con! That's it! He's coming in here pretending he's rich so he can pull some sort of scam on me! Get my place away from me!"

Glav looked around Quark's establishment with barely concealed disdain. "Why would I possibly want it? Look, Quark . . . you don't have to believe *me*. Run a thorough check on me using the Ferengi Bureau of Audit. I'm listed on the exchange; my net worth is no secret. I'm proud of it—wouldn't you be?"

He stepped forward and took Quark firmly by the shoulders. Quark flinched, still expecting a sudden blow to land on the top of his head.

"Luck was with you, Quark. With both of us," said Glav. "Bear you ill will? Pfaw! In a way, I owe you everything. As I said, check me out. Satisfy yourself through as many different sources as possible. I'll keep my distance from you until you're ready to talk with me. Because once you are ready, Quark, I'm going to make you a very, very rich Ferengi."

He released Quark and stepped back. He nodded slightly toward Odo and said, "Thank you, sir. I can find my way from here." And he turned and strolled casually down the Promenade, hands clasped behind his back, looking for all the world like someone who had everything he could possibly want.

Quark watched him go and then muttered, "I don't trust him for a second."

"No reason you should," said Odo. "We know how far we can trust Ferengi."

"Yes, we know how . . ." Quark began to echo, but

then he caught himself and gave Odo a dirty look. Odo walked away without further comment.

"You have been doing a most impressive job with the station, Commander," said the Cardassian. "Gul Dukat is most impressed."

They were sitting in Sisko's office. Sisko was more than aware of the occasional look of utter revulsion that Kira delivered in the Cardassian's general direction. Wisely, however, she kept silent, not particularly trusting herself.

Sisko nodded. "Thank you, Gotto. And you may report to Gul Dukat that he is welcome here at any time."

Gotto smiled thinly at that. "Oh . . . Gul Dukat hardly believes that to be the case. That is why he has sent me, his trusted envoy, to do his business for him."

"And his business is . . . ?"

"His."

"I see." He paused. "And Deep Space Nine is my business. And where those two overlap . . . I do not like being unaware."

They regarded each other for a moment, and then Gotto shrugged. "Oh, it's of no consequence, truly. Gul Dukat simply likes to keep all those aboard this station subtly aware of the Cardassian presence. To do otherwise would be a sign of weakness. I am instructed to spend the next several days mingling, chatting, making myself seen. That is really the extent of it. You do not have a problem with that, do you, Commander?"

"Of course not," said Sisko calmly. "As long as that is all you intend to do. Who could possibly find fault with that?"

"We have an understanding, then." The Cardassian slapped his thighs and rose from the chair.

At that moment Dr. Bashir walked into Sisko's office. "You wanted to see me, sir?" he asked.

"Dr. Bashir . . . Gotto Lon," said Sisko. "Gotto Lon was just leaving."

"A pleasure as always," said Gotto, and he walked out of the office.

As the Cardassian left, Sisko motioned for Bashir to sit. "Doctor, how well informed are you on Edemians?"

Bashir smiled. If there was one thing on which he prided himself, besides his looks, it was his expertise in multi-species medicine. Indeed, his encyclopedic knowledge amazed Sisko, although he tried not to let on.

"Fairly conversant, sir," he said. "They're a fairly hardy race."

"Would you know a sick one if you saw him?"

"Just on sight? Possibly. If I examined him, definitely."

"A group of them just arrived on DS-Nine. One of them—the youngest—seems a bit . . . off. Nothing I can put my finger on . . ."

"Was he bleeding? Coughing? Anything overt?"

"No," admitted Sisko. "Nothing overt, but . . . well, Doctor, all I can tell you is that when you're a parent, you develop a sixth sense about these things."

"It happens occasionally to doctors, too," Bashir said soberly. "Do you want me to go to their quarters?"

"Not yet. I'm still uncertain enough about this that I don't want to make too much of it. The Edemians shouldn't be difficult to spot; they'll probably set up shop in the Promenade and try to do missionary work among the poor godless denizens therein."

"Indeed? Then they have their work cut out for them."

"I agree. I want you to get close to them. Observe what you can. And if you deem it necessary, bring the youngest one to the infirmary for in-depth testing."

"And if they object?"

"They do not have that option. This is a closed

environment, Doctor. I'm in favor of being tactful, but the bottom line is . . . if the boy is carrying a disease, we'll have to isolate him. I have no desire to see another virus get loose in this station. Do you?"

"No, sir," said Bashir, shuddering inside. Not long ago an aphasia virus had gripped the entire station. That nightmare had nearly resulted in the death of practically everyone on board. The only ones who had proven immune were Quark and Odo.

Odo had privately told Bashir that for him, the possibility of everyone on the station dying was only part of the problem. The true horror for Odo was his concern that he and Quark were both carriers . . . which meant that they could not leave DS9. Ever. With the station quarantined, and with no way of filtering the virus out of the air, Odo and Quark would have been stuck together forever on the empty station, each being the only living individual for the other to converse with. "You, at least, would have been dead," Odo had informed Bashir archly. "For me, the nightmare would have just begun."

"All right, then, Doctor," said Sisko. "Thank you. That's all. And keep me apprised."

"Yes, sir. Of course."

Several other travelers—two humans, a Tellarite, and a Boffin—stopped at Deep Space Nine for a variety of reasons. None of them were particularly pleased to learn that the wormhole was closed to passage until further notice, but all seemed willing to make the best of a difficult situation.

And down in one of the ships that had docked along the great outer ring of Deep Space Nine . . .

A suitcase began to move.

It seemed to melt, becoming a thick mass of gelatinous goo. And then it oozed forward.

It flowed out of the ship and into the airlock. The seal

into the docking bay was airtight, but the mass did not attempt to break it. Instead it moved up and along the paneling until it found a section that seemed weak enough.

The slime drew back, as if coalescing for a fleeting moment into a fist, and then it punched through the paneling. The panel crumbled under the impact, and the mass seeped through and around the heavy docking clamps.

Within seconds it had made its way along the clamps and reached the far end of the airlock. It was only a moment's work for the slime to push out another panel and trickle down onto the floor.

Then the mass started to come together, to re-form. It became a small tower of ooze, and then it assumed form and definition.

Within moments it had morphed into a passable imitation of a humanoid.

It looked down at its hands, touched its face, and nodded in satisfaction.

The metamorph walked away from the docking bay. Within minutes it had reached the Promenade deck and was mingling freely with the other denizens of the station.

Deep Space Nine was under siege.

But no one knew it yet.

CHAPTER
5

"Come! Come freely and experience the word of K'olkr!"

The Edemians had set up shop in an empty booth along the Promenade. Mas Marko rang a large, re-sounding chime to attract the attention of passersby. It worked to the degree that it got people to glance the Edemians' way. But it did nothing to get anyone to take them seriously.

Sisko, far more familiar with the parade of life that was the Promenade, had gone over some ground rules with Mas Marko. There was to be no physical accosting of people; no getting in their way; no attempt, in any way, shape, or form to force their beliefs on the denizens of Deep Space Nine. The reason for that was simple: Sisko was looking to avoid starting a fight.

Fortunately for all concerned, Mas Marko readily accepted Sisko's rules. "Only those who willingly embrace the word of K'olkr can truly understand," he had replied. "We can but expose individuals to those thoughts. K'olkr teaches us that his way is the way of acceptance. Acceptance in all things, Commander. You cannot quarrel with that, certainly."

Indeed, Sisko could not.

So now Mas Marko stood in the Promenade, trying to appeal to that which was worthwhile and decent and good in the Promenade's browsers. Which was not, unfortunately, a lot.

He was surrounded by his entourage, who were trying to hand out treatises on the greatness of K'olkr. No one seemed particularly interested.

Bashir stood a short distance away, watching carefully. In particular, he was watching the boy, Rasa.

From his knowledge of Edemian physiology, he determined that the boy was roughly ten earth years in age. Edemians were almost indefatigable. Marko and his followers had been calling to people nonstop for several hours now.

All except Rasa. He remained quiet, listless. The prodding from his mother to participate in their endeavors was met with indifference.

And she was worried.

Even from where he was watching, Bashir could see her anxiety. But was she worried about something and did not know what? Or was she genuinely concerned about something in particular?

Either way, Bashir felt it was worth his time to find out.

And he knew of a very simple way to do it.

He walked very casually toward the Edemians. As he got within range, he saw that Azira was still urging the boy to take part in what they were doing. Bashir was lucky enough to make eye contact with the unenthusiastic lad, and he raised an eyebrow to indicate interest.

"Have you heard the word of K'olkr?" asked Rasa. His voice was high-pitched, not at all like the stentorian tones of his father. Up close, Bashir could even see some of what Sisko had already picked up. One didn't have to be an expert in alien medicine to see that Rasa looked . . . diminished, somehow. His eyes, rather than the softly glowing red of the others, were mere flickers, like smothered embers.

Furthermore his skin was not the solid ebony of the others, but instead was inconsistently colored. Looking closely, Bashir could even see signs of splotching.

All this he noted in a second. Covering his clinical assessment smoothly, he said, "Why, no. I haven't. The word of K'olkr?"

His response caught the attention of the others. They turned toward him, but Bashir deliberately didn't look at them, instead focusing entirely on Rasa. He wanted to make it painfully clear that the dialogue was between him and the boy. "Who is K'olkr?" he asked. "A friend of yours?"

"Uh . . ." Clearly the boy hadn't expected any response. He licked his lips and looked nervously to his father for guidance.

"He asked you, son. Tell him," came Marko's response.

"Uh . . ." Rasa looked back to Bashir. "K'olkr is . . . is all." It was clear that the words his father had drilled into him were slowly coming back to him, out of reflex . . . or perhaps out of a sense of self-preservation. "K'olkr loves us. K'olkr protects us. He . . ." He looked once more to his father, who merely nodded in calm surety. "He guides us," said Rasa. "By trusting ourselves to the fate decreed by K'olkr, we have that much more security in ourselves."

"Trusting yourselves to the fate K'olkr decrees?" said Bashir. "So you believe purely in predestination? Or do you accept the notion of free will?"

Rasa looked somewhat surprised at this. It was as if he hadn't been certain until just this moment that Bashir was actually paying attention to what he was saying. Automatically he said, "Free will when it comes to dealing in mortal affairs. But trusting in the wisdom of K'olkr when it comes to those matters that are the affairs of gods."

Bashir suddenly snapped his fingers. "Blast! You know, this is so interesting . . . but I have to get to my duties."

"Oh." Rasa looked deflated. He glanced apologetically at his father.

"That is a pity," said Mas Marko. "It is clear to me that your conversation with my son is of interest to you, Mister . . ."

Bashir was about to correct him out of habit by saying, "Doctor," but some internal warning sense stopped him. Instead he said simply, "Bashir. Julian Bashir."

"Mr. Bashir. Must you leave so abruptly?"

"I'm afraid so. Although . . ." and he paused, as if just coming up with the idea. But then he said dismissively, "No. Forget it."

"What?" said Rasa, momentarily forgetting that his father was supposed to take the lead in discussions. Marko, however, did not remonstrate with him. He was obviously proud to see his son actually taking charge of a situation.

"Well," Bashir said, "perhaps this young man would be interested in accompanying me. Much of my job, I hate to admit, is somewhat drudgery-filled. Certainly some stimulating conversation would be a vast improvement for me. Although . . . well, he's probably helping you far too much here."

"To be honest, sir," said Mas Marko, "we have been here for some hours and have not had much success in attracting more than sniggering looks. That being the case, I would hate to lose momentum with you. Rasa, would you care to accompany the gentleman?"

"Yes, sir," said Rasa immediately.

But at almost the same moment Azira said, "I don't think so."

Rasa looked from one to the other, as did Bashir.

Something was definitely going on between the boy's parents. Their faces were absolutely unreadable. But whatever was happening, it was quite clear to Bashir that Mas Marko was still in charge. Azira held his gaze for only a moment before lowering her eyes.

Marko spoke to her in a voice that seemed filled with understanding and a very faint sorrow. "Like all of us, the boy must accomplish all that is possible during his time in this sphere. You must be willing to let him go."

"That is what I do," she said. It wasn't a comment that Bashir fully understood, but Azira turned to Rasa and said, "Make K'olkr proud."

"Of course I will, Mother," he said.

Deciding that further conversation would only delay matters—and possibly shift them in a different direction—the doctor started walking without further hesitation. "So how do we know when we are operating under our own free will . . . and when we are to leave matters in the hands of K'olkr?"

Rasa immediately fell into step next to Bashir. "Well," he said, "we have a set of laws called Siilar that enable us to study situations and make determinations. . . ."

Their voices faded, mixing into the general babble and buzzing of the surrounding voices.

"He will make us proud," said Mas Marko firmly. He did not look at Azira or even seem to be addressing her.

Azira said nothing.

The matter already apparently concluded, Mas Marko spoke with even more fervor to the next person who happened by. As if encouraged by the apparent success his son was having with the Starfleet man, he said, "Sir, the words of K'olkr would be of interest to your life—"

"Unless the words happen to be 'profit,' 'money,' and 'greed,' I seriously doubt it," said Glav, and he walked away from the Edemians.

As he neared Quark's establishment, he slowed down his brisk pace . . . and then, very deliberately, gave the place a wide berth. He saw Quark busily attending to customers, being his usual servile self. Glav managed to angle himself to just within Quark's view and then started to walk away.

Quark, however, moved like lightning. "Glav!" he shouted. He practically leapt over a table and barreled across the Promenade, knocking people aside to get to Glav as quickly as he could.

He struck another very distinctive Ferengi posture the moment that he was at Glav's side: he bent over slightly so that his eye level was just below Glav's. This was a body-language method of saying, "I acknowledge the greatness of your place in the universe. How may I serve you so that you may enrich me?"

The body language said all that. Quark, for his part, licked his lips with anticipation and purred, "Glav, old fellow, where *have* you been? I've tried repeatedly to reach you in your quarters. You weren't there."

"Oh . . . I've been looking around this fascinating station of yours," he said, turning in a slow circle so that he bore a passing resemblance to an antique conning tower. "This is quite an amazing situation you people have here. But enough of me, Quark. Let's talk about you. What do you think of me?"

Quark bobbed his head in appreciation and gave a high-pitched laugh. "Ah, Glav . . . no one can tell a centuries-old joke like you."

"That's extraordinarily obsequious of you, Quark."

"Thank you," said Quark, bobbing his head appreciatively. "I strive for perfection in all matters."

"So tell me, Quark . . . am I correct in assuming that you have checked out my . . . status?"

"Thoroughly," said Quark. "Very thoroughly. Glav, dear fellow . . . you've managed to keep a rather low profile personally, haven't you."

"I have tried to do so," agreed Glav. "Oh, if you do research under my name, it is quite easy to find my net worth. Otherwise, though, I've managed to be fairly subtle about it."

"Exceptionally subtle," crowed Quark. "Subtle as the whispering winds of space. Subtle as—"

"Quark."

"Yes, Glav?"

"You're overdoing it."

Quark stepped back and bowed slightly. "I apologize."

"It's no matter," said Glav. "To be honest, Quark, I expected no less of you."

"Then it is my honor to live down to your expectations."

Glav put a hand on Quark's shoulder. "We can do business, Quark."

Quark gasped in amazement and pleasure, not to mention fulfilled hope. "How can I, from my lowly station in life, hope to aid you? My humble business is barely worth your notice."

Glav looked around and then gestured toward a nearby table and chairs at the outskirts of Quark's Place. He sat down, Quark opposite him.

Elbows on the table, head propped up, looking the soul of disingenuousness, Glav said, "You have connections."

"I do?" Quark looked momentarily confused. But then he cleared his throat and, recapturing his self-possession, said, "Well . . . of course I do. But not . . . I mean, how could the people whom I have connections with possibly compare to the scope of—"

"It's the individuals whom you are connected with,"

said Glav. He sighed and lowered his gaze. "I have a confession to make, Quark."

Quark looked at him questioningly.

"When I came to this station," he said, "I was . . . Well, my motives were not particularly honorable."

"So?" The concept of honorable motives did not have much importance in Quark's worldview.

"I came here," sighed Glav, "because I was very much looking forward to rubbing my good fortune in your face. I wanted to parade my success before you, make you squirm, perhaps even dangle a business proposition in your face . . . and then depart. It was . . ." He shook his head. "It was petty vindictiveness."

"It's understandable," said Quark.

Glav looked up in surprise. "Why, Quark . . . you're not even being obsequious. You really *do* understand."

"Squirming, vindictiveness . . . pfaw. What's not to understand?"

"If you understand that, then certainly the subsequent events will be well within your comprehension as well. For as I was walking around this incredible station, I had a realization. And my greed, I will admit, came bubbling to the surface. It was a heady feeling, Quark. With the amount of money at my command, my sense of pure greed had become . . . stilted. Lost."

Quark gasped. "You poor bastard."

"You know, I hadn't even realized I'd lost it. That's the truly tragic thing. It's far too simple to become content. Beware contentment, Quark. It can lead to your undoing."

Quark shifted uneasily in his chair. "Well, I am . . . I am happy with my situation in life. But," he said more firmly, "but content? No. No, never. I always dream of riches. Of *the deal,*" he said reverently.

"The deal," said Glav, "sits before you. Look at me, Quark. I hold the key to the deal."

Quark stared at him for a long moment.

And then suspicion played across his face.

"This *is* a scam," he said slowly.

Glav looked confused. "What?"

"It is!"

"Quark! I have been honest with you!"

"Ah, but here it comes!" Quark raised his voice in anger and alarm. "The scam! The sting! Put me off my guard with sweet words and then persuade me to participate in some insane enterprise in the hope of improving my station in life. When, in fact, your real intention is to deprive me of—"

"I'm not going to deprive you of anything!" said Glav in confusion.

Quark sat back, his fingers interlaced, looking confident and smug. "How much?" he said. "How much were you going to ask me to contribute to whatever scheme you were launching? Eh? Enough to put my entire establishment at risk? Or—"

"Nothing!" cried Glav. "Nothing, I swear! I . . ." His face turned dead serious. "I swear on Amorphous, the shaper of Ferengi dreams of avarice, that I was not going to ask you to put your establishment—or any of your personal fortune, however paltry that might be—at risk in any way."

Quark's jaw dropped. A Ferengi did not swear by Amorphous lightly. Even among the Ferengi, certain things were simply not done, and lying to another Ferengi in the name of Amorphous was one of them. It was enough to restore Quark's confidence to some degree.

"All right," he said slowly. "All right. What can I contribute? I don't understand."

"This station," said Glav, barely able to repress his rising excitement. "This station . . . for pity's sake, Quark, look at it. The potential, Quark. The *potential!* I've been doing a study of it. Projecting across the probable expansion of the business that will come through here as a result of the Bajoran wormhole. Furthermore, I've been analyzing the percentage of effectiveness in the way that business is being done here. Would you like to know what I've found?"

Quark nodded eagerly.

"There is potential here," he said, "for increasing profits . . . thirteen hundred percent!" Upon Quark's startled intake of breath, he nodded his head. "Yes, you heard me right. Under the right management . . . under the right mind-set . . . this station could be the single largest profit generator in this entire sector."

"Under the right management? But the Federation—"

"The Federation!" Glav laughed coarsely. "The Federation! Oh, please, Quark. If you want a painfully boring continuation of the status quo, you call in the Federation. But if you want profit"—he tapped his chest—"you call a Ferengi."

"But . . . no one called us."

"We Ferengi do not sit around waiting for the deal to come to us. We find the deal. We exploit the deal. We"—he thumped his fist on the tabletop to emphasize each word—"we make . . . the . . . deal. There are those in this universe to whom things happen. And there are others who make things happen. Which would you be, Quark?"

"Well . . . obviously, the latter."

"Then you will help me?"

"Help you what?"

"What! Isn't it obvious?" He smiled toothily. "I want to buy Deep Space Nine."

Quark stared at him skeptically for a moment. "You . . . you aren't serious?"

"Why wouldn't I be serious?"

"Well, because . . . for pity's sake, Glav! It's not for sale!"

"Have you asked?"

"No! Of course not."

"Ah," said Glav, leaning forward, "but you see, it's amazing what's for sale if the price is right. And I'll tell you right now, Quark, what we Ferengi already know: when the price is right, *anything* is for sale. That is where you come in."

"It is?" Quark sounded less than enthusiastic.

"Yes. Because you are going to be able to use your influence to help." For a moment he seemed uncertain. "You *do* have influence, don't you?"

"Uh . . . why, yes, of course." Quark gathered his composure. "The fact of the matter is that I am one of the major influences on this station. Why," he continued, becoming more full of himself by the moment, "just last month, all the station personnel were ill. Whom did they turn to in their hour of need?" He thumped his chest proudly. "I ran the entire station single-handed."

"Now you're boasting."

"I swear! There I was, all alone in Ops, holding things together. And then there was the time when I became the very first source of relics brought through the wormhole. I held an auction here that they're still talking about throughout the sector."

"Then you can help me."

"I—"

At that moment, an irritated Orion shouted, "Quark! You call this a drink?"

Seeing the source of the complaint, Quark turned to Glav apologetically. "I hate to break off, but I fear I really must attend to this. The last time an Orion was dissatisfied, the damage took me a week to repair."

"I understand fully. We'll talk later."

Quark slid off the chair and headed toward the disgruntled Orion. Glav, for his part, walked away humming to himself, looking around the station as if trying to figure out where he was going to redecorate.

And the table that they'd been sitting at, unseen by either of them, shifted. Within moments it had dissolved into a puddle and then built itself back up again to become the distinctive form of the station's security officer.

Odo shook his head.

"What fools these Ferengi be," he muttered.

Rasa looked around the infirmary with curiosity. "What is this place?" he asked.

"It's where we treat the sick," Bashir told him, trying to look casual. He watched as Rasa opened a cabinet and stared in fascination at the contents. "Certainly you've seen places like this before."

"No," said Rasa. "I've never had the need."

"Hmm. Well, you're a lucky young man. Never to be sick a day in your life."

He waited until Rasa's interest in the cabinets seemed to flag and then he said, "You know what this is?" And he tapped the monitors up on the wall over a bed.

Rasa shook his head.

"All sorts of lights come on," said Bashir. "Here . . . watch. Hop up onto this bed and lie down."

Rasa, curious about the equipment, did as he was told. As he lay back, the bioscan units came on. Readings immediately began feeding into the diagnostic files of the computers. Oblivious of what was happening, Rasa twisted around so that he could see the blinking lights and the source of the noises. "What's that thumping sound?" he asked.

"That's your heartbeat. It . . . sounds a little fast," said Bashir, still endeavoring to seem casual. "Fast for an Edemian, at any rate. Tell me, Rasa, does your head ever hurt?"

"Sometimes."

"When?"

"Oh . . . in the morning. And a little at night. And . . . sometimes in the middle of the day." Rasa was starting to sound uncomfortable. "I thought you wanted to talk about K'olkr."

"Well," said Bashir reasonably, "if I'm supposed to learn a bit about your life . . . seems only fair that you learn a bit about mine, don't you think?"

Rasa started to sit up, and Bashir moved quickly to his side, holding his shoulder down gently to prevent him from rising. "Let me go!" shouted Rasa, but he didn't have the strength to back up his command.

And then he started to cough.

It was a deep, hacking sound. The exertion had cost him, and he coughed more and more violently. Within seconds the hacking became so fierce that his legs flexed upward while his upper torso cramped over, as if he were curling into a fetal position with each sudden expulsion of air.

"Nurse!" called Bashir. He started to order a hypo that would settle Rasa down, but ultimately it proved unnecessary. Rasa stopped of his own accord, the coughing settling down until the fit simply ended. Rasa looked up at Bashir then, and the glow in his eyes seemed just a bit dimmer.

"Are you all right?" asked Bashir.

Rasa nodded. But he didn't look all right, and he didn't sound all right.

"I didn't mean to upset you," the doctor said.

"It's all right," said Rasa. He swung his legs over and slid off the biobed. "I . . . think I'd better go back to my parents now."

"Don't you want to discuss K'olkr?"

Rasa studied him. "I . . . don't really think that you do."

"How about you?"

The boy let out a long sigh that Bashir feared, for a moment, would set off another fit. But instead Rasa simply shrugged fatalistically.

"No. Not really."

And he walked out of the infirmary.

Lobb studied the passersby carefully to see who might be amenable to hearing the message, the word, the glory, of K'olkr.

The follower of Mas Marko then thought he saw a likely candidate—an attractive young woman who looked lost and adrift on the sea of humanoid consciousness.

She was walking away from Quark's, holding a drink as if it were her last friend in the cosmos. Merely looking upon her, Lobb felt tremendous empathy.

K'olkr seemed to whisper to Lobb, saying, "Yes! Yes! She is one for whom you've been waiting. She will be your first convert to the wisdom of K'olkr. You can do it. Steady. Speak to her in soft, alluring terms that will draw her to you."

As she passed nearby, Lobb raised his voice in vehemence that surprised even him. "K'olkr wants you!" he called out. "K'olkr loves you! You, young woman!"

She stopped in her tracks. She turned her head slowly to stare at him.

"Your life," he said, his fervor rising, "can be a beautiful and splendid thing. Your life can be beyond anything you might have imagined possible. Your life can be sanctified, glorified, purified, if you accept, understand, and embrace the wisdom of K'olkr!"

He stretched out a hand to her, gesturing for her to come over to him.

She regarded him for a moment more and then— slowly, ever so slowly—approached him . . .

And then she raised the glass and hurled its contents at him.

The liquid hit Lobb square in the chest. A huge stain spread in no time, the red liquid pouring down his chest and trickling to his waist. He stared at it in stupefaction.

"My life is fine as it is, fool," she said tartly. "Maybe you're the one who should be reevaluating your life. Standing around shouting things at people who didn't ask you to come and don't want you here."

She turned on her heel and walked away.

Lobb stood there, unmoving, not certain what to say or do. He felt utterly humiliated in front of Mas Marko. He was all too aware of his leader and mentor's presence looming over him.

Sadly, Mas Marko put a hand on Lobb's shoulder. "I'm sorry, Lobb. I'm afraid that the realities of our mission aren't going to be particularly easy to deal with."

"Why . . ." Lobb seemed to grope for words. "Why do they hate us so much?"

"They hate themselves," Mas Marko told him. "We hold up a mirror to the emptiness and misery of their lives. They see what they have . . . see the meaninglessness and misery of a life without the spirit of K'olkr . . . and the vast majority of them react with hostility. The truth can be very difficult to accept, but a very small number will see what we have to offer and be drawn to it. It is for those few that we commit our lives to constant labor."

Lobb nodded understandingly. Unfortunately none of it made him feel any drier or any less humiliated.

Azira had listened without comment to all her husband had said. But now she perked up slightly as she saw Rasa heading across the great open area of the Promenade. "Rasa," she called. "Darling! Over here!" And she waved.

63

"He knows where we are, Azira," said Marko. He didn't sound harsh or angry, but something in his voice indicated quite clearly that he found her behavior inappropriate.

Azira folded her hands into her gown, accepting her husband's mild rebuke. But when Rasa walked up to them, Azira put an arm around him protectively and gazed up at her husband with an expression that might have been called deliberately blank.

Mas Marko ignored it. "Rasa," he asked, "how did it go with the Starfleet man?"

Rasa didn't say anything at first. Marko looked at him curiously and then said, with more firmness in his voice, "Rasa, I believe I asked you a question."

"I don't know, Father."

"You don't know how it went?"

"No, Father."

Marko was silent for a long moment. "Is there something you're not telling me?"

"Mas Marko," Azira said, choosing to use the full formal address since they were out in public. "I think the boy is too tired to concentrate right at this moment."

"Is that the case, boy? That you are too tired?"

The boy looked down at the toes of his boots with great interest. "Yes, Father."

"I see. Very well." He turned to Lobb. "Would you be so kind as to escort Rasa back to our quarters and make certain that he settles down for some rest? You can take the opportunity to go to your own quarters as well and change to something . . . drier."

"Thank you, Mas Marko," said Lobb. He was just starting to feel the uncomfortable dampness and chill from the liquid, and was rather eager to change out of the sodden clothes.

They walked away, and as Mas Marko watched them

go, he was aware of Azira stepping a bit closer to him than was typical for public behavior. But he did nothing to discourage her, for he knew what was on her mind, and he was not, after all, without feelings or heart.

"He looks so small," she whispered. "So small."

Mas Marko shook his great head. "K'olkr moves in mysterious ways," he said. He tried to keep the sadness from his voice, but was only partially successful.

Rasa had settled down easily enough. Indeed, "settled down" might have been too mild a phrase. When the boy lay down on his bed, Lobb saw that Rasa was asleep almost before his head hit the pillow.

Satisfied that his mission had been successfully completed, Lobb stepped out of the quarters that Mas Marko was sharing with his wife and son and started to head to his own across the hall.

There was a man standing there.

He had thick red hair, and his face was fixed in a sullen deadpan. His chin came to a point; indeed, his entire face looked like a perfect triangle. He was not particularly tall, not particularly short, not particularly anything.

He simply stared.

"Can I help you?" asked Lobb.

The man said nothing.

"Are you interested in learning the wisdom of K'olkr?"

Nothing.

Out of reflex Lobb was going to press the point further, but then he became more aware of the sogginess of his clothes. The dampness was becoming uncomfortable, and a chill began to spread through him . . . although some of that chill was possibly a result of the sullen, fixed scrutiny that he was receiving from this odd red-haired man.

"Perhaps we can discuss matters later," he said, not really feeling like prolonging the encounter. He stepped past the red-haired man and, for some reason that he could not readily pinpoint, suddenly tensed as if he expected an abrupt attack.

But there was nothing. The red-haired man made no motion at all, and a few seconds later Lobb was safe in his room.

Safe?

What an odd word to occur to him. Safe. Had he been in danger just then?

The red-haired man had been unarmed and unassuming. What possible threat could he have posed?

Lobb stared into a mirror, looking sadly at the mess on the front of his robe. No wonder he felt paranoid about someone as unthreatening as the red-haired man. Certainly he had not expected to be assaulted by the charming woman whom he had been trying to help. So it wasn't surprising that he was starting to give a second look to everyone he ran into.

Maybe that wasn't such a bad thing. It might help him stay one step ahead of those who would like to see people like him come to harm.

And then he heard something.

It was like . . . something dripping, something thick and gelatinous, slurping around. . . .

He spun.

The door was not airtight. Through the joints now poured some sort of bizarre . . . *stuff*.

"What in the . . ." he managed to get out.

It was viscous and red, bubbling into a large puddle on the floor. Lobb was afraid to touch it, for he had no idea what it might do to him. But it was blocking the exit. If it started to seep toward him, how would he get around it to safety?

He took a step to the side, trying to figure out a way to maneuver around it.

And then, in defiance of any logic, the mass began to grow.

It was as if a tower were rising underneath it, and it took Lobb a few moments to understand that, in fact, the mass was reshaping *itself.*

It grew, expanded, began to fill out, and then took on definition. He could see the outlines of arms close to the sides of a body, a head starting to form, features coming into existence.

The red-haired man.

Lobb rubbed his eyes, trying to deny what they had already told him.

The glubbing and slurping sounds ceased. The man was now fully formed in Lobb's room, studying him with detached interest.

"Who in the name of K'olkr are you?" whispered Lobb. "What do you want?"

The red-haired man gave a reply . . . but it was not verbal.

He drew back his right arm, and it re-formed.

It became a cube-shaped mass, square and gleaming, like a solid block of metal.

Lobb gaped, not comprehending.

And the red-haired man took four quick steps forward, like a bowler about to release a ball. The movement of his right arm was fast, smooth, and liquid as he slammed it forward.

Lobb had just enough time to emit a high-pitched, terrified scream. And then the hand-weapon took him squarely in the face, driving the young Edemian back. And then it kept on going, before Lobb even had a chance to scream, and connected solidly with the wall. Lobb's cranium, unable to offer the slightest resistance, collapsed with the sound of a crushed melon.

The red-haired man remained in that position for a moment, as if admiring his work or waiting for photographers to take pictures. Then he withdrew the anvillike

PETER DAVID

fist, paying no attention to the sickening thud of Lobb's remains to the floor. The red of the drink that had been tossed onto Lobb's robe now mingled with the dark tint of his life's blood.

A massive smear of blood had spread over the wall.

The killer stared at it for a moment and then extended a finger toward it.

And he began to write.

CHAPTER
6

"HE WANTS TO WHAT?"

Sisko seemed unsure whether to laugh or not. Odo, for his part, tended to take everything seriously. No one could quite recall ever hearing him laugh at anything.

They were in the commander's office, and now Sisko was indeed starting to laugh. But it was more of an abrupt bark of amusement. "He wants to what?" he said again.

"You heard me, Sisko," said Odo sharply. "He wants to buy Deep Space Nine."

Sisko pondered that a moment. "What sort of offer is he planning to make?"

Odo tilted his head, not quite understanding. Seeing the shapeshifter's confused look, Sisko said, "Well . . . we want to know if he's going to make it worth our while. How much do you think we can get for this station?"

"Sisko!"

"Well, you don't think we should simply dismiss the offer out of hand, do you? Where would the sense be in that?"

Odo looked hard at him. "This is one of those joke things, isn't it?"

"Well . . . I admit I'm not being entirely serious, if that's what you mean. Perhaps the Ferengi were playing a joke on you, Constable. Is it possible they knew you were there?"

"Hardly." Odo sniffed.

"Ah, well." Sisko allowed a smile. "Relax, Constable. You have to admit, with all the difficulties we've had to deal with on DS-Nine, handling a Ferengi who wants to buy it from us is rather lightweight."

"I suppose," allowed Odo. "It is fairly nonsensical. Of all the Ferengi schemes I've had to short-circuit in the past, this is certainly one of the most ludicrous."

"It's not even a scheme. It won't require your intervention," said Sisko. "Let them come, make their offer. I'll listen politely, tell them the station's not for sale, and that should be that."

"If I know Quark—and believe me, no one knows him better than I—that is rarely, if ever, that."

Sisko gave the matter some thought. "Have you ever wondered, Constable, what it would be like to be unscrupulous?"

"No," said Odo, sounding faintly puzzled. "Why would I wonder about something like that?"

"Well, imagine it," said Sisko. "We agree to sell the station, fabricate official documents transferring ownership, and then . . . I think the old phrase is 'take the money and run.'"

"I think you're losing your mind, Sisko."

Sisko sighed. "No. Not losing my mind. Just . . . always pondering the possibilities." He eased back in his chair, but did not look comfortable.

Odo wasn't quite sure what to say. Clearly Sisko had something on his mind, but Odo wasn't sure it was something the Starfleet commander wanted to talk about. And even if it was, why should Odo waste his time with it? Let Sisko unburden himself to Dax or someone else. Odo regarded Sisko as, at best, a necessary evil. At worst, a nuisance. A living symbol of an organization whose members wore a holier-than-thou attitude on their uniform sleeves.

Still . . .

"It's Jake, isn't it?" Odo said, feeling some reluctance about mixing into this.

But Sisko actually seemed grateful for the opening, and Odo rationalized it to himself by concluding that ingratiating himself with Sisko now might prove useful in the future, so that Odo would be free to do his job his way.

"It's not easy," said Sisko slowly, "to make decisions in life that you know are right for you . . . when you constantly have to worry about how they're affecting someone else."

"It's Jake," said Odo firmly, his question answered. "Sisko, he's a boy. He knows nothing from nothing."

"He knows he's unhappy. He knows he's scared."

"Of what?"

"Of growing up alone. Of having no friends. Of losing me. I mean, DS-Nine holds challenge for me. What does it hold for him? What does a life in Starfleet hold for him?"

Odo said nothing.

Sisko rose, feeling his temper bubbling, and he suppressed it. Instead he turned it into bleak humor. "I should do it. Sell the station to the Ferengi, then take the money and run. To hell with it."

"I'd probably have to arrest you," said Odo.

Sisko regarded him with mild interest. "I'd like to see you try. I warn you, Constable . . . you'd have your work cut out for you."

"I think I could handle you," Odo told him.

"Don't be so sure. You're looking at the meanest phaser this side of the asteroid belt. Do you know what they called me in Starfleet Academy?"

"Just a guess here: Sisko?"

"They called me Dead-Eye. That was because . . ."

"You were blind in one eye?"

"Nooo. Because I was the best shot there. You're looking at the inventor of the two-cushion phaser ricochet shot. I'd set up a mirror, bounce a phaser shot off it, and still hit the target."

"I see. I don't imagine you've heard the adage about the shortest distance between two points being a straight line."

Sisko stared sadly at Odo. "Constable, you have no sense of adventure at all."

"There are more subtle ways to deal with things than by shooting them, trick shots or no," said Odo. "Unless, of course, you plan to knock some sense into your son's head by bouncing a phaser beam off his cranium."

"That would hardly solve the problem."

"No," Odo said reasonably, "but it would stop him from whining about it."

Before Sisko could respond to that rather mean-spirited comment, Dr. Bashir stuck his head into the office. "Do you have a moment, Commander?"

"We were finished," said Odo, before Sisko could reply. He rose and walked out into the main Ops area.

As Odo passed O'Brien, the chief engineer suddenly said, "Constable!"

"Yes, Chief?"

"Remember how you nailed my sleight of hand before?"

"Yes."

"You have to give me a chance to even things up."

"I do? Why would I have to do that?"

"Because if I can do a trick that will fool you, then I can certainly do tricks to fool Molly."

"Ah. You feel that I have the same deductive capabilities as your tot. I see."

But O'Brien wasn't listening. He had produced a deck of cards and was rapidly shuffling them. Before Odo could make clear that he wasn't remotely interested in participating, O'Brien held the cards up in a fan. "Pick a card," he said.

"Why?"

"So I can do the trick."

"Oh, very well." He pointed to one card, facing down like all the others. "That one."

"All right. Look at the card."

Odo stared at it.

From nearby, Dax watched in mild amusement. Kira tuned out the entire business, concentrating on charting the flux in the emissions from the wormhole.

"What are you doing?" asked O'Brien, barely hiding his impatience.

"I'm looking at the card," replied Odo, who was making no effort at all to hide his impatience.

"I *meant* take it out of the deck and look at it," said O'Brien, and then added quickly, "and then replace it without telling me which one it is."

Odo did as he was told. O'Brien then reshuffled the deck, fanned the cards once more, and then triumphantly produced a seven of hearts.

"Is this your card?" he asked.

"No," said Odo.

O'Brien's face fell, but only for a moment. He gamely sorted through the deck once more and this time produced the two of clubs. "Is this your card?"

"No."

They stared at each other.

"Devil take it," muttered O'Brien. "Maybe I should just take up juggling."

* * *

Bashir held his medical padd in front of him as if it were a shield. On it were all the medical records that the biobed had discerned from young Rasa and the diagnosis that Bashir had developed in tandem with the resources of the computer.

"Are you sure?" Sisko asked him.

"Yes, sir," said Bashir. "It's called panoria. It's a viral condition, and extremely debilitating. Most Edemians have a natural immunity to it. About three percent do not. The short-term effects of this illness are general malaise, easy exhaustion, and an overall negative effect on the metabolism. In the long term . . . it is much worse. In less than a year it causes a gradual shutdown of the entire metabolic process. The patient becomes an invalid . . . for the brief period of time that is left him."

"It's terminal, then." Sisko's voice sounded like the chime of doom, even to him.

"If left untreated, yes. Most definitely."

"I'll order Rasa quarantined immediately."

"Not necessary, sir," Bashir said with conviction. "Panoria is unique to Edemians and two other races, neither of whom are present in Deep Space Nine; for that matter, they don't even possess sufficient technological capabilities to travel this far. Rasa may be a danger to himself . . . but not to others."

"You said, 'if left untreated.' Does that mean the boy can be saved?"

"Absolutely," said Bashir firmly. "I've checked over our medical stock, and I can very easily synthesize the elements required. We would have to start him on medication immediately. Ideally, it should have been started several weeks ago."

"Several *weeks?* Doctor, how long has the boy been ill?"

"The symptoms would have easily been noticeable" —Bashir paused, counting backwards in terms of the usual known progress of the disease—"three weeks ago.

Elevated pulse rate, nausea, fever, malaise, aches and pains . . ."

"Why in the world hasn't the boy been treated already?"

"I'm hardly in a position to answer that, sir," said Bashir.

"In that case, let's go ask the people who are."

He rose and came from around his desk, but as he and Bashir approached the office exit, Odo appeared in the doorway.

"Another problem, Constable?" asked Sisko.

"That," said Odo, "is putting it mildly."

One of Odo's security men was standing there at the entrance to Lobb's quarters arguing with Mas Marko when Odo, Sisko, and Bashir walked up. The security man, Meyer by name, looked relieved upon Odo's arrival.

Marko turned to face Sisko and Odo. "Commander," he rumbled, "your man is being uncooperative." He pointed a large ebony finger at Meyer.

"Following your orders, sir," Meyer said flatly. "No civilians in or out. Boyajian and Tang are in there now with the . . . victim."

"Who filed the report?"

"Passerby, sir. Said she heard a scream. We checked it out and found . . . the situation."

"This is the quarters of one of my people," said Mas Marko firmly, his voice rising and sounding more and more dangerous. "If one of them has been injured or is in any sort of peril, I must go in immediately. Now, in the name of K'olkr, let me pass!"

Sisko didn't exactly ignore him. But he was clearly not about to be intimidated by him, either.

"Is the room secure?" Odo asked.

"Yes, sir," Meyer said. "No one was seen leaving, and our people have the room sealed off."

"All right," said Sisko. "Let us in. Mas Marko, wait out here, please."

"I—"

Sisko's glare was palpable. "Wait out here, please." His tone was flat and unyielding.

Marko said nothing. He did, however, glower more fiercely than anyone Sisko had ever met, with the possible exception of Odo himself.

Odo seemed to have forgotten Marko entirely. He entered the room with Sisko and Bashir right behind him. The door rolled shut.

Sisko was immediately hit by the stench of death. He had encountered it so many times in his life that it seemed to be permanently embroidered on the inside of his nostrils.

But this . . .

This was beyond the pale.

Boyajian and Tang were going over the quarters with tricorders, trying to stay as far from the body as possible. Bashir leaned over the corpse, running his medical tricorder over it and clearly fighting to maintain his medical dispassion. That was not easy.

It was hard to find anywhere on the floor to step that was not thick with blood. The head had been crushed beyond recognition—as brutal and hideous a death as Bashir had witnessed in his brief medical career.

"I take it cause of death is the obvious?" Sisko tried not to shudder as he looked upon Lobb's corpse.

"Massive, catastrophic head trauma," said Bashir. "The victim was definitely one of the Edemians."

"Before we let Mas Marko in here," observed Odo, "we'd better make damned sure he has a strong stomach. Boyajian, Tang . . . go over every centimeter of this place. Take it apart molecule by molecule if you have to. I want this killer found, and found immediately. Nobody gets away with this on my station. Nobody."

"Constable," said Sisko, "what, precisely, do you make of this?"

Odo stepped over to the wall, to see what Sisko was pointing at. "I saw it the second we came in," he said in a low voice. "It was impossible to miss."

On the wall, etched with Lobb's own blood, was a large number one.

"Crosshatch followed by an Arabic numeral," said Sisko. "The killer was human."

"Either that," said Odo, "or the killer wanted to make sure that the human commander of this station got the message."

"And in your opinion, Constable . . . what is that message?" But he was afraid he already knew the answer, and Odo confirmed it.

"Where there's a number one," said Odo slowly, "there's usually a number two, a number three, and so on. Sisko . . . we'd better catch this lunatic fast. We might very well have a serial killer loose on Deep Space Nine."

CHAPTER
7

MAS MARKO AND AZIRA sat in their quarters. There was a dim expression of shock on Azira's face, but Mas Marko had his carefully neutral mein on display.

Bashir sat facing them, while Sisko and Odo stood slightly behind him.

"Poor Lobb," Azira was saying in a hushed voice. "It . . . it doesn't even seem possible. We . . . we just saw him. K'olkr . . . Marko, we're responsible."

"Don't be absurd," Mas Marko said calmly.

"How do you figure that, Azira?" asked Sisko.

Her hands moved in vague, undefined patterns. "We . . . we sent him back here with Rasa. We sent him to where his murderer was waiting for him. If it hadn't been for us—"

"You can't blame yourself," said Sisko. "There was no way that you—that anyone—could possibly have known."

"Listen to the commander, Azira," Mas Marko told her.

Marko had been all bluster earlier when Sisko finally emerged from the quarters and agreed to let him in. But upon entering, he had become very quiet. He had knelt over the lifeless body of his follower and murmured prayers for five minutes, asking K'olkr to accept and cleanse the soul of the extremely worthy, extremely young, and extremely unfortunate missionary. He had spoken with such fervor that Sisko had found himself rather moved.

Faith, thought Sisko, was a nice thing to be able to cling to in a universe where nothing made any sense.

Kind of a shame he still had trouble with the concept.

Mas Marko turned back to Sisko. "Do you have any clues as to the murderer yet?"

Sisko turned toward Odo. "We have some promising leads," said Odo confidently.

Sisko knew this was total fabrication. Odo's security guards had been over every inch of the place. They had not turned up even the slightest clue as to who might have gained entry into the quarters, killed Lobb, and escaped. "It might as well have been a ghost, for all we know," Odo had said in irritation.

But Odo spoke with confidence now. "It's only a matter of time. That's certain."

"Commander," Mas Marko said gravely, "we have a slight situation on our hands. Our beliefs call for a funeral within twelve of your hours after the deceased's soul has passed to be with K'olkr. We would like to return to Edema—"

"I'm afraid that's not possible," said Sisko.

They stared at him. "Whyever not?" asked Azira.

It was Odo who responded. "We're in the midst of a murder investigation," he said sharply. "No one will be allowed to depart the station until we have our killer safely locked up."

"You . . ." Azira looked stunned. "You would . . . *keep* us here? With some madman running around, capable of such . . . such hideous deeds, you would force us to stay here and be at risk?" She turned to her husband pleadingly. "Marko, tell them they can't do this."

But Marko was studying Odo thoughtfully. "You were lying before, weren't you, sir?" he said. "You don't have the slightest idea who was responsible for Lobb's death. I, my wife, Del . . . everyone on board this station is equally likely to be the perpetrator. You can't let us go because you have no more reason to believe that we did not do this . . . this hideous thing . . . than the lowliest of the liquor-guzzling slime that crawls through your Promenade. Isn't that so?"

"We have several promising leads," Sisko said flatly. "But with something like this, Starfleet has very, very specific procedures that we must follow. And we will follow them, even if it means keeping you here."

"And exposing us to the same hideous fate that claimed Lobb," said Azira tonelessly. "How . . . how could you—"

But Mas Marko put up a hand, and Azira once again lapsed into silence. Then his voice resonated in the quarters, as if he were giving a benediction. "If this is how you must proceed, Commander, then that is the way it must be. We are followers of the word of K'olkr. We trust that he will guide us through this . . . this dreadful business, just as he will guide you to the heartless creature that perpetrated this crime. And when he does . . . we will ask K'olkr to forgive him."

"Praise K'olkr in all things," whispered Azira, her hands wrapped around Mas Marko's arm. It was a far more overt action than she would have taken normally with outsiders present, but clearly she felt confused and frightened by the entire business.

"But if we are to be confined here, Commander . . . then I must request that we be allowed to conduct funeral services for Lobb." He looked saddened. "To be truthful, he had no family. No loved ones, besides those within the Order. No one except us, truly, to mourn for him. Perhaps, indeed, it is part of K'olkr's grand plan that he be interred here in space . . . to wander forever, in body if not spirit. Would that be acceptable to you, Commander?"

"Of course," said Sisko. "Tell me what your requirements are, and I'll made the arrangements."

"If we're done here," Odo said, "I have a murder investigation to conduct."

Sisko nodded to him, and Odo walked out.

Mas Marko looked at the Starfleet men with a slight question on his face, clearly not understanding why they were still there.

Sisko looked to Bashir significantly, giving a silent cue as to what he was going to say next. Bashir nodded, showing that he understood. "Mas Marko," said Sisko, "Azira . . . there is something else we must discuss."

"Something else?" said Marko, sounding suddenly tired. "More joyous news to share with us?"

"It's . . . about your son. Dr. Bashir here—"

"Doctor?" Marko looked up at him, and his eyes narrowed. "Ah. Now, isn't that a remarkable coincidence."

"What do you mean?"

"Nothing, Commander. Pray continue." But his face hardened, and Sisko suddenly felt a chill pass through him.

"Your son and I were in the infirmary chatting," said Bashir. "Did Rasa tell you?"

"No."

"Yes, well . . . one thing led to another, and I happened to run a standard exam on him . . ."

"Indeed. Doctor"—Mas Marko rose, towering over the two men—"shall we end this shadow dance? Will you tell me what you found . . . or shall I tell you?"

Sisko and Bashir looked at each other. This wasn't precisely the way they had anticipated this going.

"Panoria," said Bashir flatly. "It's a viral infection, potentially deadly."

"Is that the name for it?" said Marko, sounding only mildly interested. "Thank you for telling us."

"Were you aware of your son's condition?" asked Sisko.

"We were aware that he is not the healthy young man he once was," said Marko. "That, we knew."

"Well, there's good news, then," said Bashir. "You're lucky that we caught it. That we were able to diagnose the illness. Bring Rasa to the infirmary, and I can start him on medication immediately. We'll have him out of danger in no time at all."

"As out of danger as he could be, considering that there's a capricious murderer stalking your station," Marko said.

"That's hardly the point."

"Yes. Yes, you are quite right, Commander. Indeed, not the point at all." Marko steepled his fingers, as if trying to determine how best to phrase what was going through his mind. "Gentlemen, your . . . zeal is appreciated. But I must ask you not to interfere."

It took a moment for his comment to sink in fully. Sisko tried not to gape, but he was quite clearly stunned. "I . . . beg your pardon?"

"I said you must not interfere," repeated Marko. "That is not too difficult for you to understand, is it?"

"Mas Marko," said Sisko carefully, "perhaps Dr. Bashir did not make himself clear. Without treatment . . . your son will die."

Mas Marko laughed.

It was not a cold, unfeeling laugh, but rather one that seemed to speak of a bitter, ironic grasp of the situation. "And you are saying that, if he receives this treatment, he will never die? Is that it?"

"Of course not," Bashir spoke up. "We're not saying

he'll *never* die. That's absurd. We're saying that it need not happen now. That's all."

"These things happen in their own time and in the time that is accorded to them by K'olkr. Isn't that right, Azira?"

"As you say, Marko," she said. It was the softest that Sisko had ever heard a woman speak.

"Mas Marko . . . you're saying that you do *not* want us to aid your son?"

"That is correct."

"But . . . *why?*"

"He is in the best of all possible hands," said Mas Marko serenely. "He is in the hands of K'olkr. K'olkr will determine his fate, as he will determine the fate of all things."

"This is absurd!" Bashir snapped.

Sisko said warningly, "Doctor . . ."

But Bashir didn't seem to be listening. "You want me to just stand aside and *let* him die? When medicine can still save him? What . . . what sort of monster are you?"

"Doctor," Sisko said again, this time in a tone so dangerous that it caught Bashir's attention. But the young surgeon was still clearly roiling with barely suppressed anger.

"Apparently you are having difficulty understanding this," said Mas Marko. "I do not see why, however. Certainly the concept of noninterference should not be alien to you, Doctor. Nor to you, Commander. I have some passing familiarity with the ways of the Federation and Starfleet. And, as I recall, doesn't your primary law stipulate noninterference?"

Sisko nodded.

"And it is a good law. A solid law. A law that is in existence," said Marko, "to prevent you from unknowingly forcing your own unasked-for assistance upon others. It is a law in which you are saying, in essence: we will not mix into those affairs that may not be ours to understand. Is that not right?"

"In a manner of speaking," said Sisko.

"We are guided by similar beliefs, Commander. Matters of sickness and health, life and death . . . these are within the purview of K'olkr. We may not gainsay him. We may not interfere with him. That is clear. All life comes from K'olkr. He decides when we are put into this sphere, and he decides when we depart it. And no one—not you, not my beloved Azira—no one has the right to question him on matters such as these."

"I'm not asking you to question your god's actions."

"He's your god, too, Doctor," said Marko serenely. "You simply aren't aware of that yet."

"Fine, whatever. But as I said, I'm not asking you to question his actions. I don't want you to compromise your beliefs. All I'm asking you to do is save your son."

"K'olkr gave us our son," Mas Marko said. "If K'olkr chooses to take our son as well, then that is the affair of K'olkr. We must have faith that his decision is based on his great understanding of his master plan."

"*What* master plan?" said Bashir. "You don't know what this master plan is."

"Exactly the point, Doctor. If we knew what the master plan was, why . . . we would be K'olkr. But we are not, quite obviously. We are mere mortals. And it is not fit for us to interfere with that plan. If we were to do so," he said gravely, "it would be an indication to K'olkr that we had lost faith in him. That we did not believe there was a master plan. That we had acted against his wishes."

"Mas Marko, I have a son, too," said Sisko. "I know how I would feel if he were dying."

"Don't seek to compare your sorrow to mine, Commander," said Mas Marko. "Mine is no less than yours. Do not presume to think that my son is less dear to me than yours is to you."

"He's your son, dammit!"

"And he's K'olkr's as well." Mas Marko no longer seemed upset, but merely sad—sad that Sisko and Bashir had so much difficulty grasping a simple truth that was so clear and unvarnished to him. "K'olkr loves Rasa no less than I. In truth, he loves him more. After all, Azira and I could but ask for a son to be given to us. K'olkr was the one who actually gave him. And if K'olkr chooses to take him back, then all we can do is praise him and be grateful for the time he gave us with Rasa. And I am afraid, Commander, that that is really all we have to say on the subject."

Bashir turned to Azira, trying to fight down the desperation he felt creeping through him. "Azira, do you agree with this . . . this philosophy? The child grew in you. He—"

"That's enough, Doctor," Sisko said.

"I hold my beliefs no less dear than my husband does," said Azira softly. "No less dear, I would think, than you do your own, Doctor. I do not think you would appreciate it if I stood here and exhorted you to violate your doctrines. I would ask you, then, to extend me the same consideration."

And she said nothing more.

They strode down the corridor, Bashir walking double time to keep up with Sisko's long, determined stride. "You're supposed to be the expert," Sisko was saying. "How could you be so familiar with the Edemian race and still be totally unaware that their religion would prevent you from treating their illnesses?"

"I'm a doctor, not a theologian," Bashir said, a bit more sharply than he would have liked. "You're not just going to let this happen?"

"I have no choice," Sisko shot back. "You know that, Doctor."

"But—"

"Look, Doctor, we both know that you cannot proceed with any sort of treatment if it's against the wishes of a parent."

"What about Rasa himself? What if—"

"The *parent,* Doctor. And the parents have chosen to invoke the Prime Directive."

"And you're just going to stand aside! What if it were Jake? What if—"

Sisko turned on him, his eyes blazing with anger. "Starfleet Command personnel always have some degree of latitude when it comes to the Prime Directive, Doctor," he said, his voice cold and inflectionless. "We are allowed to use our judgment in cases where there is some room for maneuvering. But this, Doctor, is not one of those times. As much as you and I may dislike the situation, we have been told in no uncertain terms to butt out. This request comes directly from the tenets of their society. We haven't a leg to stand on here. The Prime Directive isn't there for us to obey when we agree with it and ignore it when we don't. You will not ignore the Prime Directive, and you had damned well better not ignore me. Is that understood, Dr. Bashir?"

Bashir felt as if Sisko's glare might bore a hole through his face. He rallied his determination and said simply, "Understood, sir."

"Good. Oh . . . and further tasteless comparisons to my own parental situation will not be appreciated. Is that understood as well." It was not a question.

"Good," Sisko repeated. He walked away, feeling as angry and helpless as Bashir . . . but managing to hide it a lot better.

He walked past a red-haired man and entered the turbolift. The door hissed shut behind him.

The red-haired man watched him go.

CHAPTER
8

KIRA LOOKED UP from her station as the turbolift disgorged its two passengers into Ops. Her face wrinkled in distaste. "Quark, what the hell are you doing up here? And who's your . . . friend?"

"Be on your best behavior, Major," said Quark. "He may very well be your next landlord."

Kira made an exasperated sound and went back to what she was doing. This did not deter Quark and Glav from getting as close to her as they could before she fixed them in their place with a deadly stare.

"Glav, this is Major Kira Nerys," Quark said after a moment, when it became evident that Kira was not going to volunteer any further conversation. "Major, this is Glav." And then, as if he were delivering some major piece of news, he said triumphantly, "Glav has a major business deal in the making."

"Ferengi always have major business dealings in the making," said Kira disdainfully. "If a Ferengi were lying on his deathbed, he'd be saying that he couldn't go because he has to close a deal."

Glav and Quark exchanged astounded looks. "How

does she know our sacred Ferengi death rituals?" whispered Glav.

"Lucky guess. Had to be."

"If you are waiting for the commander," Dax said as she walked by, "I'm not sure when he'll be back. If you'd like, you can set up an appointment to speak with him."

"Yes. Until then, move off, Quark," said Kira in annoyance. "You're clogging up Ops."

But Glav wasn't paying attention to Kira anymore. He was staring fixedly at Dax. She went about her business, but slowly became aware of Glav's intent stare. Slowly she turned to face him. "May I help you?" she asked politely.

"In ways that you could not possibly dream," said Glav.

"This is Lieutenant Dax. Dax, this is Glav."

"A beautiful woman," said Glav admiringly, "covered from head to toe in clothing. You Starfleet women certainly know how to tease."

Dax cocked her head in curiosity. "Kira is fully clothed as well. You made no such remarks about her."

Kira looked up in mild surprise at Dax's comment.

Glav blew air out through his lips. "Bajoran women —ice princesses, the lot of them." Lowering his voice to imply confidentiality, he purred, "It's said their noses look that way because they're so used to wrinkling them in disgust at the thought of sex."

"Okay, that's it!" said Kira. "Security!"

A security guard stepped forward, obviously itching to eject the Ferengi not only from Ops but possibly out of a docking ring airlock.

Sisko picked that moment to return to Ops.

"Commander!" Quark called out even as the security guard advanced on him. "We wanted to have a word with you!"

The security guard stopped in his tracks, unsure whether to carry out Kira's order now that the ranking officer had reappeared in Ops. Sisko, however, was immediately aware that he'd walked in on the middle of something.

He turned to Kira. "Problem, Major?"

"I was having them removed from Ops."

"Why?"

"Because they're unauthorized personnel. Because they're interfering with the smooth running of this station. And because they're obnoxious."

"Good enough. Good day, gentlemen."

The security guard advanced on the Ferengi once more.

Quark stabbed a finger at Sisko and called out, "You don't know what you're passing up here, Sisko! The opportunity of a lifetime! Of a hundred lifetimes!"

Sisko was already heading up to his office, but stopped to face the Ferengi. "The station isn't for sale," he said.

Their faces fell. And as the guard pushed them toward the turbolift, Quark suddenly began to shout, "All right! What was he *this* time? The chair? A glass? Wait . . . the table! Damn! I thought it looked too new! I should have spilled something on it when I had the chance! Can't I have a single private meeting anymore? What sort of station are you running here, Sis—"

His protests were cut off as the turbolift dropped out of sight, although unintelligible shouting was still discernible for some moments after the lift had departed.

Moments later Odo arrived and entered Sisko's office. Sisko summoned Kira in as well, closing the door behind her for privacy.

As first officer, Kira had been apprised of the situation, and she was clearly apprehensive about the threat to the smooth operation of Deep Space Nine. Unfortunately, Odo couldn't do much to allay those concerns. It was clear from the security's man angered expression that he had nothing to offer.

"We're combing the priors of everyone on the station," he said, "but at the moment we've got a full house. In addition to the regular residents, we have over two hundred transients stacked up—some because the wormhole is shut down and others conducting the usual run of slimy business. One thing we don't need, Sisko, is more people piling in here, giving our unwanted resident new targets."

"I'm ahead of you," said Kira. "In addition to the advisories about the wormhole being impassable, I've sent out an update that states we're already filled to capacity and new arrivals will not be welcome." She paused and then said to Sisko, "I hope I did not overstep my bounds, sir. You seemed busy, and I felt that speed was—"

"You could have checked via communicator," said Sisko mildly. "However, Major, since I rely on your judgment in many matters, I hardly see why you shouldn't rely on that selfsame judgment."

Kira nodded briskly in acknowledgment. Even after all this time, she still felt as if she were walking on eggshells with Sisko, never knowing what he was going to take in stride and what he was going to consider a breach of protocol. The man was a complete mystery to her. Then again, so were most humans. For that matter, so were most men.

She thought about Glav's offhand insult to all Bajoran women, and she felt a quick flash of anger. But just as quickly, she suppressed it.

Odo paused, switching gears. "Sisko, rumors are already flying all over the station. Have you considered when you're going to handle the announcement of our little problem?"

"Yes. Right now, as a matter of fact."

"I hope you're not going to tell people to shut themselves up in their quarters until it all blows over."

Sisko looked at him curiously. "Actually, I was going to advise something rather close to that."

Kira also seemed puzzled. "They would be most secure in quarters, wouldn't they? Out of harm's way?"

"Yes, you would think that, wouldn't you?" Odo did not look particularly thrilled. "Sisko . . . Major . . . the one thing I can tell you for certain is that Lobb had locked his door behind him. The killer gained access, murdered him, and then vanished . . . and the door remained sealed from the inside the entire time."

"Ohhh, dear." Sisko leaned forward, rubbing the bridge of his nose. "Not again."

"Again," said Odo. "Advertising that we have another locked-room murder on our hands could very well cause a repeat of what I had to go through last month. I'm not particularly eager for that to happen. Have you ever tried conducting a murder investigation when everyone concerned is shouting for your head?"

"No."

"No. But I have, and we all know that it's not exactly the best way to handle one's affairs. I don't need a station full of paranoid personnel deciding that the only way the murder could have been done is if the killer had the ability to ooze through the cracks in the door. And I wonder who on this station might possess the ability to do such a thing, eh?"

"What are you saying, Odo?" asked Kira. "That we should put people at risk by telling them to conduct business as usual?"

"What risk?" said Odo. "Lobb was killed in the privacy of his room. Whoever or . . . whatever," he added reluctantly, "was responsible for this, it's clear that a locked door probably isn't going to be any protection at all. Safety in numbers, on the other hand, is always advisable . . . whereas panic never is."

Kira and Sisko exchanged looks.

"He has a point, sir," admitted Kira.

"I know," said Sisko. "It goes against my first impulse, but the important thing is not to adopt a siege mentality. If we do, we'll accomplish nothing . . . and we might quite possibly do a great deal of harm."

"Well, whatever we're going to do, we'd better do it quickly, Sisko," Odo advised. "Rumors are already all over the place."

"There are always rumors, Constable." Sisko thought about it a moment more and then rose from his chair. "All right. Business faces, people."

He walked out of his office and down to the operations console. "Attention, all hands," he said.

Immediately Sisko's voice was heard throughout Deep Space Nine. Such wide-ranging pronouncements were rare enough that his voice brought people up short. They attended as if being addressed by the voice of God.

Except, of course, the Edemians, who knew precisely what the voice of God sounded like, and it was definitely not Benjamin Sisko. Mas Marko, his family, and his single remaining retainer were in Marko's quarters praying for guidance and basking in the glow of the inner spirit of K'olkr.

Everyone else was listening to Sisko.

"There has been an incident on DS-Nine," he said. "A body was discovered in the habitat ring, in private quarters in section fourteen. The victim was an Edemian named Lobb. His death"—Sisko paused only a moment before deciding the best way to phrase it—"was not due to natural causes. Suicide has not been ruled out . . . nor has homicide. Security Chief Odo is conducting a full investigation. If anyone has any information pertaining to this occurrence, please report directly to Security Chief Odo. Your cooperation will be appreciated. Please go on about your business. Sisko out."

He stepped back and found Odo looking at him curiously. In a low voice, Odo said, " 'Suicide has not been ruled out'? Sisko, I assume you were simply being coy. You saw the man's skull, or what was left of it. How could that possibly have been suicide? What did he do? Run into the wall head first at warp one?"

"I prefer the word 'discreet' to 'coy,' actually."

"Whatever," said Odo dismissively. "All right. I'm off to see what leads I can turn up in the Promenade. The place is rife with the scum of the sector. If there's anything to be learned, it will probably be there."

"All right."

Sisko started to head back to his office, but O'Brien intercepted him. "Sir, could I speak to you for a moment? A couple of requests . . ."

"Of course, Chief. Oh, and, Constable," he called out just before Odo stepped onto the turbolift. "When you're making your inquiries . . ."

Odo looked at him. "Yes?"

"Try to be coy."

Quark and Glav sat disconsolately in Quark's casino, Glav staring at Quark in a manner that simply dripped disdain.

"Well, that was a superb use of influence," he said. "What the devil happened? I thought you said—"

"It's that Odo's fault," said Quark in irritation. "He hates me. He's always hated me. And that blasted shapeshifter found out about your intentions and had time to go to Sisko and poison him on the whole idea. It doesn't matter how influential I am. If Sisko is unwilling to give the proposal a fair hearing, there's only so much I can do."

"How do you know it was Odo?"

"Because it's *always* Odo," Quark told him, making no effort to keep the exasperation out of his voice. "He's made me his hobby . . . and his hobby is making my life miserable."

"But why, for pity's sake?"

"He hates me," said Quark flatly. "That's all. He just hates me. The fact is . . . he's jealous of me." He turned and spoke a bit louder. "Hear that, Odo? I hope you're disguised as something! I want you to know I'm on to your game!" Bringing his voice back down to normal, he grunted, "It should be obvious why. When people think of Quark, they think of fun. Good company. Good business. Good gaming. Good times. People from all over the station seek me out, and why shouldn't they? Quark's is where the action is.

"But Odo? Nobody's ever happy to see Odo, because when he's heading your way, the chances are that he's coming to arrest you. He's got these beady little eyes that make you feel guilty even if you aren't doing something illicit."

"Remarkable," said Glav. "He's actually made you feel that way?"

"Well . . . not me, specifically," said Quark. "I mean, to be honest . . . there's never been a time when I *wasn't* doing something illicit. But that's not the point. The point is that, with him around to sow the seeds of distrust, it will be difficult, if not impossible, to get anything done."

"He's the only problem?"

"Yes," said Quark firmly.

"Hmm." Glav scratched his chin. "Actually, the Bajoran woman didn't seem particularly fond of you, either."

"Oh, blame that all on me, why don't you! You didn't exactly endear yourself to her with those ice queen comments."

Glav grunted. "It may have been a bit ill-timed," he

acknowledged. "That other woman . . . What was her name? Dax?"

"One of Sisko's closest advisers," said Quark. "She's been by here several times. Very accessible. A marvelous listener."

"Hehh." It was a coarse, nasty laugh—typically Ferengi. "You fancy her."

"I have had my fantasies about her," said Quark. Whereas most individuals of taste kept such things to themselves, the Ferengi paraded their most lewd sexual thoughts in a constant attempt to outdo one another by proving who was more base. "There's one," he said, "in which I have her wrapped from head to toe in robes a foot thick. You can't see any of her flesh. Then I—"

"Quark," said Glav patiently, "we're getting off the track here. Is there anyone else in Ops who works closely with Sisko and who might prove an ally?"

Quark gave it some thought. "Well . . . the most likely candidate is—"

"G'day, Quark," said O'Brien as he walked past.

Quark stood up so quickly he almost knocked the table over. "O'Brien!" he called. "We were just talking about you! Come! Join us!"

"Can't right now," he replied. "In a rush. Maybe later."

"Free drink in it for you!"

O'Brien grinned lopsidedly. "It's a date."

As O'Brien walked away, Quark turned back to Glav and rubbed his hands together zealously. "O'Brien is perfect. He's the chief of operations. His home life is stressed so he tends to hang out here after hours more than the others do. I've given him some advice from time to time. One time"—and he tried not to laugh—"he even wound up risking his life, almost getting his fool head shot off, because of something I said to him."

"He must hang on your every word!"

"He's probably our best shot. The doctor, Bashir,

might also help. He's young and easily influenced. The silver tongue of a Ferengi might persuade him to help us out."

"This sounds promising, Quark." Glav smiled. "Very promising."

Quark looked around uneasily. There was an empty glass on a table next to them. His eyes narrowed. No one was at the table. Just a glass, sitting there, looking rather suspicious.

Abruptly Quark sprang forward, snatched the glass up, and shouted into it. "You hear that, Odo!" he shouted, loud enough to catch the attention of nearby imbibers. "Listen all you want! We have nothing to hide! And you're going to regret the way you've treated me! Do you hear me? Regret it!"

"I hear you perfectly well," said Odo.

Quark blinked, staring at the glass. Then he looked up.

Odo was standing nearby, fixing him with a piercing stare. "The way you were shouting, the entire station probably heard you."

Trying to maintain as much of his somewhat tarnished dignity as he could, Odo picked up a napkin and cleaned out the glass. "Just testing," he said.

Odo stepped forward. "I want to talk with you," he said.

Something in Odo's voice appealed to Quark's nastier nature. He sat himself back down and spread his arms expansively. "I'm here. You're here. You can talk. I can listen. How can I be of service to Deep Space Nine's soon-to-be-former head of security?"

Odo ignored the comment. "I want you to keep your eyes open," he said.

"I generally do," Quark said calmly. "It helps me avoid bumping into furniture."

"I mean," Odo said testily, "that—as much as I hate to admit it—all those who come to this station general-

ly wind up connecting with you in some way, shape, or
form in order to undertake their underhanded dealings.
Quark's has always been something of a watering hole
for the slime and refuse of this sector.''

"They're drawn to the ambience.''

"Yes, as are carrion eaters to corpses. The point is,
Quark, I want you to watch out for anyone who doesn't
seem to have any business dealings here. Someone who
does not contribute to the overall air of depravity that is
so characteristic of your regular clientele. Someone
who, in short, does not fit in.''

For a moment a look of concentration passed over his
face. Then Quark actually started to look excited. "You
know, I have seen someone like that!''

Odo couldn't believe it was going to be that easy.
"Who?''

"You.''

And Quark once again laughed that incredibly irritating Ferengi laugh. This time Glav joined him.

Odo strode away in disgust. And the thing that
disgusted him most was that he had walked right into it.
He had indeed, unknowingly, described himself.

No wonder people seemed suspicious of him. He was
the most suspicious individual on the station. And once
again he had that old feeling of isolation that had been
hammered home to him when he first arrived on Bajor.
Back when he had been considered by one and all to be
nothing more than a freak.

He realized now how little things had changed. Oh,
he had developed more polish, more style. He had
managed to cover his fundamental feeling of isolation
with biting sarcasm and a general disdain for most
things humanoid. All of it contributed to making his
life a bit more livable.

But it didn't make him one bit less of a freak. Just a
smug, self-righteous, self-confident freak.

He walked briskly across the Promenade, passing by

one of the cross-corridors. And he had already gone
past it when something registered on him that he had
glimpsed only out of the corner of his eye.

There had been a man there.

That's all. A man. Nothing special about him. Odo
had glimpsed reddish hair and a sort of angular face, he
thought.

But he had seemed to give Odo a weird sort of look as
he walked past.

That's all.

A weird look.

It was nothing that Odo should have given a second
thought to. Indeed, he was quite used to puzzled stares.
His face had a sort of unfinished look to it that
frequently prompted double takes as unknowing individuals tried to figure out what race he belonged to.

A weird look.

So quick. So . . . so . . .

All of it flashed through Odo's mind as he took
another step on his way. And by the time he had taken
the next step and was already stopping in his tracks, his
mind had processed it.

Recognition.

It hadn't seemed the typical look where someone
stared at Odo in puzzlement, trying to place him,
confused by his bizarre appearance.

This man had looked as if, just for a moment, he
recognized Odo.

But it wasn't someone Odo recognized. Which meant
that it wasn't someone Odo had met, because his
memory for faces bordered on the supernatural.

The entire thought process had taken a grand total of
three seconds. In that time, Odo had skidded to a halt,
backtracked, and stepped into the open end of the
cross-corridor.

No one.

Odo started down the corridor. He walked slowly, taking measured strides.

"Hello," he called to the air. "Excuse me. I'd like to talk with you for a moment."

He followed the corridor until he got to the first junction, and then he stopped. He looked as far to the left and right as he could, and then down the hallway that the red-haired man would have taken if he'd kept going straight ahead.

Nothing. Which meant that he could be just about anywhere.

Odo had absolutely no reason to suspect the man of any wrongdoing. He'd made no threatening gesture, said nothing suspicious . . . nothing at all, in fact. Odo didn't even have enough to seriously question the man, should he find him.

But Odo had long ago learned to trust his instincts. And his instincts were screaming at him that the man he'd spotted was . . . off, somehow. Maybe not by a lot . . . but off.

He tapped his comm badge. "Odo to security," he said. "I want you to keep an eye out for a red-haired man. Somewhat triangular face. Wearing a red jumpsuit with a black crew neck. If you find him, detain him. I'd like to chat with him for a few minutes."

Boyajian's voice came back over the badge. "Is he a suspect, sir?" he asked.

"He's an itch, Boyajian," said Odo. "An itch I want to scratch."

He stood there a moment or two more and then walked away. But moments later, when he rounded a corner, he suddenly swung his head back quickly, as if hoping to catch someone who might now come out of hiding.

Nothing. The corridor remained vacant.

With an annoyed sigh, he left the area.

Long moments passed.

And then a gelatinous ooze started to pour from a vent positioned directly above the intersection of the corridors.

It moved down to the floor, making not the slightest sound. No one was around to see it as it seemed to create a pillar of itself. Then the pillar started to re-form, to acquire shape. . . .

CHAPTER
9

KEIKO COULD NOT UNDERSTAND why her husband was hovering near the doorway to her schoolroom. He'd never shown any inclination toward meeting her there when classes were over. What in the world had gotten into him?

Keiko had been having trouble obtaining regular child care lately, so Molly had been coming with her to the school. It was working out better than she had thought. Molly had her own table, of course. She watched in delight as color shapes flashed in front of her eyes, and she manipulated the controls to get them to overlap properly.

Jake Sisko was maintaining polite interest in Keiko's classes. He was a bit of an erratic student. His general and obvious dissatisfaction with his situation in life acted as something of a barrier. When she managed to find ways to get around that and penetrate his mind—to touch his imagination and his interest—he could do excellent work. Keiko regarded his attitude not as a failure on his part—discontentment aboard Deep Space Nine was something with which she could easily empathize—but rather as an ongoing challenge for herself as a teacher.

Nog had not deigned to show up this day. Jake said Nog had mentioned that he felt sick. Keiko had a feeling that what made Nog ill was, quite simply, school. Still, she felt encouraged by one aspect of the situation: Commander Sisko had expressed concern to her, privately, that the Ferengi boy, Nog, was having an adverse effect on Jake. On the one hand Sisko wanted to terminate the association; on the other, how could he forbid Jake to see the one kid who was close to his age?

But if Nog was cutting school and Jake was there, then it would seem to indicate that Jake wasn't always immediately in Nog's orbit, that he was capable of thinking for himself. If that was the case, then perhaps Sisko could worry a little less . . . at least about this.

Other children would show up or not show up, depending on whether their parents felt they had something more pressing for them to do. But one regular was a nine-year-old Bajoran girl named Dina. Her mother, Bena, was unmarried and had been eking out a living as a day worker in the mines. She was now working heavy loaders in the docking ring. Keiko's heart would always go out to Bena whenever she saw her at the end of the day looking tired and haggard. She wished she could do more for the woman than simply teach the child. Then again, it was more than anyone else seemed to be doing for her.

She glanced again at Miles, who was trying his best to look nonchalant. But at the same time he had an air of vigilance about him as if he was preparing for some sort of attack at any moment.

Keiko put her husband out of her mind for a moment as she turned back to the class. "All right," she said. "That's all for today. You worked very hard. Don't forget the homework, and I'll see you all tomorrow."

There were nods and mumbled thank-yous from all

around. As the students filed out, Miles O'Brien stepped aside to let them pass. Keiko stopped Dina and said, "Your mother isn't here again to pick you up?"

Dina shook her head. "No . . . but it's okay, Mrs. O'Brien. She told me she'd probably be working overtime. I'll be fine."

"How about I walk you?" said Miles.

But Jake Sisko, overhearing the conversation, stopped and said, "It's okay. I'll take her home. She doesn't live too far from me anyway."

"Would you, Jake?" asked Keiko. "I'd appreciate it. Thank you."

He took the young girl by the hand. "C'mon," he said. "I'll show you a shortcut." He walked off with her, and Keiko smiled as she watched them go.

"He's a good kid," she said. "He really is." She walked over to Molly, shutting off the computer for her. "So, Miles . . . this is a surprise. What are you doing here?"

He tried to look surprised. "What, is there a rule that I can't walk my wife home if I feel like it?"

"No. No rule," she said carefully, taking Molly by the hand. They headed for the door, and she continued, "But there is such thing as habit. And it hasn't exactly been your habit to meet me at school."

"So where is it written that a man can't change the way he does things?"

She stopped and faced him, clutching Molly's hand and stopping her from wandering away. "This has to do with that announcement that Commander Sisko made earlier, doesn't it?"

"No! No, of course not!"

"Miles, you're lying."

"I know."

Despite the seriousness of the situation, she smiled. Every so often she ran into one of those things that reminded her of why she'd fallen in love with O'Brien in the first place. And one of them happened to be that she thought it marvelous that O'Brien could flawlessly bluff his way through a poker game with serious money on the table but was utterly incapable of lying to her with any conviction at all.

"So . . ." She lowered her voice, not wanting to be heard by anyone walking past. "So . . . how bad is it? Really?"

"Bad enough," he said, putting an arm around her, "that I wanted to escort you home . . . and maybe review procedures with you on how to use this."

He held up a small phaser.

Keiko gaped at it. "You can't be serious. Where did you—"

"I got special permission from Commander Sisko. I've rigged it so that it's locked in on stun. That should be more than sufficient in case something happens. Here . . . take it."

He tried to press the weapon into her hand, but she held it carefully with her thumb and forefinger, keeping it a foot or so away from her as if it were a bag of waste material. "My God," she whispered. "Miles, what's happening around here?"

"Some things that you're not going to like," he said. "And I'll be damned if I don't do whatever is required to make sure my family is okay."

Jake Sisko and Dina chatted pleasantly as they headed for the habitat ring. As they approached Dina's quarters, Jake slowed down.

A small girl was walking slowly toward them, regarding them with curiosity. Her hair was short and red, her face a little pouty. Jake didn't recognize her and figured she must have arrived with one of the ships that were being forced to stay at the station until the wormhole opened up.

"Hi, there," he said. "You lost?"

She studied him for a moment and then slowly shook her head. She turned to Dina and seemed extremely curious about her.

"Hi, my name's Dina. What's yours?"

"Meta," replied the girl.

"Ooh. That's an interesting name," said Dina. "And this is Jake. He's walking me home."

"Are your parents around here, Meta?" asked Jake.

"Oh, yes." Meta sounded quite confident for a girl so young. "Yes, they're around."

"Want to do something together?" Dina asked. "I've got some games in my quarters."

"Sure," replied Meta.

"Well," said Jake. "That's good, then. You guys hang out together." He ushered them into Dina's quarters and then added, "Oh . . . and keep the door locked up, okay? You heard that announcement my dad made. If somebody got killed or something, then you can't be too careful."

"No, you can't," said Meta.

The door rolled shut, closing the two girls into the room.

Dina turned to Meta and said, "So . . . what would you like to do first?"

And Meta smiled.

"Ha! I win again!" Gotto crowed.

The Cardassian scooped up his winnings as other players around Quark's gaming wheel turned away in disgust. Quark, squeezing his hands together in the standard Ferengi pose of subservience, said, "It is quite clear that this is definitely your day, Gotto. A truly amazing run of luck."

"Thank you, Quark," said Gotto. "You know . . . Gul Dukat is most interested in you."

"Is he, now?" Quark tried to sound humble. "What could I possibly have done to attract the attention of such a mighty individual as the great Dukat?"

"He remembers you from the days before the Federation took over this . . . establishment," he said. "You were someone who could always be bought."

"I pride myself on my standards," Quark replied.

Gotto looked left and right. "Can we talk a moment?" he asked.

"Of course!" Quark quickly gestured for one of his employees to take over the wheel, and he moved away, sticking close by Gotto's side.

Out of the corner of his eye, Quark noticed that Glav was coming toward him but stopped when he saw who Quark was with. Then Glav grinned, nodded, and gave a signal of approval. The Cardassians were *the* military power in the area. If they could be swayed over to the Ferengi's plan . . .

Quark acknowledged Glav's presence with a silent gesture, but indicated that Glav should keep his distance so that the Cardassian wouldn't feel outnumbered. That was not generally the way they liked to operate. Introducing another player into things at the moment could cause aggravation. Glav, who was hardly a stranger to business dealings, hung back.

"This way," said Quark, wanting to proceed with caution . . . and most particularly not wanting to have yet another conversation within earshot of wherever Odo might be hiding.

They went up the stairs and paused outside one of Quark's notorious holosex suites. Quark grinned as he turned to Gotto. "Odo never comes in here," he said. "First, the very thought of any sexual activity makes him tremble with disgust. And second . . ."

They stepped inside. The suite was small, with solid black walls and a grid of glowing yellow lines.

"There's nowhere to hide," said Quark with satisfaction. The doors hissed closed behind them. "Now . . . what can I do for you?"

"I'll be blunt, Quark," said Gotto. "When we Cardassians abandoned this station, we had no idea of the potential gold mine that it represented."

Quark gulped slightly. "You're . . . you're planning to take it back?"

"Not as of this time," said Gotto. "However, I am going to be making more frequent visits. And I want a contact man, Quark. Someone to keep his eyes and ears open. Someone who can keep us apprised of just what the Federation is up to."

"You want me to be your spy?" said Quark.

"'Spy' is such a nasty term," Gotto said. "There's always gossip, isn't there? Think of yourself as a paid gossipmonger."

"Paid."

"Of course," Gotto told him. "You don't really think we expected you to do it for . . ."

"Free."

Gotto couldn't believe he'd heard correctly. "I'm sorry . . . did you say—"

"No charge," said Quark easily. "You're looking for cooperation from me, and I am perfectly happy to provide it."

"Nooo," said Gotto suspiciously. "No Ferengi does anything gratis. What's the catch, Quark?"

Quark rubbed his palms together. "The catch is . . . we'll cooperate with you, and you'll cooperate with us." Figuring that the best idea was to imply that a number of people were involved, Quark continued, "Some associates of mine and I are undertaking plans to purchase this station."

"Purchase it?" Gotto laughed. "Purchase it from whom?"

"Why, from the Federation."

"Don't be absurd. The Federation doesn't own Deep Space Nine. The Bajorans do. And they're welcome to it," he added with a snort. "We took everything useful out of it . . . although, again, if we'd known about that damned wormhole . . ."

"But . . ." Quark was stunned. "I assumed that there was some sort of under-the-table negotiation."

"Nothing. The Bajorans asked the Federation to administer the station while they are lobbying for full Federation membership."

"Member, schmember," said Quark. "What's in it for the Federation? Bajor must be paying them *something*."

"Nothing, I swear," said Gotto.

"You mean they're here out of the *goodness of their hearts?*" Quark simply could not believe it. When the switchover in power occurred, he had been positive that there must have been some sort of payoff. Something that would have prompted the Federation to come into the station in terms that he could relate to. But this! He shook his head in astonishment. "Zot! They're even more stupid than I credited them!"

"That's what the Federation is all about," said the Cardassian. "And people wonder why we have nothing but disdain for them. What's truly a wonder is why more people *don't* feel that way."

"This has been very enlightening."

"Indeed. Right now the Bajorans are hurting. As far as commercial considerations go, they might indeed be amenable to a potentially large cash flow, if the right bidder should come along."

"So I should simply ignore the Federation personnel on board Deep Space Nine and concentrate on the Bajorans?"

"Oh, no. Not at all. The Bajorans still want the

protection of the UFP, remember. They value the Starfleet presence . . . or at least some of them do. Their government is fairly splintered, and there is nothing that all of them can really agree on except that they all disagree. But a Starfleet recommendation would go a long way toward making your effort successful. Indeed, it would serve a twofold purpose. Those Bajorans who support Starfleet would pay very close attention to whatever Starfleet says. And those who wish that Starfleet would simply go away will be very inclined to do whatever it takes to get rid of them."

"The major," said Quark thoughtfully. "Major Kira. She holds no great love for Starfleet. She stomped around this place for the first several weeks after Sisko arrived. She's calmed down a bit since then . . . but she's still lukewarm in her support."

"Ah, yes. Kira. The Bajoran woman." The Cardassian smiled lopsidedly. "I've known some Bajoran women in my time . . . if you understand my meaning."

Quark nodded eagerly . . . although he felt something deep within him start to twist uncomfortably. But he forced it away, and said, "So . . . if our effort is successful, we can look to our neighbors, the Cardassians, to . . . ?" He let the sentence dangle, giving Gotto the opportunity to complete it.

Gotto took advantage of it. "You can count on us," he said, "to lend support wherever and however we can. You see, Quark, we have no particular love of the Federation either. We would far prefer to deal with someone who can be . . . oh, what's the word?"

"Bribed?"

"That's it!" Gotto said, pointing at Quark. "That's it exactly. Things are so much easier when both sides of a particular situation speak the same language, don't you think?"

"Oh, beyond question." Quark extended a hand, which the Cardassian shook. "It will be a pleasure doing business with you."

Bena checked her chronometer and moaned. It was later than she had thought.

She'd had a rough shift in the docking ring. First there had been the additional delay caused by the extended shutdown of the wormhole. Then word had come down, just to make things even more aggravating, that no one was being permitted to depart Deep Space Nine. The rumors were circulating that no one would be permitted to budge until the Feds got through investigating some sort of incident. Apparently they didn't want to take the chance of anybody slipping out on them.

As a result, the transients' extended stay was causing a lot of aggravation. Most of the docking bays were now occupied. And a number of people, due to the extended stay, were requesting that their cargo be moved to the newly repaired storage facilities. It had been a ton of work for Bena and the other dock rats, as they called themselves. No, definitely not one of the easier days.

Even so, all days—even the worst—came to an end. And the Bajoran woman was about to depart when she saw one of the oddest things she'd observed in quite some time.

Several Edemians had entered the docking bay. With them were Benjamin Sisko and Dr. Bashir.

They were walking slowly, taking measured steps. They were heading for the vast open loading doors, which had a forceshield in effect to maintain the atmosphere in the docking bay and make it possible to function without, for example, being sucked out into the void of space.

The lead Edemian walked nearly to the edge of the

bay, until it seemed as if his next steps would take him straight out into space.

He stopped just short of that, though. "Will we be able to see from here, Commander?" he asked. His voice was deep and full, and seemed to reverberate throughout the bay.

"Yes, Mas Marko," replied Sisko.

"Very well." The Edemian stared out into space and then intoned, "Let it be done."

Sisko tapped his comm badge. "Sisko to Major Kira. You are cleared for takeoff, Major. And stay away from the wormhole. You know how temperamental it's been."

For a long moment nothing happened. And then one of the runabouts, lifting off its pad on the habitat ring, hurtled past the docking ring. It moved off from the station, and now Bena could see that it seemed to be towing something. . . . Yes, it was an old casing of some sort. The runabout had no tractors, of course. But in the jury-rigged tradition of Deep Space Nine, someone had actually managed to find a length of cable and had used it to anchor the casing to the runabout.

"As K'olkr welcomes us into life," Mas Marko was intoning, "so does he welcome us into death. For death is as life, and life is as death. Death is not the end of existence but merely the end of this cycle. The end of a life does not matter, but only how we lived it. Lobb Sorbel lived his life as a good and faithful servant of K'olkr. May K'olkr welcome his spirit with empty and loving arms. May he send the spirit of Lobb onward, ever onward, through his journey into full understanding of the wisdom of K'olkr. So say we all."

"So say we all," echoed the other Edemians.

There was a moment of silence, and then Sisko said into his comm badge, "All right, Major. Cut him loose."

The runabout snapped around like a whip, and the

cable line was severed. The casing went free and hurtled away. Obeying the laws of physics dictating that an object in motion tended to stay in motion, the casing kept going. It was heading away from the wormhole, away from Bajor, toward open space.

"Good journey, Lobb," whispered the female Edemian.

Bena noticed that the woman was looking at the youngest Edemian in an odd way, almost with dread. The Bajoran didn't understand why, nor did she care all that much. She had her own young one to attend to.

Bena headed for the crossover bridge that would take her to the habitat ring and home. This time, she promised herself, she would manage to stay awake enough to spend some time with her daughter. She hated that Dina always seemed to get the smallest time portion of her mother's schedule, shoehorned in between work, eating and sleeping.

Not that she knew how she could possibly change it.

Meta stared with puzzlement into a mirror. Behind her, Dina was patiently combing out her hair.

"You should let it grow more," said Dina. "You'd be so pretty. Your hair is so thick."

"What difference does it make?" asked Meta. "Long or short. Why does that matter?"

"Well, you want to look your best, don't you?" Dina chirped.

"I hadn't given it much thought."

"Hah! And you call yourself a girl!" said Dina.

"Well . . . not really," said Meta. She turned to fix Dina with a very odd look. "Do you mind . . . if I watch you a bit longer. I haven't had the opportunity to spend this much time with a child. It's a . . . a learning experience."

"Ohhh," said Dina. She put down the brush and

came around to face Meta sadly. "Not a lot of kids where you are, huh?"

"Not many."

"Well," Dina told her firmly, "you're welcome to be my friend for as long as you're here on Deep Space Nine."

Meta nodded slowly and let Dina do her hair. When Dina had pulled it back into as much of a ponytail as she could make, she looked at two barrettes lying on the table in front of them—one red and one green.

"Which one do you want in your hair?" she asked.

"I don't know," replied Meta.

Dina paused a moment, then started moving a finger from one to the other, speaking as she did, and pointing back and forth between the two barrettes. Meta watched with interest as Dina chanted, "Which one, which one, will I choose? Which will win and which will lose? Do's and don'ts and don'ts and do's? This one, this one, I now choose."

She stopped on the green one, picked it up, and clamped it tightly around Meta's hair.

And Meta watched every move Dina made.

She listened to every word she spoke.

She absorbed it all, like a scholar desperate for knowledge.

And she prepared.

It was just Bena's luck that her quarters were halfway around the habitat ring. She was walking as quickly as she could, though, and she was almost there. . . .

And then, from around the corner, came a nightmare from her past.

She took a step back, gasping, her hand fluttering to her chest. She couldn't get the words out, for her throat was too full of bile and revulsion.

The Cardassian looked no less surprised. "Well!" he

said. "And here I thought that my pleasant memories were going to remain just that. Bena . . . how long has it been? Two years? Three?"

Bena pushed past him and kept on going. Gotto fell into step behind her, his much longer stride easily keeping pace with her. "No words of greeting?" he asked.

"Burn in hell."

"I was hoping for kinder words than that," he told her. "Bena . . . why are you behaving this way? After everything I did for you?"

She spun on her heel to face him. "Get away from me!"

"Well, now, this is a fine turnaround," he said. "Who helped you and your daughter out, eh? Not the Bajoran slug who fathered her, that's for certain. No, it was me. My noticing you was the best thing that ever happened to you."

She took a step toward him, clenching and unclenching her fists, naked hatred seeping from every pore. "You were the worst thing that ever happened to me. You . . . you humiliated me! The . . ." She lowered her voice, shuddering in shame. "The things you did to me . . ."

His voice was silky and insinuating. "And here I thought you enjoyed yourself."

"Enjoyed . . . ?"

She drew a hand back and slapped him as hard as she could. But his skin was coarse and hard, and she did far more damage to the palm of her hand than she did to him. In fact, he didn't so much as blink.

And then he grabbed her wrist and whispered, "I've missed you, you know."

At that moment the door to her quarters slid open. Standing there, having heard the commotion, was Dina. And next to her was a child whom Bena had never seen before.

"Mommy?" Dina's whole face was a question mark.

"Get back in the room!" she shouted. "Dina! Now! Call security!"

But the Cardassian was too quick. He shoved Bena through the door. She staggered back, tripping over a chair and sprawling on the floor. He followed her in, the door closing behind him.

"Now then," he said softly, "let's remember old times."

Dina stood there, confused and terrified. The face of the girl next to her was immobile. Now, with the door closed, Bena's exit was blocked. And Gotto made sure that she wouldn't be leaving any time soon by reaching up toward the lockpad and driving his powerful fist into it. Sparks flew, and the locking mechanism short-circuited, closing them in.

He turned toward Dina and smiled at her in a way that did nothing to encourage positive feelings. "I remember you," he said, "when you were just a little bit of a thing. But you probably don't remember me, do you?"

Dina was wide-eyed. "You're . . . you're a bad man."

Bena was on her feet, screaming, *"Get away from her!"* She charged at Gotto, fingernails clawed like a tigress. Gotto caught her easily, as if she had been moving in slow motion, and twisted her arm around and down. She cried out, feeling as if her arm had been ripped out of the socket.

"Remember this?" he asked silkily. "Cardassian fore-play?"

Dina ran toward him, punching at his legs. He kicked her aside as if she weren't there.

And then the odd little red-haired girl stepped in between them, insinuated herself. Gotto didn't know her, didn't care about her. He grabbed her by the arm to yank her aside.

Her arm came off.

Or rather it seemed to come off.

Gotto gasped in shock before he realized that her skin and bones had just . . . just *melted* in his grip.

Dina shrieked, high-pitched terror. Bena had pulled away from Gotto and was now gaping in shock, too overcome to make any sound at all.

The little girl was melting, becoming a shapeshifting red slime. Her face, her hair, her entire body, simply dissolved, making an odd sucking noise as it pulled apart and re-formed into a substance with the consistency of molasses.

Gotto still had his arm in the middle of it, and now there was no trace of the child at all. Instead, the stuff was creeping up his arm, up his shoulder, starting to envelop him.

Gotto screamed.

Which was a mistake.

The red slime seeped up into his mouth, into his nose, cutting off all forms of air intake. Gotto began to choke, coughing up red slime.

He staggered against the wall, clawing at the air, reaching for something to fight against. He started to thump at his chest, as if hoping he might be able to reach in and pull out whatever it was, in the name of every Cardassian god that had ever been, that was filling up his lungs, his entire chest cavity.

He went to his knees, reaching for Bena, imploring her to help him. *Help me, for God's sake, get it out of me!*

He got his wish.

The creature exited. Abruptly.

Jake Sisko was a bit nervous.

He kept thinking that maybe he hadn't done the job thoroughly enough. He'd dropped Dina off, sure. Gotten her squared away. But her mother hadn't been there . . . and not only that, but he'd left her with some stranger. Oh, sure, a child. Probably some kid who would wind up being Dina's best friend in the entire world.

But still . . .

He sat and stared at his homework, and finally said to himself, "Ah. Couldn't hurt to make sure everything's okay." What he did not say out loud—or even to himself, really—was that he would have seized upon any excuse to get away from his homework.

He exited the rooms he shared with his father and headed down the hallway to Dina's quarters. Moments later he was standing outside the door.

He raised his hand to ring the buzzer.

And then he heard a scream . . . and what sounded like some sort of explosion.

"Dina!" he shouted. He hit the buzzer, but got no response. "Dina!" he called again.

And then he looked down.

Blood was seeping out from under the door.

Jake lunged for the comm pad on the wall, hit it, and shouted, "Security! Security alert! Somebody get down to habitat ring, level five, corridor thirty-nine-A! Hurry!"

His alarmed summons was immediately heard in Ops by Odo . . . and also by Sisko himself.

"That was Jake!" said Sisko.

"Security team to habitat ring, level five, corridor thirty-nine-A!" Odo barked the order through his comm unit even as he bolted for the transporter pad. Sisko was just ahead of him.

"Commander, I can handle—" began Odo.

But Sisko wasn't listening. He stepped onto the pad, spun, and called out, "Chief! Beam us over there *now!*"

O'Brien, who had just gotten back from escorting Keiko to their quarters, fought down the flash of concern for his own family's safety. His rooms were not that far from section 39A. But he forced his professionalism to the forefront and, the moment Odo was on the pad, manipulated the controls with practiced skill.

Within seconds Odo and Sisko materialized two feet away from Jake. Sisko was immediately relieved to see that his son was in one piece. He strode forward quickly and, all business, said, "What's happening—"

Jake pointed wordlessly, and then Sisko saw it, as did Odo. The dark, viscous liquid that could only be blood.

Even as two security guards charged toward them, Sisko hit his comm badge. "Sisko to infirmary. A medical team to habitat ring, section thirty-nine-A, immediately!"

Odo was trying to force the door open, but it wasn't budging. He spun and said, "It's locked from the inside. I think the mechanism is destroyed. I can't override it."

"Have your men phaser it open," said Sisko.

They heard another scream from within, and Odo said sharply to his men, "Give me ten seconds to get through and then do as Sisko says."

"Get through? Constable, what—"

But Odo wasn't looking at him anymore. He flattened himself against the door . . .

And promptly went liquid.

Bena was whimpering in terror. Dina sat there in slack-jawed shock, unable to deal with what she was seeing. Both of them had blood spattered all over them. In their hair, in their clothes . . . everywhere.

The Cardassian was still intact, but only from the waist down. From the waist up, the force of the metamorph's exit had simply blown Gotto apart, as if a giant balloon had been inflated inside him to the point where his body couldn't contain it any longer. There were identifiable portions of him, but not in any great number and not anywhere near each other.

Meta had resumed her little-girl shape. Calmly and collectedly, she was smearing a large "#2" on the wall, just above something that bore a passing resemblance to a piece of the Cardassian's forehead.

Dina was making a faintly human noise. She was whimpering. Acting more out of automatic impulse than any conscious maternal instinct, Bena pulled her daughter's head close to her chest.

Meta finished drawing the number and then turned and looked sadly at Bena and Dina. When she spoke, it was in that same little-girl voice, which made her words all the more chilling.

"I really should kill both of you, too," she said. "I'm sorry. It's nothing personal. It's . . . just the way I am. Killing things is what I do. I like to watch them die. It makes me that much more appreciative of life. Now . . . the only question is . . . which of you do I kill first?"

Crouched in a corner, clutching her daughter like a life preserver, Bena whispered in a tear-filled voice, "Please . . . please don't . . ."

Meta thought about it a moment and then pointed at Bena. Bena screamed.

And Meta began, "Which one, which one, will I choose? Which will win and which will lose? Do's and don'ts and don'ts and do's? This one, this one, I now ch—"

Then Meta whirled.

Something was coming through the crack between the doors. It was slow, because the space was tight. But it was coming, thick and viscous.

Meta took a step back, her eyes going wide. She looked around, a tinge of desperation in her face, and then she leapt upward, her body dissolving as she did so. It was as if she were exploding out the top of a volcano, a tower of lava hurtling skyward.

Meta went up into an overhead vent, seeping through it and vanishing into the ceiling.

Bena hadn't seen what Meta was reacting to. All she knew was that all of a sudden the creature wasn't there anymore. She had no idea what to expect, no clue as to why they had been spared.

And then she saw something oozing through the door. At first she wasn't able to get any noise out through her throat. It felt as if her vocal cords had become completely constricted. And then she managed to get something out—just a little squeak of scream, but it was enough to open the floodgates. She started screaming again, loudly, uncontrollably, as more and more of the creature seeped in, piling up on the floor and oozing toward them.

It reached the middle of the floor and started to re-form, and Bena went into complete hysterics. The hysteria broke through her fear, and she started grabbing things and hurling them at the creature that was reconstituting itself in her room.

Odo pulled himself up to a standing position and then ducked his head, avoiding the small statue that sailed past him. "Madam," he said stiffly, "control yourself!"

She gaped, not understanding at first what her eyes were telling her. And then she said, "It's a trick! *It's a trick!*"

Her histrionics made little impression on Odo. He went over to Bena and quickly ascertained that the blood she was covered with was most definitely not hers or her child's. He said urgently, "Who did this? Where is he?"

But now Bena was saying nothing. She was just trembling, staring at Odo with overwhelming terror in her eyes. She looked as if she were trying to escape into her own body.

"Where is he?" Odo repeated more forcefully. But he quickly realized he wouldn't get anything out of her. She had lapsed into shock. The little girl looked flat-out comatose.

He tapped his comm badge and said, "Sisko. The

woman and child in here are all right. But it appears"—
he looked down at what was left of Gotto—"as if a
Cardassian in here has seen better days. I suggest you
send your son away unless he has an extreme tolerance
for gore."

It was the work of a few seconds to crosswire the lock
and get the doors opened. But the moment they slid
apart, Odo blocked the exit. "Computer!" he called.
"Seal off corridor thirty-nine-A, habitat level five!" he
said.

"Seal confirmed," said the computer calmly.

Odo turned and faced his men. "Proceed with extreme caution," he said. "There's no sign of the perpetrator. But if he's got some sort of personal cloaking
field, as the Tosk did, he may still be hiding somewhere
in these quarters. Carstairs, Hicks . . . do a detailed
sensor sweep of the inside. The seals will keep him in
the area in case he slips past us. Careful now."

The security men entered, weapons and detection
devices at the ready. They were followed by Bashir and
his medical team. Sisko was right behind him, having
taken Odo's advice and sent Jake back to their quarters.

He looked down at the remains of the Cardassian.
"Dear Lord," he whispered. "What happened?"

"It appears," deadpanned Odo, "that he died a
broken man."

"My God, Constable—"

"Don't throw your gods in my face, Sisko," snapped
Odo. "I've dealt with enough of these vile Cardassians
to last me a lifetime. I will not shed one tear for the
demise of any of their number. However," he said with
even greater conviction, "it doesn't matter to me who
or what the victim of a crime was; if there was a crime,
then there will be arrest and punishment. There will be
justice"—he glanced once more at the Cardassian—
"even for the unjust."

Carstairs came forward with a tricorder, shaking his

head. "Nothing here, sir," he said. "Even if the killer were invisible, we'd detect energy readings, body signs . . . something." Moments later Hicks reported similar findings in the corridor.

In a black fury, Odo snarled, "He couldn't have just disappeared into thin air."

"Of course he could," replied Sisko. "Some sort of personal transporter device. But if that's the case, he'll leave an energy trail. Scattered ions. Traceable. We'll find him."

Bashir's medical team was taking the two Bajoran females out. "Get them cleaned off and calmed down," Bashir said as he was going over the remains of the Cardassian with his medical tricorder.

"I'll want to talk with them as soon as they're capable," said Odo.

Bashir nodded, but he appeared distracted, and he was shaking his head. "Nothing. Still nothing. Damn. I don't understand this. No DNA traces. No nothing. How can anyone do this sort of thing and not leave any hint of himself behind? No bits of tissue, no follicles . . . nothing."

And then they heard screaming again.

Immediately they charged out into the hallway, expecting to see the worst.

But instead what they saw was Bena. She was struggling now, the initial shock seemingly having passed from her. The medtechs were trying to keep her calm, but were not having tremendous success. Bashir removed a spray hypo from his kit, ready to give her a sedative.

She did not look ready to be sedated, however. She was pointing with a quavering finger as Odo emerged from the quarters behind Bashir.

"It was him!" she shrieked. "Him!"

Sisko had met the woman several times during loading bay procedures. He knew her in passing, and he tried to sound reasonable now. "Bena," he said, "it couldn't have been Odo. He was with us—with *me*—the whole time. On the bridge, then down here. A dozen people saw him." He took her firmly by the arms. "Do you hear what I'm saying? Do you think I'm lying?"

She looked frantically from Sisko back to Odo. "It was . . . the same. . . . It was . . ."

Odo was careful not to approach the woman. From a safe distance, he said, "Are you saying the killer looked like me? As I do now?"

She shook her head frantically. "No, the . . . It was . . . red and slimy, and . . . and it was a little girl, and then it wasn't, and . . ." And then she crushed her face against Sisko's uniform, sobbing uncontrollably. As gently as he could, Bashir gave her a sedative. The effects were almost immediate, and within moments she had been led away by the medical personnel. Dina had made no sound at all, but merely watched the entire thing with glassy, vacant eyes.

Sisko looked down at his uniform shirt, which was now smeared with blood. "It would seem, Constable," he said slowly, weighing the impact of his words, "that we have another shapeshifter on board."

Odo nodded, his face expressionless.

And, in the ceiling . . .

Meta quietly oozed away through the infrastructure of DS9.

CHAPTER
10

MAS MARKO stood in the middle of Ops, tall and sullen and not looking the least bit cooperative. Del, as always, stood nearby and to the side.

Kira, who practically had to crane her neck to look up at Marko, said, "Sir . . . I'm trying to be accommodating, but I don't know when Commander Sisko will be back, and we simply cannot have unauthorized personnel hanging about Ops. Now unless you want me to call security . . ."

He looked down at her from his great height. "I would think," he rumbled, "that your security forces would have more pressing matters than me to occupy them—for example, trying to track down a murderer."

"Sir . . ."

At that moment Sisko returned via the turbolift. Odo was not with him, having stayed behind to comb the area for some trace of the intruder. Seeing Mas Marko standing there, the commander had a feeling that he wasn't going to be exactly thrilled with this particular conversation.

"Mas Marko," he said, "this is not an especially good time."

"Perhaps, Commander. I understand your situation. But you must now understand mine. And my situation is that one of my trusted followers was murdered. I want to know what you're doing about it."

"In my office, then."

Moments later they were in Sisko's office. Marko chose to stand rather than squeeze his bulk into a human-sized chair. Del stood just outside the office. As usual, he contributed nothing to the conversation, but seemed content merely to bask in the presence of his leader.

"So," Marko began, "how goes the investigation? Have you learned anything yet?"

Why, yes—that we have a shapeshifting serial killer who murders without rhyme or reason.

"Nothing just yet," said Sisko carefully. "We do, however, have some—"

"Promising leads, yes, I know. How promising?"

"Very promising."

Mas Marko studied him for a moment and then said, "You know, Commander . . . it may be my imagination, but it seems to me that you are being somewhat evasive in this matter."

"You're correct, Mas Marko," said Sisko. "It's your imagination."

Marko smiled thinly. "Yes. Well . . . there's something you should understand, Commander: a crime has been perpetrated against an Edemian missionary —a murder most foul. I trust that you will do the right thing when it comes to the disposition of the murderer."

"We haven't caught him yet, Mas Marko. I think disposition is a bit premature."

"Not if, as you say, you have some promising leads. Commander, the Edemians will be expecting satisfaction in this matter. We are firm believers in justice. The teachings of K'olkr are quite specific. The killer must be found, and he must be turned over to us. You see, there's no other option."

"I see," said Sisko tightly, fighting once more to keep his temper under control, "that you have an opinion, Mas Marko. Your opinion has been noted. Keep in mind, however, that this is a Bajoran station—property of Bajor, administered by the Federation. There are jurisdictional questions to be sorted out."

And Mas Marko looked more dangerous than Sisko had ever seen him.

"I don't care about jurisdiction," he said tightly. "I care about right and wrong. It is our right to see justice done by Edemian law. It is wrong to ignore that consideration."

"I'm not ignoring it, Mas Marko," said Sisko. "I simply cannot make any promises."

The air seemed to crackle with danger, and then Mas Marko told him, "Perhaps you cannot make promises, Commander, but I can. And I can promise you . . . that you will not like what happens if you cross my people and their proprietary claims."

Kira appeared at the door of Sisko's office. "Sir," she said, and there was a look of concern on her face. "Gul Dukat is calling."

Aw, hell, thought Sisko. But his face remained inscrutable as he said, "Hold him, please. Mas Marko . . . I must attend to other business."

Marko inclined his head slightly. "As you wish, Commander."

He left the office, ducking his head, as always, to avoid hitting it. Del followed him, and the moment they were out of earshot, Sisko called, "All right. Put him through."

On his personal screen, the image of Gul Dukat materialized.

As usual, Dukat looked relaxed, even convivial. Sisko knew, of course, that the Cardassian commander was as crafty, and as difficult, a customer as he had ever dealt with. Dukat was a master of making himself look like the injured party, no matter how overt his own actions were in leading to a crisis.

The problem was, in this case, that he now had a legitimate grievance—unless, by some miracle, Dukat was calling about something else entirely.

"Commander," said Dukat.

Sisko returned the greeting in kind. "What can I do for you?" he asked.

"You can answer a question for me, actually," said Dukat. "I seem to have lost touch with my man, Gotto."

"Lost touch?" said Sisko.

"Yes. He was to report in regularly during his business at Deep Space Nine, and he has missed his check-in. I have endeavored to contact him directly and have had no success. I have spoken to your own people, your charming Major Kira—who, by the way, makes no effort to hide her disdain for Cardassians in general and for me in particular. You should talk to her about that."

"I'll encourage her to make a greater effort to hide her disdain in the future," Sisko replied solemnly.

"Please do. At any rate, Major Kira said that I should speak to you if I have any questions about Gotto."

Sisko glanced in Kira's direction. She was looking straight at him, watching the conversation. Although he had no proof, and she wouldn't admit to it, Sisko had a sneaking suspicion that Kira was a fairly skilled lip-reader. He raised a questioning eyebrow toward her, and she gestured in a manner that seemed to say, *What was I supposed to tell him?*

"Commander Sisko," continued Dukat, and the edge in his voice served notice to Sisko that the danger Dukat represented should not be ignored. "Where is Gotto?"

For a moment Sisko contemplated either lying or

pleading ignorance to buy some time. On the other hand, if Dukat already knew what had happened and was playing some sort of mental chess game with Sisko, then Sisko was not going to look particularly good getting caught in a bald-faced lie.

And even if Dukat didn't know the truth . . . well, he was going to find out sooner or later. And there was a good chance that he would hear the facts from some source other than Sisko. It would probably be better if Sisko presented the news himself, as gently as he could.

That was the theory, at least.

"Commander," prodded Dukat, "what's going on out there at that busy little station of yours?"

Sisko cleared his throat.

"There's been a . . . mishap," he began.

A frustrated Bashir walked through the Promenade to try to clear his head.

What sort of creature would do such things? Was the killer truly similar to Odo? He had seen the security chief's expression upon learning of that possibility, and it had not been a pleasant one.

The murderer had left no traces. None. For all the luck that Bashir was having in tracking down hard information about it, it might as well have been a ghost.

Then he heard a female voice calling out familiar words: "Come, learn the glory of K'olkr."

There were the Edemians at their usual station. There was Rasa, looking spent and wasted. In fact, he was dozing in his chair, oblivious of everything going on around him. There was Azira, calling to passersby, trying to interest them in partaking of the wonders of K'olkr. There was . . .

There was . . . nobody else. The elder Edemian males were nowhere around.

And then Azira, in mid-sentence, caught sight of him.

They exchanged glances for a long moment, and then she looked away.

But there had been something in the way she had looked at him. Something unspoken that seemed to cry out to him. Something . . . something that he could not quite qualify. But, nevertheless, it was something that he felt moved to act upon.

Without giving any thought whatsoever to his actions —indeed, without having a clue as to what he was going to say or do—Bashir walked with conviction toward Azira.

She continued not to look at him, but now her manner was far more forced. Obviously she saw him. Obviously she knew he was there. But she was refusing to make eye contact.

Fear, perhaps? Or . . . shame?

"Azira," he said.

At first she didn't say anything. He repeated his salutation, and this time she afforded him a brief glance. "Doctor," she said deferentially, "is there something I can do for you?"

Just wade in! his mind told him. He put on his most charming expression and said, "Nooo . . . but there's something I can do for you."

"Oh, really? What might that be?"

Very deliberately, he hardened his voice. "I can save your son."

She sighed. "Doctor . . . my son is already saved." She sounded content, at peace. "He believes in and embraces K'olkr, as do I. As long as he has that, then he is saved beyond anything your medicines can offer."

She didn't believe it.

Of that Bashir was certain. If there was one thing he prided himself on, it was his understanding of women. And everything about Azira—*everything*—screamed to Bashir that she was as much at peace with her son's illness as the Cardassians were at peace with Bajor—which was to say, not at all.

"Are you sure?" he asked.

"Yes."

"Well, it's a good thing that you're sure," he said forcefully. "Because, you know, if you're wrong, then you're throwing away this boy's life. You do realize that."

"I'm not throwing away anything."

"Maybe you're right," he said. "Maybe, just maybe, you lucked out. Of the thousands of religions in the galaxy, you may just have been lucky enough to fall in with the right one."

Bashir had done some reading up on Edemian culture. His annoying lack of knowledge about what made their minds work had drastically undercut his awareness of their physiology. "Maybe Rasa's spirit will go to the Sparkling World. Maybe he'll see the unadorned glory of K'olkr and bask in its brightness and warmth. Maybe K'olkr will take him under his great wings and then bless him and send him on his journey to cosmic oneness."

Then his voice grew harsh. He hated to speak that way; the chivalry that pervaded every fiber of him shuddered at the notion of verbally abusing a woman. Nevertheless, he had no choice. "But then again . . . maybe you're wrong. Maybe when Rasa dies, his spirit will go nowhere. Maybe his body will be just a sack of lifeless meat. The body and spirit will be deprived of the opportunity to grow to manhood—"

"Stop it," she said sharply.

"All because you were willing to throw away his life when I could have saved it. Will you feel proud, then?"

"I said *stop it!*"

She put her hands over her ears, trying to turn away. Relentlessly, Bashir kept hammering at her. "Just you and his father and his little coffin. Are you going to pitch that out into space, too? Let his dead body float around until it's drawn into some planet's atmosphere where it can plummet to the surface and burn? Or maybe some Klingons will use it for target practice. I hear that's a favorite Klingon pastime, taking potshots at debris. His small, wasted body, blown to bits—"

And Azira's scream filled the Promenade.

"Stoppp it! Stop it, stop it, stop it, stop it, stop iiiiitt!" Rasa didn't stir. Didn't so much as move.

But Bashir did. He spun in a 180-degree semicircle as Mas Marko appeared behind him and swung him around to face him. A cold fury emanated from Mas Marko, and if he could have ripped Bashir's heart out with the power of his glance, he would have done so at that moment.

Bashir said the first thing that occurred to him: "Don't hurt my hands."

Mas Marko lifted him clear off the floor, holding him high over his head with just the one hand. Del was just behind him, looking on in amazement. He had never seen his master so angry.

"What do you think you are doing?" he demanded, shaking Bashir as if he weighed nothing.

"Sp-speaking to your wife."

"Who gave you the *right?* How *dare* you seek to undermine my authority? To offend our god?"

Bashir's life flashed before his eyes, and he allowed himself a moment to reflect that, overall, it had been pretty damned good.

And at that moment Odo's hand clamped firmly down on Mas Marko's wrist.

Because of Marko's considerable height, there was no reasonable way that Odo should have been able to seize his arm so casually. Bashir suspected that, in moments such as this, Odo subtly altered his height and made himself taller. Not that he was, in any way, disparaging the effort.

Slowly Marko lowered Bashir to the floor. The doctor stood on unsteady feet for a moment. Then, pulling himself together, he cast a glance at Azira.

She had said nothing during the entire altercation. In fact, she wasn't even looking at Bashir. She was staring fixedly and determinedly at the floor, as if frightened that looking at Bashir might cause some abrupt loss of nerve.

"You," Marko said, his voice thundering with barely contained anger, "you, Doctor, are an unwelcome obstacle."

"An obstacle to what?" Bashir said hoarsely, rubbing his throat. "An obstacle to your son's death?"

Marko took a step forward, but Odo interposed himself. His shoulders were squared, his gaze determined.

"If I throw you into confinement for assault, Mas Marko," Odo said, unruffled by the Edemian's ire, "the good doctor will be free to chat with your wife all day if he so desires, and you won't be around to stop it. If that is your wish, then by all means"—he stepped aside—"try to hit him."

Bashir looked nervously from Odo to Mas Marko and back. Odo was simply standing there, his arms folded. "Go ahead," he said challengingly. "Try your best. If you think you can hit him before I stop you, then give it a whirl. But I *will* stop you. And you don't have to connect to be held for assault. All you have to do is try. Go on. Try."

Mas Marko seemed to consider it for a moment, to Bashir's obvious discomfiture. Then he backed away, clearly making an effort to compose himself before landing in serious difficulty.

Still staring fixedly and grimly at Bashir, Mas Marko raised his voice and, once more, began to sing the praises of the holy K'olkr.

A crowd had gathered, out of curiosity, to see if the

Federation doctor would get his brains splattered all over the Promenade. In fact, bets were being placed on just how far Bashir's head would roll if Mas Marko knocked it off his shoulders. Seeing that the show was over, though, and that the Edemians were going back to their usual task of trying to stir up interest in their tired old god, the crowd rapidly dispersed.

Odo led Bashir away, heading toward his office. Bashir was thanking the security officer for his intervention, but Odo didn't seem remotely interested in hearing it. He pulled Bashir into his office and, the moment the door slid shut behind them, turned on the doctor and snapped, "Would you mind telling me what the hell you were doing out there?"

Bashir felt a twinge of annoyance. "I don't appreciate the way you're talking to me, Mr. Odo."

"*You* don't appreciate— Doctor, *I* don't appreciate having Starfleet personnel stir up a situation that's already threatening to become as raw and explosive as any I've ever encountered. Do you think Commander Sisko would look kindly upon this little fracas? I seem to recall something about your being instructed to keep your nose out of the Edemians' business. Well . . .?"

Bashir grunted in acknowledgment, "The commander would probably be less than ecstatic. I can just imagine what he'd say."

"This is an outrage! *An outrage!*"

It wasn't Sisko who was speaking. Rather, it was the enraged Cardassian commander, Gul Dukat. He looked ready to punch his fist right through the communications screen.

"I share your anger at the situation, Commander," began Sisko.

"Situation? Commander Sisko, this is not a *situation*. This is an *incident,* and incidents can have very serious consequences for all concerned."

Sisko's voice became dangerously silky as he stared at Gul Dukat on the screen. "Are you threatening me, Commander?"

"I am saying, Commander Sisko," replied Gul Dukat, "that I want to see a full report on this *situation* by this time tomorrow. Furthermore, as soon as the murderer of Gotto is apprehended, he is to be turned over to the Cardassians for processing."

" 'Processing'? Meaning execution?"

"Meaning none of your damned business," said Gul Dukat. His affability had vanished, swept away by the assault on his second-in-command. "We consider this a direct provocation against the Cardassians."

"No, Commander," Sisko shot back, his voice becoming more heated. "This is an unfortunate occurrence of your man being in the wrong place at the wrong time. Furthermore, from the little we've managed to get out of the woman and child since the incident, it seems that your man was about to force himself, violently, on a Bajoran woman. If Gotto hadn't been there, the killer—who appears to act purely out of opportunity—would have slaughtered mere Bajorans, and you and I wouldn't be having this conversation."

"Oh, and don't think for a moment, Commander Sisko, that I am less than ecstatic whenever we have an opportunity to chat." Dukat was speaking with infinite sarcasm. "Force himself? Honestly. Am I supposed to accept, on faith, the calumnies of some Bajoran bitch? I assure you, Commander, that my man was an innocent victim, probably of yet another Bajoran terrorist plot."

"An innocent victim, then," said Sisko, "for the sake of argument. Unfortunately, in the real world, innocent people sometimes suffer. That's a sad reality. You can't interpret Gotto's murder as a personal assault."

"I don't agree with you there, Commander, but you are quite right in saying that the death of *mere* Bajorans would have been of no interest to us. Why should we care about them? Lord knows they were more than happy to attack us, to wage guerrilla war on us, whenever they had the opportunity. We would mourn their death about as enthusiastically as they would mourn the death of one of us. But this was the death of a Cardassian, Commander—moreover, a high-ranking Cardassian who was on a mission from me. I know you say that this was one of a series of murders. I hope, for your sake, that it will be the last.

"But," he continued fiercely, "I don't care if your little psychopath slaughters every Bajoran on that station, up to and including your first officer. The fact is, there is a dead Cardassian on Deep Space Nine, and that situation must be attended to. We demand justice, and we will have it. We will have the murderer, and we will not wait forever to obtain him."

"Meaning . . .?"

"Meaning that if the killer is not apprehended and turned over to us within a reasonable period of time, we will come in and conduct our own investigation."

"That," said Sisko flatly, "is not an option. This is a Federation matter."

"That all depends on your point of view. To us, it is a Cardassian matter. And Cardassians look after their own."

"Gul Dukat, we are in favor of continued peaceful relations with the Cardassians. But we cannot permit you to bring your own people in here to troop through Deep Space Nine and take over the investigation. That would only make matters worse."

"What will make matters worse," replied Dukat, "is if you endeavor to interfere. If you will not permit us aboard the station to exact vengeance upon the perpetrator, then we will have to play it safe."

"And how do you propose to do that?"

"Why, quite simply, Commander." Gul Dukat seemed to relax again—which was more than enough to make Sisko tense. "We would not want to take any chance of the killer escaping. So we would, quite simply, blow the station to kingdom come. Oh, true, several hundred Bajorans and other life-forms— including you humans, I'm afraid—would die. But at least we'd be assured that the murderer had suffered as well."

"That's insane!" Sisko almost shouted, fighting to keep himself, and the situation, under control.

"Are you questioning my sanity, Commander?"

"I'm questioning your tactics. To ensure the death of one being, you'd slaughter hundreds of innocent people . . ."

The moment the words were out of Sisko's mouth, he knew exactly what Dukat was going to say. And he was right.

"Why, Commander!" said Dukat, twisting the knife. "I'm surprised at you. Don't you know that in the real world, innocent people sometimes suffer? That's a sad reality. You can't interpret it as a personal assault."

"Very funny, Commander," said Sisko.

Dukat smiled thinly. "Notice, Commander . . . that I'm not laughing."

The screen snapped off. Sisko sat back in his chair, rubbing his temples with his fingers.

Dax stuck her head in. "Problem, Benjamin?"

"Don't ask, old man," said Sisko tiredly. "Don't ask."

Odo took a seat behind his desk and placed his hands flat on the desktop. "I'm willing to keep this matter between us, Doctor . . . but I do not need you making my job any harder than it already is. And it's pretty miserable right now." He shook his head. "I've got every available man combing every inch of this station —talking to people, running scans on inanimate objects to see if they have life readings, trying to detect the small expenditure of energy that might accompany sudden shapeshifting, in the same manner that I do. . . ." He paused, and then repeated bitterly, "In the same manner . . ."

Bashir looked at him, full of curiosity. "Do you really think that this shapeshifter is just like you? I mean . . . one of your people?"

Odo leaned forward, propping his elbows on the desk. "What do you know about me, Doctor?"

"Only what I've read in the files—how you were found, how you don't have any idea where you come from, that sort of thing."

"It is a rare occasion," said Odo, "when you can read someone's file and learn just as much about him from them as he knows about himself. That's my whole life right there, Doctor. The facts in that file . . . and the duties of this job." He looked despondent. "It would have to happen this way, wouldn't it?"

"Wouldn't what?"

Clearly Odo weighed answering the doctor. He wasn't automatically inclined to, but he felt the need to vent his spleen to *some*body. Kira was too hardened by a difficult life to be all that sympathetic, despite the occasional efforts she made. Sisko he still didn't trust. Dax was a puzzle. O'Brien had been getting on his nerves lately. And Quark . . .

"Don't make me laugh," he said bitterly.

"What?"

"Nothing." He shook his head. "It's just that . . . well, it's just my luck that I should finally encounter a creature that might be one of my own kind. I don't know for sure that it is. There *are* other shapeshifting species in the galaxy. Perhaps it's an offshoot from my people—presuming I have a people. As I said, I don't know. But of all things, this possible first relative of mine turns out to be a psychopathic random killer. And I have absolutely no idea where to start looking for him.

This station has thirty-five levels, Doctor. Its diameter is about one-point-four kilometers. And hidden somewhere in this maze is a being who—if it's just like me—could be disguised as a stick of furniture or a discarded hatch . . . *anything.*"

Bashir nodded sympathetically. "It must be a very difficult situation to be in. Very frustrating."

"Yes, it is."

"Almost like . . . oh . . ." Bashir made a tremendous show of giving it a great deal of thought. "Almost like, say . . . watching a boy die when you know that you could help him."

Odo didn't look remotely amused. "Some of us, Doctor, are able to put aside our personal feelings and do our jobs."

"How fortunate for some of us," said Bashir dryly.

"Security to Odo!" Meyer's voice crackled over Odo's comm badge.

"Odo here," he said. He had a sick feeling he knew what Meyer was going to say.

"Cargo bay, level twenty-two, sir!"

He didn't even have to ask. "I'm on my way." He rose quickly and said to Bashir, "I have the unfortunate feeling that you're going to be needed, Doctor."

"I have the unfortunate feeling," said Bashir, "that I'm going to be too late."

"Juggling?" Sisko looked at Dax skeptically. "Now why in the world should I take up juggling?"

"You need something to relax you, Benjamin," said Dax reasonably. "I heard Chief O'Brien mention it the other day."

"But . . . juggling?" He shook his head. "I can't see it. I've got my occasional baseball outings . . ."

"Yes, yes, I know. Holosuite forays in which you bring up baseball greats and play against them. But there's that sense of competition again. You should try to master something for the pure enjoyment of doing it. Also, juggling would suit your environment."

"My environment?" He looked around. "Are you implying," he said, "that this station resembles a circus?"

"No. You're inferring that. I'm simply saying that a lot of things are happening right now. You have to deal with many disparate individuals and keep them all satisfied. In that respect—"

"I have to keep a lot of balls in the air at the same time." He smiled slightly. "Interesting parallel, Dax. I'll keep it in mind. Not too seriously in mind, of course. But—"

"Odo to Commander Sisko."

He tapped his comm badge. "Sisko here, Constable."

Odo was as terse as his own man had been earlier. "Cargo bay, level twenty-two."

"On my way."

People weren't sure of her last name. Everyone had simply called her Old Kelsi. Speculation was that she had been called that since she was a teenager and had simply grown into the name.

Old Kelsi was the premier traffic manager in the bay area. She kept things moving, running smoothly. She had been there so long that there was open speculation that she predated the space station—that Deep Space Nine had, in fact, been built around her.

Need something moved? Run it past Kelsi.

Need something found? Ask Kelsi. It didn't matter how fully loaded the bay area was or how many ships might be passing through at any given time. The Bajoran woman had an incredible gift for remembering precisely where everything was at any moment. She never even had to consult computer logs; she just *knew*. She was one of the few Bajorans for whom even the Cardassians had respect, because she didn't react to them with hatred and contempt, as other Bajorans did. She seemed to be above politics—or perhaps she just didn't give a damn about it. The cargo bay of Deep Space Nine was her entire reason for existence.

Granted, it wasn't the most impressive of reasons, and certainly not one of the galaxy's hot spots. But she had carved out her niche, and she held on to it like a pit bull.

And she had done her job more efficiently than anyone could ever have hoped.

She was one of the true Deep Space Nine mainstays. Many regarded her as a permanent part of the station.

And now she was.

Her lifeblood was smeared all over one of the inner bulkheads, an immutable part of the decor; repeated scrubbings would never fully manage to get it out. The rest of her had simply been torn apart. Not a scream had been heard out of her; something had smothered her so thoroughly that her final, hideous assault had not alerted a single one of the workers in the cargo bays.

The screams had come later, upon the discovery of her remains. One of the cargo workers had stumbled over her . . . literally. He had been rearranging things in a corner and had tripped over her leg, which was no longer affixed to the customary place on her body.

The rest of her was lying in something of a puddle. And smeared on the wall, unmistakably, was "#3."

"Same as the others," Bashir whispered, studying the readings off his tricorder.

Odo could barely contain his fury. "Comb the area," he told his men. "I want this . . . this *obscenity* found, immediately." He turned toward the security guards. "Everything is to be tested. Do you understand? I want every single molecule of this station checked out. Now move. *Move!*"

Several dockworkers were looking on in shock and horror, muttering to themselves, the pitch of their voices rising. Sisko turned to them and said, "All right, people. As you were."

"As we *were?*" said one worker incredulously. But when he saw the look on Sisko's face, he said nothing further.

"You realize, Sisko, that our problem has just gotten even worse," Odo told him in a low voice. "At least the other murders were committed in private quarters, so that we managed to keep the details under wraps. But this . . . The particulars of this incident will spread like wildfire."

"I know," said Sisko grimly. "Believe me, I know." He lowered his voice and said, "Are we any closer, Constable? *Any* closer to ending this?"

"No, but it *will* end, Sisko," shot back Odo fiercely. "I will find the one who did this. That's a certainty. Every passing second brings us closer to that moment."

"I accept that, Constable," Sisko told him. But his tone was grim. "I just hope that the reason it ends is not because the killer runs out of victims."

CHAPTER
11

THE BUBBLING PANIC HAD BEGUN.

The main floor of the Promenade was a surging mass of people shouting, vying for attention, trying desperately not to let alarm overtake them, and not succeeding all that well.

Sisko stood on the upper level, looking down upon the crowd and feeling for all the world like some sort of planetary overseer, speaking from on high.

He would have been unable to make himself heard under ordinary circumstances. But he had keyed his voice through his comm badge, so that his words echoed throughout the station's intraship public address system.

"The matter," he was saying, his voice rolling like waves, "is under investigation!"

"Investigate it on your own time!" someone shouted. "I want to get the hell off this station!"

"Me too!"

That refrain was rapidly taken up throughout the Promenade. Sisko put up his hands, trying to bring them under control. "That is not possible."

"Why not?"

And then, before Sisko could respond, someone else shouted, "They say the murderer is a shapeshifter like Odo! Is it true?"

Sisko paused. He saw Odo in the crowd, his security crew trying to restore some semblance of order. Odo had heard the shouted question, too, and he was looking up at Sisko with interest, clearly curious as to how the commander was going to answer it.

"That is a working theory," said Sisko.

Immediately the area around Odo began to widen a bit. People pulled back from him, as if he'd suddenly become infected with some hideous disease.

Each word that Sisko spoke was slow and loaded with anger. "I will not," he said, "stand still for another wave of accusations against the constable. We went through this after the faked murder of Ibudan. I will not see a repeat. Security Chief Odo is not a suspect. Far too many witnesses, including myself, can place him elsewhere at the time of the murders. Furthermore, if you treat him like a suspect, you will simply prolong this matter, because it is *his* job to solve these murders. We need full cooperation from all of you. Besides, there are several known shapeshifting species throughout the galaxy. There is no reason for suspicion to fall automatically on Chief Odo, and every reason for it not to."

He paused a moment, taking a breath, and in that time, someone called out, "We still want to get off this station! You can't make us stay here! We're at risk every moment we're here!"

"You're forcing us to stick our heads into the dragon's mouth," shouted another.

"I'm forcing you to stay," said Sisko, "for two reasons. First, we have no desire to allow the murderer to leave DS-Nine during a mass emigration—"

"That's *your* problem, Sisko," someone shouted.

Sisko noticed that the people seemed a lot braver and

more likely to mouth off when they were together in one large crowd. Security in numbers.

"No," countered Sisko, "it's *your* problem. Because that brings me to the second reason. Let us say, for argument's sake, that we are indeed dealing with a shapeshifter. That means that it could be disguised as one of you. Your copilot or a crew member. It could be among your cargo or your personal belongings."

This caused a great deal of unease among the crowd. They started looking apprehensively at each other and even at their own clothing as if waiting for their shoes to make a false move.

"If I allow you people to leave," continued Sisko, "there's a perfectly good chance that the killer will leave with you. In your endeavor to escape, you might very well take the murderer along with you for the ride. Here on the station there's safety in numbers. Out in the depths of space—particularly for you one- and two-man cargo runners—there will be no one and nothing except a real possibility of a very lonely death."

Not a word was being spoken.

"Now," said Sisko serenely, "who is interested in bucking those odds? Hmm? Show of hands, please."

No one seemed particularly anxious to volunteer.

"Good," Sisko said. "That will be all. If any of you have further questions, feel free to pose them in an orderly manner. If Security Chief Odo wants to talk with you, kindly give him your full cooperation. Thank you."

He then turned away, headed for the turbolift shaft, and moments later was being whisked away to Ops. The moment the lift doors had closed, he leaned against the turbolift walls and let out a long sigh.

"There's got to be an easier way to earn a living," he muttered.

As soon as he stepped out onto the bridge, he went straight to O'Brien. "Chief," he said, "can you order a systems-wide shutdown of the airlock doors to all docked ships?"

"Are you kidding?" asked O'Brien. "The way these systems are set up, it's a miracle the airlocks work at all. Shutting them down is no problem. What's tough is keeping them operational."

"Good. Do it."

"Taking no chances, Commander?" asked Kira.

"Exactly right, Major. I'm not going to risk another near-disaster like the one we had with Captain Jaheel. If we hadn't been lucky, we would have lost half the docking ring that time he tried to take off without clearance. We learn from our mistakes, Major."

"Yes, sir." She looked, though, as if she wanted to say something else.

"Yes, Major?" he prompted.

She shook her head. "It's . . . well, Old Kelsi was one of the first people I met when I arrived here. I . . . She deserved better, that's all."

"I don't know of anyone who *deserves* what has happened in the past several days," Sisko replied.

But he could tell from Kira's look that she knew who deserved such a death. Oh, yes, she knew. Definitely.

Cardassians.

He did not, however, pursue the subject. Instead he went to his station to study the reports and information being routed through his command computer.

He gazed around Ops and reflected bleakly on the fact that the creature might be right here. Right in front of him. It could be one of his people. It could be a piece of equipment. Anything. Anywhere.

He headed for his office, but it seemed as if he'd barely sat down when O'Brien appeared in the doorway. "Sir," he said, "I hate to intrude, but with school letting out soon, I was hoping that—"

Angrier than he wanted to be, Sisko slammed a fist down on his desk. "Is this going to be a regular thing with you, Chief? What next? If your wife feels like going shopping along the Promenade, are you going to request time off to serve as her bodyguard? Did you do this on the *Enterprise,* too?"

"No, sir," O'Brien shot back. "We felt safe on the *Enterprise.*"

"Oh, really? When, Chief? During the Borg attack? During the skirmishes along the Neutral Zone? Fighting Cardassians? When precisely did you feel at ease?"

O'Brien, who lately had been picturing a hideous scenario—coming home to find his wife and child splattered all over their grungy quarters—came perilously close to blowing his top.

"When? When we were off duty," he snapped, "and I wasn't constantly being called away because some other bloody thing had broken. When we were with our friends, back when we had friends. When we had time to breathe, and our lungs weren't filled with stale air because the atmosphere regulators were designed for Cardassians and I haven't managed to convert them all over yet. When we always had more than enough of whatever we needed. Back when we *had a life!*"

There was dead silence.

They realized that all talk had ceased in Ops. Sisko glanced out through his door and saw that every eye was upon them. Quickly all of the crew members went back to what they were doing.

Except for Dax, who was still looking at Sisko.

And Sisko remembered the times in the past when he had poured out his anger and frustration to her. He could hear his own voice saying, "If only I'd been with Jennifer. I could have saved her. If only I hadn't dragged her out into space. If only . . ."

And Jake's eyes, looking at him in that same accusatory manner . . .

O'Brien looked down. "I'm sorry, sir," he said. "It's just that . . . well, when there's an emergency—if we're fighting to keep the station from blowing up or being sucked into the wormhole or some such—I'm right in there up to my elbows. I'm able to put everything out of my mind except getting the job done. But with something like this . . . with this madman running around, there's nothing for me to do except dwell on the danger and imagine the worst. And from what I've heard, the worst can be pretty bad. Molly, she'll soon have her third birthday. I want her to live to see it . . . you know?"

Sisko nodded. "Tell you what, Chief," he said softly. "I'll make you a deal."

"A deal, sir?"

"Cut yourself loose for the fifteen minutes or so it takes to get your wife and child safely squared away after school, and you don't have to keep running it past me . . . as long as you make sure that Jake gets home as well."

O'Brien smiled gamely at that. "Done, sir."

"Then get to it, Chief," said Sisko firmly. "That's an order."

"Yes, sir."

O'Brien walked out quickly, and Sisko smiled to himself. If only all of his difficulties could be solved that easily.

In the infirmary, Julian Bashir swung the cellular scanner away from the tissue samples that had been taken from Kelsi—although he rather bleakly speculated that there wasn't much left of her *except* tissue samples.

Nurse Latasa was looking over his shoulder. She saw the fatigued look on his face, and said, "Doctor . . . it's none of my business, but when was the last time you slept?"

"Oh. Sleep." He made a great show of searching his memory. "Yes . . . I remember now. That's what you do when you're not working. When you're not hoping to find some clue . . . *anything* that will help Security nail this homicidal maniac." He looked at Latasa closely.

"Doctor, is everything all right?" she asked.

He cleared the file on the bioscanner and said, "Nurse, place your hand here, please."

She was puzzled, but did as he asked, putting her hand flat on the counter. He ran a quick scan over it and quickly checked the readings against Latasa's files. "Yes, it's you, all right."

"Doctor . . .?"

Realizing how odd his behavior must have seemed just then, he said, "We're dealing with something that changes its appearance. That's a good way to turn people into raving paranoids. Nurse, we have to develop a code phrase."

Latasa laughed uncertainly. "Doctor, I hardly think we need a—"

"Yes, we do," he said firmly. "I hope some of my research will lead somewhere. But when I ask you for reports and such, I have to know that you're the genuine item and not a shapeshifter who's trying to cover his tracks by feeding me false information."

"If you say so, Doctor," she said. Her tone made it clear that she thought his request was odd. Then again, she knew what was happening around the station, and she was willing to take precautions.

"Okay. So our code word will be . . ." He gave it a moment's thought and then said, "Preganglionic. You got that, Nurse? If I say, 'What's the word?' you reply, 'Preganglionic.'" He paused and saw that she was smiling. "What's so funny?"

"I have to admit," she said, "for a moment there, I thought you were going to say that the code phrase should be something like—I don't know—'Kiss me, you fool.' You say, 'What's the word?' And I say, 'Kiss me, you fool.'"

Despite the horrific situation that had led to their current difficulties, Bashir actually laughed. "Now, Nurse, that has got to be one of the most juvenile notions I've ever heard, beyond question. Although . . . you know, I almost wish I'd thought of it. But," he sighed, "it's too late now, I suppose."

The tissue samples were still there, and Bashir rather reluctantly went back to them, hoping that something had grown there in the meantime. Something that he could actually put to use.

"It's terrible about Kelsi," said Latasa.

"About all of them," Bashir agreed. He'd discharged Bena and Dina some hours before. Odo had posted a full-time guard to them; it was the only way that Bena would leave the infirmary. Even the survivors, mused Bashir, were victims.

"I was thinking about Kelsi in particular," she said. "I mean, I'd met her. Gotten to know her. I . . . I hate to admit it, but I'm relieved that I wasn't assisting at her autopsy. I'd much rather remember her the way she was, rather than . . . than what they say she looked like when that maniac was finished with her."

"I know," said Bashir. "You have a picture in your mind of people. You don't think about . . ."

His voice trailed off as he looked up from the bioscanner.

"You know," he said. "That . . . just might do it."

"Do what, Doctor? Doctor . . . do you have some sort of clue about the killer?"

"No. No, not yet. But I have a thought about something else that's bothering me. Nurse . . . thank you. You may have been extremely helpful just now . . . more than you know."

"Oh . . ." Latasa was confused, but said gamely,

"Glad I could be of help, Doctor." And as he started to head out of the infirmary, she called after him, "Preganglionic."

He smiled, replied, "Kiss me, you fool," and walked out.

CHAPTER
12

SECURITY GUARDS Boyajian and Meyer were making their way carefully through deck 15 of the space station's core. Boyajian, in particular, felt as if they'd logged several hundred miles in just the past forty-eight hours. And every step of those miles had been nerve-racking as they watched for any sign of the intruder. Every shadow in Deep Space Nine seemed to stir these days; every corner seemed threatening. Every person required a second and even a third glance, and even then he couldn't be absolutely sure about anyone. For that matter, he had to check every possession he owned to make sure it had no bioreadings. . . .

Suddenly, from overhead, a red mass started to pour down from the ceiling.

It splattered to the floor a mere three feet in front of the two security guards. Immediately Meyer hit his comm badge and shouted, "Odo! It's here! Core level fifteen, corridor nine!"

Odo was nowhere nearby.

He was in the docking ring, grilling people in the hope that they had noticed something—*anything*—

that would be useful to him. But when he heard the alarmed call from his men, he immediately hit his comm badge. "Odo to Ops! Emergency! Lock on and beam me to core level fifteen, corridor nine . . . now!"

"Benjamin, they've got a sighting," called Dax, stepping in for O'Brien. She quickly manipulated the transporter controls as Sisko came out of his office and charged down into Ops. "I'm beaming him over there now!"

"Send me along," he ordered, stepping onto the pad.

For a moment Dax wanted to argue, to state that Sisko could serve far better by staying at Ops and keeping out of the way of Security.

But she knew better. She knew *him* better.

So she simply said, "Energizing," and a moment later Sisko vanished.

O'Brien was heading for the turbolift to return to Ops when he heard from behind him, "O'Brien! Just the man I wanted to see!"

"Not now, Quark," he said, and he kept up his stride.

Quark fell into step on one side of him, Glav on the other. "Now, come on, O'Brien . . . I always make time for you. You haven't got a spare moment for me? Remember that free drink? Eh?"

O'Brien hesitated and then said, "Look . . . ten seconds. What is it? What do you need fixed? Tell me, because I really have to get back up to Ops."

"Fixed? Nothing like that! O'Brien, you have to expand your horizons! You have to—"

"Five seconds and counting."

"We want to buy Deep Space Nine."

O'Brien laughed. "Fine," he said. "You have my vote." And he walked away.

"Hah!" Quark crowed to Glav. "You see? The chief of operations supports us!"

"I don't know," said Glav doubtfully. "I always have difficulty reading human sarcasm. Maybe he wasn't being serious."

"Of course he was!" retorted Quark. "The whole key was his saying that we have his vote. Humans don't talk lightly of such things. They're very much into discussing this and considering that and voting on the whole package. It's practically a religion to them! Believe me, O'Brien has no reason to love Starfleet. They booted him off one of their prestigious starships and put him here . . . back before they knew that anyone was going to be remotely interested in the place. We have him on our side, pressing our case to Sisko. I guarantee that O'Brien will sway him. And Sisko, in turn, will help convince the Bajorans. It's going to work, I'm telling you. In fact," he said, lowering his voice, "this entire murder business—while certainly a gruesome and deplorable happenstance—has made the property that much more obtainable. It wouldn't surprise me at all if the Federation and Bajor wouldn't *love* to get rid of the place after everything they've been through."

Glav grinned. "You're right, Quark! Trust you to take death, slaughter, and misery . . . and find the up side! Your mind never stops working. Very well. Despite the rather distressing setback of Gotto being slaughtered, I'm still maintaining high hopes for this! In fact, this calls for celebration! Join me in a drink?"

"Drinks? Hah! I can do better than that," said Quark. "Tell me . . . have I introduced you yet to the wonders of my holosex suites?"

Glav displayed even more teeth. "Nooo . . ."

"Well, then"—Quark patted him on the back—"you're long overdue."

And they went off together, chortling in that way that Ferengi had.

Without paying the least bit of attention, they walked

153

past a red-haired Bajoran man. He watched them with curiosity . . .

And followed them.

Odo looked only mildly surprised when he materialized to find Sisko standing next to him. They didn't have time for any exchange of words, for they found themselves facing a huge red gelatinous mass that was seeping down from a bent ceiling plate.

Meyer and Boyajian had their phasers out, but they didn't know where to shoot. The security guards were tough, but this was beyond anything they had ever confronted. Hearing the whine of the transporter, Meyer glanced back as Odo and Sisko strode forward. "Sir! Watch out!"

The red stuff was accumulating faster and faster, spreading outward in a huge disgusting puddle. Meyer and Boyajian stepped back as it almost snared their feet. Visions of winding up like the thing's previous victims were racing through their heads. "Sir!" Boyajian called out.

Sisko frowned in confusion, because Odo wasn't moving. Odo was simply staring at it. For just the briefest moment—a moment that Sisko would never admit to anyone—he wondered if Odo felt reluctant to take on a being that might very well be just like him. Despite the creature's murderous intent, was it remotely possible that Odo felt closer to it than to the people with whom he worked?

He wiped the notion out of his mind as quickly as it had come. Odo might be arrogant, smug, and even condescending, but when it came to reliability in getting the job done, he was second to none.

Still . . . why the hell was he just standing there?

The glop had become a circle five feet in diameter and was spreading faster than ever. At any moment it would doubtless coalesce into some fearsome form and then . . .

But Odo wasn't waiting. He strode forward, pushing his own men aside, squatted down, and stared at the red mass. It surged forward, around his feet.

"Constable!" shouted Sisko.

Odo dipped his fingers into the slime, held a glob of it up, rubbed it between his fingers, brought it to his nose, and sniffed it.

"Coolant," he said, "mixed with some sort of gelatin, I think."

"Wh-what?"

Odo didn't respond to Sisko's confused question. Instead he stepped back and looked up at the ceiling.

And Odo's body dissolved.

Sisko gasped. He'd never actually seen Odo shift his shape before. He knew what the security chief could do, but knowing it was quite different from actually witnessing it.

Starting from the top down, Odo began to transmute into his natural state. But his legs were the last to go, and as they did he sprang up off them, giving him the slight lift he needed to propel himself up into the ceiling crack from which the ooze was still pouring.

"This way," said Quark.

"I've been here before, Quark," Glav said as they stepped into the holosuite. The door shut behind them. "We had a conference in here, remember?"

"Ahh," said Quark, "but you've never seen the holos in action before. Computer," he called out, "Run program XXX-three."

The air seemed to shimmer around them, and then a blast of hot air hit them.

They were in a large and elaborately decorated tent. Great tables were laid out with food of all types and colors. Some sort of poultry was roasting on a spit, the crackling sound as real and the aroma as convincing as if it were the genuine article rather than a holodeck re-creation.

"This technology," said Glav, "never fails to amaze me."

"It gets better," Quark assured him. He dropped down onto a large pile of pillows, then reached up and pulled Glav down next to him. "Watch."

There was the tinkling of gentle bells, and the entrance curtains of the tent were pushed aside. In swayed two dancing girls, clad in multicolored gauze that did little to obscure the specifics of their bodies and nothing to obscure their curves. Their faces were covered with veils as well.

They posed in front of Glav and Quark, frozen in position.

Glav nodded appreciatively. "They look . . . quite suitable," Glav told him.

"Better than that," Quark said. He clapped his hands together briskly.

The women removed the veils from their faces.

Glav gasped and said, "Remarkable! Is that . . . ?"

"Yesss." Quark chuckled. "It took a while to get the program just right. Dead ringers, don't you think?"

The holograms of Major Kira Nerys and Lieutenant Jadzia Dax smiled invitingly at the two Ferengi.

"I managed to tap into their personal files," he said. "Their last complete physicals . . . their measurements from when they were fitted for their uniforms. I assure you, everything is accurate."

"But isn't that sort of information confidential?"

"Hah!" chortled Quark. "Confidential except to the right people. And the right people have the right isolinear chips to find out just about whatever they want." He lowered his voice and snickered, "Wait until you see the birthmark one of them has on her . . . ah, but you can find out for yourself. Oh, ladies . . ." He clapped his hands once more.

The holo images of Kira and Dax began to dance, their bodies undulating in time to music that was coming from everywhere. In unison they started to remove the veils that covered the rest of them, and the gauze began to flutter to the floor.

On the lower level of Quark's drinking and gambling establishment, a red-haired Bajoran moved through the crowd. The customers were more subdued these days, with a general atmosphere of paranoia hanging over them. Still, despite all the nervousness in the air, no one gave the nondescript Bajoran a second look.

He looked up the stairs that led to the holosuites, and started upward.

In the crawlway above the ceiling, Odo began to re-form.

The first thing he saw was a large overturned vat positioned above the crack. The last of its contents were dripping out and down to the floor below.

And the next thing he spotted was a pair of booted feet disappearing around a corner in the crawlway.

Odo did not like to undertake one shapeshift after another in quick succession. Each time he morphed, he expended energy. Even maintaining the same shape, as he did most of the day in his humanoid form, took some effort. That was one of the reasons he had to return to his natural form and rest at the end of the day. And if he shifted too often, too fast, he could overexert himself.

The consequences of such overexertion would not be pretty.

Nevertheless, Odo gamely shifted again. His shape drew in upon itself, becoming smaller and smaller, and within seconds he was a rat.

He darted down the crawlway as fast as he could—

which wasn't as fast as a real rat could go, because a real rat didn't weigh all that much. Odo, however—due to those dreary laws of physics—could alter his shape all he wanted, but he couldn't do a thing about his mass. He now had the exterior shape of a rat, but not its interior structure. Otherwise his weight would have crushed the "rat's" skeleton and pulped its internal organs. Odo, not really having any internal organs or skeletal structure, wasn't hampered.

Even as heavy as he was, he was still far better equipped for speed in the confined area than the individual he was pursuing . . . and he already had a fairly good idea who that might be.

He heard the scuffling of elbows and knees in front of him and scooted around the corner. He saw a humanoid form ahead of him, and—yes, just as he thought—it was a Ferengi. A particular Ferengi with whom he was all too well acquainted.

The Ferengi heard a scuttling behind him and glanced back under his own arm. When he spotted the rat he let out a sigh of relief and continued on his way.

The rat, however, had other plans. It clamped its little teeth into the cuff of the fugitive's trouser leg . . . and held on.

And didn't budge.

The Ferengi fell flat, his right leg unexpectedly anchored. He craned his neck and saw, to his shock, that he was being assaulted by the heaviest damned rodent he had ever seen. He kicked at the creature furiously, but it didn't seem to notice or care.

"What the hell kind of rat are you?" screeched the Ferengi in an alarmed, high-pitched voice.

The rat suddenly began to expand. The Ferengi's eyes went wide as, within seconds, he was joined in the crawlway by the station's head of security.

"Oh, no!"

"That's 'Odo,'" he corrected. "Sounds like 'Oh, no,'

but with a very bad head cold. So . . . just not your day, is it, Nog?"

Nog moaned softly and thudded his head against the side of the crawlspace.

In the holosuite, Dax was pirouetting in place. Kira was arched backwards, her stomach muscles rippling. A considerable amount of gauze was piled up on the floor, and not much was left on the women's bodies. A fine film of sweat glistened on their skin, and their fingers moved quickly, chiming out seductive melodies with the fingertip chimes they wore.

"Ohhhh, Quark." Glav could barely contain himself. "Creating the likenesses of genuine women . . . putting all this together. I must congratulate you. You are true slime."

"Thank you," said Quark, trying to retain his modesty even as Dax and Kira cavorted, having totally abandoned theirs.

At that moment true slime began to ooze through the crack in the holosuite door.

Sisko scowled fiercely at the Ferengi boy who stood in front of him, not looking particularly contrite.

"It was just a joke," he said sullenly.

"A joke?" said Sisko, barely keeping his outrage in check.

Odo was even less successful. He grabbed Nog by one of his huge ears and said, "Would you consider it an even bigger joke if I cracked your oversized head like a walnut?"

Nog didn't appear to be listening. His eyes had crossed, and his breathing had gotten faster and raspier.

Immediately Sisko realized what the problem was. "Constable," he said, "I'd let go if I were you. They like having their ears grabbed. Remember?"

Odo promptly released the Ferengi boy with a look of

such disgust that he might just as well have shoved his hand into raw sewage. "What *was* I thinking?" he wondered.

Meyer and Boyajian were looking sheepishly at the glop that was already starting to coagulate on the floor. "Sorry, sir," said Boyajian. "Guess we handled this pretty badly."

"It was an understandable mistake," said Odo. He gripped Nog firmly by the upper arm. "What was *not* understandable was how you could possibly have thought this was funny."

"People are getting hurt, Nog," Sisko told him angrily. "People are getting killed. And causing our people to run around responding to false alarms is simply unconscionable."

Nog shrugged. He didn't even make an insincere attempt to say he was sorry, which only served to exasperate Sisko even further. "Constable," he said, "get him out of here. Take him back to his father."

"Yes, sir," said Odo. He shoved the boy in front of him. "Let's go."

Rom was working the Dabo wheel, trying to drum up interest in one of Quark's premier games.

Betting had been rather slow that day. Most of Quark's patrons were content to nurse their drinks and watch each other with a high degree of suspicion. The grim attitude seemed to be one of *Why should I gamble? I probably won't live to enjoy my winnings.*

Not an attitude that was exactly conducive to spirited gaming.

"Come on!" he called out cajolingly. "Who feels lucky?!"

"Shut up," grumbled a Tellarite.

But Rom didn't take the admonition to heart, because he saw a potential pigeon fluttering his way. "Doctor!" he summoned Bashir over. "You look lost.

You look lonely. You look like someone who may be open to a game of chance."

"Life holds enough chances without adding artificial ones," said Bashir, looking around. "Where is Quark?"

"A spin will get you an answer," purred the Ferengi.

Bashir rolled his eyes. "Oh, very well." Quickly he placed a bet.

Rom spun the wheel. He watched the ball skittle around . . . and then fall in . . . precisely where Bashir had bet that it would. He gaped and then said gamely, "Two out of three?"

"Tell you what," said Bashir. "Forget my winnings. Just tell me where Quark is."

"Well, you know it's not my place to spy on my boss," said Rom. "However, it just so happens that out of the smallest corner of my eye, I believe I saw him step into Holosuite B."

"Thank you," said Bashir, and he started to walk away.

"Doctor! I don't think Quark would particularly appreciate being disturbed in the middle of a holosuite sex fantasy . . . if you catch my meaning."

"Don't worry," Bashir shot back. "I'm a doctor, remember? I doubt there's anything in there I haven't seen before." And he headed up the steps.

Jake Sisko was bored.

He had intended to cut loose after school and have fun, but Chief O'Brien had escorted Jake to his quarters after taking Keiko and little Molly home.

Ben Sisko's admonitions about staying put had been assessed and accepted, but ultimately Jake found himself staring into the mirror and feeling utterly without anything interesting to do. There was homework, sure, but what kind of life was that? School and homework. School and homework. Wow. Fun.

And besides, he was quite aware of one great truth:

his mother had stayed put. He and his mother had both hidden in their quarters while the *Saratoga* was being pounded by the Borg.

"A fat lot of good it did us," he muttered.

The hell with it. He wasn't accomplishing anything of great importance sitting around. And he was lonely, too. Nog hadn't shown up at school the past couple of days. Oh, sure, his father, Rom, had said that he'd be bringing him to class regularly. But—surprise, surprise —the word of the Ferengi hadn't been the most dependable.

Where would Nog be about now? Not in his quarters, certainly. Nog was a mover and shaker. He didn't sit around, kept captive by his father's worries. Nog would be out. Nog would be happening. Nog would be . . .

Over at Quark's, most likely. Out in the Promenade. Which was where Jake Sisko now resolved to go.

He stepped out of his quarters, looked right and left to make sure that O'Brien wasn't hanging around to spy on him, and headed for the crossover bridge that would take him to the Promenade and the heart of Deep Space Nine.

CHAPTER
13

KIRA AND DAX wore nothing but the bracelets on their wrists and ankles.

They—or rather, their holographic counterparts—were gyrating in front of the two Ferengi. Dax's long hair hung down past her shoulders, slightly obscuring her breasts; Kira, with her short hair, wasn't hiding behind anything. Quark and Glav were practically jumping out of their skin with excitement, and Glav was stretching out grasping fingers, almost touching Dax's swaying body . . .

And directly behind the Ferengi, a small column of red protoplasmic matter had grown and was taking on shape. A second later the nondescript red-haired Bajoran was standing directly behind them. Neither of them appeared aware of him, their attention rather understandably drawn elsewhere.

The intruder's hands had disappeared, to be replaced by huge spike-studded mallets. He raised them over his head, ready to bring them smashing down . . .

And from outside, they heard a voice say firmly, "Emergency medical override on lock. Employ now." A second later the door hissed open and Bashir entered, saying, "I apologize for barging in, Quark, but there's something important I have to . . ."

"Get out!" shrieked Quark, trying to scramble to his feet so that he could block Bashir's view of the holograms.

Bashir didn't quite know where to look first.

Naturally the first things he noticed were the naked forms of Dax and Kira, twirling around in ecstasy for the dining and dancing pleasure of the two Ferengi. Since no one had told the program to stop running, the two female figures continued their activities undeterred by the doctor's advent.

However, this held his attention for only a second—a remarkable display of willpower—before he saw something that didn't fit into the hologram program at all.

A Bajoran with fists transformed into lethal maces, about to bring them smashing down onto . . . Quark's skull.

A look of pure hatred flashed across the Bajoran's face as he realized he'd been spotted.

"Quark! Behind you!" shouted Bashir.

Humans might not have moved at that point. They might have looked in confusion at whoever was shouting, perhaps even demanded clarification of the situation before taking any sort of action. They might have said, "What do you mean?" and actually looked behind them to see what was happening. Such a delay, in this instance, would have proven fatal.

Quark, however, was a Ferengi. A Ferengi proudly possessed the most highly developed sense of self-preservation in the known galaxy. And whenever a warning was hurled his way, a Ferengi ducked first and asked questions later.

Consequently, Quark acted on pure self-preservation reflex. Forgotten was his momentary outrage at Bashir's intrusion. That could wait. He immediately lunged forward, knocking over a tray of food, getting far away from whatever the hell was behind him before his mind had even fully processed the information that he was in danger.

The action saved his life.

The pseudo-Bajoran's fists slammed down right where Quark had been. Pillows, given the semblance of reality, were torn to holographic shreds.

Glav emitted a startled shriek and crawled backwards, bumping into the Dax hologram, but not caring the least bit about her lack of clothing. "It's the shapeshifter!" he squealed.

The metamorph spun in place, snarling, his focus on Quark. And Quark, his voice an octave higher, called out, "Computer! Program XXX-four! Now!"

And in an instant the room was filled with fog. From somewhere in the mist came the sound of female laughter.

Bashir didn't know where they were or what the hell was happening, but of two things he was certain: they had to get out of there, and they had to leave now.

The exit, he knew, was right behind him. He spun toward it.

But the door had automatically slid shut behind him and returned to its lock program, and he plowed straight into it.

Bashir staggered back and bumped into someone. Both of them let out a yell of fear before Bashir could make out that it was a panic-stricken Quark.

"How do I know it's you?" demanded Quark.

"How do I know it's you?" Bashir shot back.

And then he saw it, coming in quickly. The huge, mallet-shaped, spiked weapon that the shapechanger was wielding on the end of his wrist.

He shoved Quark to one side, himself to the other. The weapon smashed forward, tearing through the door. Dim light from the hallway poured into the holosuite.

"Quark!" Glav was screaming. "Quaaarrrkkk!"

"Every Ferengi for himself!" Quark shouted back as Bashir dragged him to safety.

Except it was hardly safety, for the shapeshifter—his face twisted with rage—came right after them.

Sisko accompanied Odo to Quark's casino, and Odo shoved the crestfallen Nog in front of him. Sisko's approval of the relationship Nog was developing with Jake had fallen to a new low. He felt that putting in an appearance would emphasize just how seriously he was taking this matter . . . and serve as a reminder that Nog's associating with Jake would not be particularly appreciated.

Rom looked up from the gaming table as his son approached . . . and then frowned when he saw who was accompanying Nog, and the looks on the faces of all three. Cutting to the chase, he sighed and said, "All right, what did he do this time?"

"Your son," said Odo stiffly, "performed a little stunt that could very well have gotten him killed."

Rom considered that a moment. "Was there any profit in this stunt?"

"None whatsoever," Sisko told him.

Rom promptly cuffed the boy, drawing a loud yowl from Nog. "Idiot!" he bellowed. "How many times do I have to tell you? Never risk your life if there's no hope of a payoff!" He shook his head and said discouragedly to Sisko, "Kids. You talk to them and talk to them. And they never listen. You feel like everything you say is automatically tuned out."

Sisko had to catch himself, for he was starting to nod in agreement. He cleared his throat and said sharply, "Security Chief Odo is quite correct. Your son's prank could indeed have cost him his life. He poured a substance out of a ceiling plate that he intended to be mistaken for the shapeshifter. If the security men had opened fire on the ceiling instead of waiting for Odo to take charge of the situation—"

"Yes, yes, of course. I see exactly what you mean. Fool!" And again he cuffed the boy. Once again Nog yelped loudly.

But this time Sisko was starting to get uncomfortable. He took Rom by the wrist and said chidingly, "You know, hitting the boy won't accomplish anything."

"It'll make him remember!" Rom retorted.

"It'll make him remember to fear his father, and not much beyond that."

Rom looked at Sisko skeptically. "And I suppose you'll tell me next that you don't hit your son."

"Well . . . no. I don't. And we have a better understanding for it."

"And where is your son at this moment, may I ask?"

"In his quarters, safe and sound," said Sisko.

"Really? You know, all humans look alike to me, but . . . isn't that him over there?"

Sisko turned to see where Rom was pointing . . . and sure enough, at the far end of the Promenade, there was Jake. He was ogling a woman of questionable repute. She was smiling and giving him a very distinct come-hither look.

Rom leaned forward and said helpfully, "Perhaps you should consider hitting him?"

And then, before Sisko could head in Jake's direction . . .

All hell broke loose.

"It's hiimmmmmmm!" came a hysterical voice that was unmistakably Quark's.

Sisko looked up, and there, on the upper landing of

the stairs leading to the holosuites, were Quark and Bashir. They were both running at full speed, and Bashir was in the lead.

And then Sisko saw him.

A Bajoran—red-haired but otherwise unremarkable —coming up behind them. And his right arm lashed out—literally lashed out, becoming a thin, vicious coil that snaked around Quark's waist. His left arm became another tentacle that snared Quark's throat, cutting off his air. Within seconds the terrified Ferengi was going to be ripped apart.

The dedicated patrons of Quark's reacted predictably.

They screamed and ran.

Hysteria filled the Promenade as the crowd became of one mind and started stampeding over each other in a desperate attempt to get away from the now-visible murderer stalking the station.

Bashir spun and saw Quark's distress. Despite the fact that he was courting certain death, he did not hesitate. He drew back a fist and—insanely, praying that he wouldn't hurt his hand—lunged forward, slamming a punch into the shapeshifter's face.

The creature that had called itself Meta saw the blow coming. A hole appeared in Meta's face, and Bashir's fist passed right through. Then Meta's head closed in around Bashir's arm, imprisoning it.

"Security!" shouted Odo, but he was already moving. He took a step forward, then two, and his body rippled and seemed to shrink. And as it did so, his back started to convulse and erupt, something huge emerging from it.

Then the crowd enveloped him as everyone ran away from the very place that he was trying to get to. Sisko turned, trying to spot Jake, but the boy had been swallowed up in the stampede.

Three steps, four, and then five, and Odo—half the height that he was before—exploded out of the crowd, knocking people aside. The gleaming wings that had sprouted from his back beat the air furiously, and Odo was airborne, soaring across the intervening space.

Bashir pounded at Meta's head. Meta didn't seem all that interested in him, perfectly willing to delay killing Bashir until Quark had been disposed of.

Quark, struggling at the constriction on his throat, saw Glav emerge from the holosuite. Glav, a look of terror on his face, had adopted a defensive posture— the standard Ferengi cringe.

And then there was a rush of air, and Odo slammed into the shapechanger.

The four of them went down in a tangle. Abruptly realizing the genuine threat that Odo represented, Meta released both Quark and Bashir and turned his attention to the more imminent problem.

They faced each other for the first time. Odo retracted his wings, and the mass rearranged itself into its human configuration. Moments later Odo was at his normal height and was staring eye to eye at the metamorph.

For the first time in his existence, Odo was confronted by someone who might be from his own race. Someone who might hold all the answers to his questions about his own mysterious background.

Someone Odo had been waiting for, praying for, all his life.

He said the only thing he could: "You're under arrest."

Meta's arms fused together, became a spear, and stabbed forward with unnatural speed. Before Odo could move, he was driven backwards, the spear-arms slamming through his chest and out through his back. Within seconds he was pinned against the wall.

And Meta's head became round and hard, brutal spikes appearing all over its surface. His neck extended like a spring, and his head slammed forward for the purpose of connecting with Odo's.

Odo wasn't there when it hit. He went liquid and splattered to the floor just before Meta's head connected.

Odo didn't waste a moment. He solidified and, as he did so, lunged forward. His hardening mass connected with Meta's midsection before the morph could shift into another shape.

The impact knocked Meta clear off the upper landing. For a moment he flailed about in midair, and then, as he started to fall the two stories to the floor, he shifted once more.

Odo looked on in amazement as, with no apparent effort at all, the metamorph transformed itself into a rubber ball. It hit the floor and bounced across the casino floor.

Sisko drew his phaser and fired. But the morph-as-ball bounced effortlessly over the phaser beam and rolled under the Boja table.

Odo sagged against a wall. Bashir said, "Are you all right?"

"Fine. Fine. I just need to rest for a moment."

The Boja table was knocked clean over, and from underneath it, roaring in defiance, lunged a mugato. Its face was red, and its white apelike body shook as it roared in fury.

"Rest time's over," said Odo.

Odo stepped over the still-shaking body of Quark and charged down the stairs. The mugato howled defiantly. Odo came to a halt several steps away and announced, "You're not impressing anyone!"

Sisko fired his phaser from less than ten feet away. He fired on wide beam, which lessened the overall strength.

But it also meant that the creature couldn't anticipate the blast and morph a hole around it, allowing it to pass harmlessly through.

The mugato staggered but did not come close to falling. Then suddenly the creature shrieked in surprise as Odo thrust his hands into the mugato's chest. But now it was Odo who had transformed his hands into spears. The impact brought him face to face with the creature.

"Sauce for the goose," grated Odo.

The mugato brought its head down and speared Odo straight between the eyes with its horn.

Odo staggered, momentarily unable to see. Then eye stalks grew up and around from the rear of his skull so that he literally had eyes in the back of his head.

But the maneuver gave the Mugato enough time to swing its head back and forth. His horn savaged Odo's cranium, and Odo completely lost orientation.

Desperately he went liquid again. The mugato spun to face Sisko, and the commander brought his phaser up and fired once more.

The mugato skated out of the way, its clawed feet having shifted into wheels.

It sped across the Promenade, which had now emptied of many of its regulars. Sisko fired again, but the mugato darted out of the way . . . and crashed solidly into Jake Sisko.

"Jake!" shouted his father.

In a flash Meta was on his feet, having dropped the mugato configuration. He had reassumed the red-haired human appearance, but he was looking somewhat haggard. The rapid shifting was no less of a strain on him than it was on Odo.

Still, he had enough strength for another partial transmutation, which would buy him a few minutes' breathing space.

He grabbed Jake Sisko, yanked him to his feet, and brought his right hand up across the boy's throat. The hand glistened, having become a vicious-looking blade.

"Stay back!" he shouted.

Odo had been coming up on the right, and he froze where he was. Sisko, facing Meta straight on, did likewise. But Sisko had his phaser out and was pointing it straight at the metamorph.

"Both of you . . . stay where you are," Meta warned.

"You can't escape," Odo informed him. "You're on a space station. Where do you think you can go?"

"Wherever I want," replied Meta.

Sisko kept his phaser aimed unwaveringly at the shapeshifter. "Let the boy go," he thundered.

"I don't think so." Meta was as calm as Sisko was angry. "And I suggest, Commander, that you point that elsewhere. Otherwise this little human gets to be number four."

"Why are you doing this?" Sisko demanded.

"It's what I do," replied Meta.

He pressed the blade closer to the boy's throat, and Jake yelped. A thin trickle of blood started running from just under his chin.

"Point . . . the phaser . . . elsewhere," said Meta. "Better yet . . . drop it."

Sisko suspected that the shapeshifter was tired and was trying to buy time. A phaser beam at this point— particularly a full-strength pinpoint blast—might actually do it damage, especially if the creature couldn't morph a hole around the beam fast enough.

But he was holding Jake in front of him, giving Sisko no room to maneuver.

Odo was off to the side and had a better angle . . . but Odo never carried a phaser. Sisko cursed that inwardly and glanced Odo's way.

And Odo was transforming himself, rearranging his molecules once more . . . into . . .

172

Sisko blinked, not believing what he was seeing. Odo had changed himself into a full-length mirror.

The question as to what possible reason the security officer could have for doing that was quickly followed by the answer.

Ohhhh, my God . . . thought Sisko.

But even as Sisko's mind recoiled at the plan, he was already putting it into action.

He thumbed the control on the phaser as he said, "All right. I'm holding my weapon away from you, and I'm going to put it down. Okay? Just don't hurt the boy."

Slowly, ever so slowly, Sisko kept his arm straight but pointed the phaser away from Meta. Meta was concentrating on watching Sisko and so wasn't really looking at where the commander was aiming. Nor was he aware that Sisko had just reconfigured the blast into a narrow beam.

Sisko was now aiming the phaser straight at Odo.

Some inner instinct—a sixth sense, *something*—started to warn Meta. He turned to glance at where Sisko was now pointing the phaser.

Breathing a prayer to a God that he had been somewhat on the outs with as of late, Sisko fired.

The beam stabbed out, struck Odo's mirrored surface, and ricocheted.

Meta's head exploded as the beam smashed right through it. Where his head had been, there was now a red mass, a stump that was his neck, oozing and seething.

Jake shoved as hard as he could, knocking the metamorph back, and then he dropped to the floor.

Sisko fired again before the metamorph could pull himself together. Meta was knocked clear off his feet, hitting the floor hard and dissolving.

He made straight for a floor vent and started pouring down it as fast as it could.

"No!" shouted Odo, half-phased out of his mirror

form. But his voice was ragged, exhausted, and he staggered forward and fell. Angry, frustrated, he tried to pull himself forward with his arms, to reach the escaping Meta.

Too slow, and too late. The metamorph vanished down the floor vent.

"Constable, don't!" Sisko called out even as he went to Jake to make sure the boy was all right. "The vents branch out in all directions under there! You'll never find him . . . and even if you do, you'll be too tired to get him."

"He has to be stopped, Sisko!"

Sisko had never seen Odo so frustrated, so angry. "He *will* be, Constable. We'll get him."

Odo allowed a nod, and transformed the last parts of him that had been the freestanding mirror.

At that moment several of Odo's security people came charging in belatedly. The massive exodus had slowed down their response time by a tremendous margin.

Odo thumped the floor in frustration. "We have to find some way to seal off all crawl spaces with forcefields, just as we've done with the hallways," he raged. "It never seemed necessary before, but who could have predicted this? No . . . *I* should have predicted this. I should have seen this as a possibility."

Anxious to raise the spirits of his thwarted security chief, Sisko said, "That was quick thinking by the way, Constable. That mirror business. I owe you my son's life."

Shaken from the experience but recovering quickly, Jake said, "Hey, you were no slouch, Dad. That was great shooting."

"Didn't you hear?" said Odo, managing to recapture some of his sardonic tone of voice. "When your father was in the Academy, they called him Dead-Eye. I have to admit, Sisko . . . I was banking on the hope that you were telling the truth about that. I was concerned that maybe you'd been exaggerating—about your marksmanship, I mean."

"Yeah, well . . . I was," admitted Sisko. "In fact, I was lying through my teeth." He paused and then added, "Good move, though."

CHAPTER
14

QUARK WAS STANDING behind his own bar, his hands trembling as he held his fourth synthale in the past hour. He raised it to his mouth, trying not to spill any of it. Across from him sat Glav, shaking his head. "I thought you were dead," he admitted.

"You thought I was dead? No one was more convinced than I was," replied Quark. "And I thought you were dead."

"If you hadn't conjured up that smoke screen, I would have been. What was that, anyway?"

"Dantus-Three. The fog is so perpetually thick there that the natives communicate entirely through the sense of touch."

"Sounds charming."

"It is . . . under the right circumstances." He gulped down the drink. "I tell you, Glav, nothing makes you more aware of your own mortality than a brush with death."

"This was more than a brush," said Glav. "If it hadn't been for that Starfleet man . . ."

"Yes. That's quite correct."

They turned to see that Bashir was standing nearby, listening, a look of quiet confidence in his eye.

"Doctor!" Quark called out. "How excellent to see you! Come! Come over here! Glav, make room for our most excellent friend!"

Bashir smiled appreciatively at Quark's reaction and sidled up to the bar. Glav patted him on the back. "You, sir, are our savior."

"Yes! What Glav just said is true," confirmed Quark. "At first, I must admit, I did not appreciate the disruption of my personal activities. But for obvious reasons I'm not exactly in a position to take you to task for interrupting us. A drink, on the house!"

"Very kind of you," said Bashir.

As Quark pushed a synthale over to him, he asked Bashir, "You . . . you don't think that creature is lurking about, do you?"

"I hope not," replied Bashir. "Now . . . I need to talk to you about something, Quark. The way I see it . . . you owe me."

Quark frowned. "I just gave you a free drink. Doesn't that make us even?"

Bashir gaped at him. "Are you saying your life is worth only one drink?"

Glav and Quark exchanged looks. "He's got a point," said Glav. "Maybe you should give him a second drink."

Bashir pushed the drink aside. "I'm not looking for free drinks."

"Well, what, then?" demanded Quark. Then suddenly his eyes narrowed and he took a step back suspiciously. "Wait . . . how do I know that *you're* not the creature?"

"If I were the creature," Bashir pointed out, "I could kill you easily right now. I'm sitting barely a foot away. Furthermore, if I am, it won't do you any harm to discuss what I want, because if I'm not Dr. Bashir, then nothing we agree to will be binding."

Quark considered the reasoning in that. "All right. That seems acceptable. So what do you want, Doctor?"

"I want you to program one of the holosuites with a special program that I will describe."

Quark licked his lips. "How . . . sexual is it? If I can make use of it after you're done . . . or make it available to customers . . ."

Bashir looked at him as if he'd grown a third eye. "It's not sexual at all. Not remotely. It may, however, do someone some good."

"Pfaw," snorted Quark. "Do you know how difficult it is to program a new holosimulation from scratch? It takes time, and time is valuable—particularly my time. Besides, I'm not sure I want my holosuites tainted by something pristine."

"Quark, I saved your life!"

"All right!" sighed Quark. "Free drinks at Quark's for the next year, not to exceed one per day. That's my best offer."

Glav nodded approvingly. "I'd take it, if I were you."

"I do have my standards, after all," affirmed Quark.

Bashir's lips thinned almost to nonexistence. "And do your standards," he inquired, "include erotic representations of Deep Space Nine personnel? Hmm?"

"I don't know what you're talking about," Quark said fairly convincingly.

He wasn't nearly convincing enough, though. "Quark," said Bashir calmly. "How do you think Lieutenant Dax and Major Kira would react if they found out about your activities?"

"Doctor," said Quark pleadingly, "you . . . you wouldn't. It was . . . it was just a harmless pursuit, that's all. No insult was meant by it. In fact, when you think about it, it was actually flattering to them!"

"Indeed. In that case, I'll make sure they know just how enthusiastically you were flattering them."

Bashir began to slide off his seat, but Quark quickly grabbed his forearm. "Wait!"

"Yes, Quark?"

Quark muttered some obscenities in his native tongue. "All right, Doctor. You drive a hard bargain. It makes me wonder if you're not part Ferengi. At any rate, I'll program whatever you want. Free of charge. Use it for however long you want. Use it until you choke!" he added vehemently.

"Thank you, Quark. I'll get you the specifications immediately. Oh, and Quark . . ."

"Yes?" said Quark tiredly. He despised being bested in a deal, even when the deal was with a man to whom he owed his craven life.

"What is the code name of that program with Dax and Kira?"

Quark perked up. "Ahhh. XXX-three. It's from my private stock, but if you're interested . . ."

"I want it erased."

"Doctor!"

"I mean it, Quark. I want it gone. Adios. And if you try anything like that again with any station personnel, then all bets are off. I'll blab the whole thing. And I can assure you that when Dax and Kira—particularly Kira—get through with you, you'll wish the metamorph *had* gotten you. Understood?"

"Understood," grunted Quark.

"Good. Because I'll check."

Quark gave him a sullen look. "Yes. Somehow I knew you would."

"Ops to Dr. Bashir," came Kira's voice over Bashir's badge. "Can you spare a moment, Doctor?"

"On my way."

He nodded once more to Quark and then rose and headed toward the turbolifts.

Glav made a scolding noise. "You didn't once mention to him our plan to buy the—"

"Oh, shut up," said Quark irritably.

"How in hell am I supposed to tell people they can't leave this station?" demanded Sisko.

They were grouped around the operations console: Sisko, Kira, Dax, Odo, O'Brien, and Bashir. Sisko's eyes were angry as he surveyed his people.

"At first we thought we could keep it under control," said Sisko. "But you saw what that creature—"

"Would you kindly refrain from referring to 'it' as a 'creature,' Sisko?" Odo's tone was cutting. He was attempting to cover up his personal affront and not doing a terribly good job of it.

Sisko nodded. "My sincere apologies, Constable. Very well . . . we all saw what that individual could do. More to the point, he caused a panic in the Promenade. It's a miracle that no one was trampled. We have to start getting people out of here."

"And the metamorph goes out with them," said Kira.

"Not necessarily," said Bashir. "We can run life scans on the ships' equipment to make sure he's not hiding on board any of the departing vessels."

"Not good enough," said Odo firmly. "He's devious. He could manage to get aboard after a ship's been scanned. Hell, he could disguise himself as the scanner and inform you that the ship is clean."

"If only we were within beaming distance of Bajor," said Dax. "We could transport them off the station."

Questioningly, Sisko turned to O'Brien.

O'Brien looked to be in genuine pain. "You're . . . going to tell me to find a way to move the station *back,* aren't you?" said O'Brien. It was not something that he would be thrilled to do. "Sir . . . the station really isn't *designed* for that. There's a forty percent chance that the increased stress could rip DS-Nine apart if we put her through that again."

"That would solve the problem," Odo said sarcastically, "although in a rather more terminal fashion than we would like."

"It may be a moot point," observed Sisko. "Could we be sure that we wouldn't beam down a disguised metamorph to Bajor's surface? I somehow doubt they'd be any happier to have that . . . that individual running around down there than we are having it here."

"We could be sure of those people on whom I have medical information," said Bashir firmly. "I'd have something to compare it to. I could run a med scan and confirm their identities."

"In other words," said Sisko dryly, "all Starfleet personnel."

"That's correct."

"Oh, that'll look just wonderful," said Odo. "Starfleet abandons Deep Space Nine while all the transients and Bajorans have to stay put."

"Are we supposed to balance lives against 'how things will look'?" asked Bashir.

"If Starfleet is going to pull this sector together, we can't simply cut our losses and bolt when danger threatens," said Sisko. "But, just out of curiosity . . . would you be willing to leave, Doctor? Head down to Bajor, and safety?"

Bashir looked down. "No," he said softly. "I couldn't see myself doing that."

"How about you, Lieutenant?"

Dax smiled slightly. "You know the answer to that, Benjamin."

"Major?"

"One of the freedom fighters in Bajoran history was a man named Ayvon of the Seven," said Kira. "He had many famous sayings, and I think that paraphrasing one here would be appropriate: I'm not Starfleet, I'm not a coward, and I'm not going."

Sisko glanced over to O'Brien. "Chief?"

"I don't cut and run from anyone, sir," said O'Brien. "Oh, I wouldn't mind shipping my family down . . . but I don't see Keiko leaving if I'm staying."

"Anyone else?" Sisko looked around Ops and was pleased to see firm shaking of heads. These were Starfleet personnel. They wouldn't scamper under any circumstances. "All right, then," he said proudly. "We're in this together, then. But we're back where we started: how do we catch him?"

"How about this?" said O'Brien. "He seems to favor getting here and about through the air ducts. Suppose we shut down the entire station—docking ring, habitat, everything—and seal everyone in the upper levels of the core. With everyone all together, a stranger would stick out like a sore thumb. Then we vent the air ducts—blow the atmosphere out of the whole damned station. He needs air to breathe like anyone else. He should be easy enough to find when he's passed out."

"Not necessarily," said Odo. "Presuming, just for the sake of argument, that he's like me, the lack of atmosphere isn't going to deter him. I don't have internal organs in any sense you'd understand. I don't draw air into lungs or require it to oxygenate blood. Air permeates my entire mass and remains there for some time. Indefinitely, insofar as I've been able to determine. So the chances are that he could survive quite nicely until we restore atmosphere to the station."

"Still, the air-vent escape method he uses is certainly his greatest weapon against us," said Sisko. "If we could figure out some way to deprive him of that . . ."

"All right," said O'Brien, not sounding the least bit deterred. His brow wrinkled for a moment, and then he said, "How about this? By cross-wiring key circuit junctures and wiring them through the security field generators, I could ionize the air in the ducts. Give him one hell of a jolt. How would something like that affect you, Mr. Odo?"

"I wouldn't like it," said Odo.

"Okay," said O'Brien, his spirits rising. Contemplating all sorts of hideous possibilities was not the way he liked to spend his time. When he had a problem to solve through technological maneuvering, however, he was supremely happy. "Now, I'd have to shut off circulation throughout the station. That won't present any sort of immediate problem, as long as we bring the circulators back on line within a reasonable period. The other problem is that I'll have to cross-wire every circuit juncture individually. Even with all my men on it, it's going to take time."

"How much time?"

"Well," said O'Brien with slightly diminished enthusiasm, "that's the rub. There are over two hundred circuit junctures throughout the station, and two-thirds of them are not in the greatest of shape. That's one of the reasons things keep screwing up around the station. Hot-wiring the lot of 'em would take at least twelve hours, maybe longer."

"Then the sooner you start, the sooner you'll finish."

"Yes, sir."

"But before you go," said Sisko, turning toward Bashir, "Dr. Bashir will run a med scan on you to verify your identity. On all of us, just to play it safe."

There were nods from all around, but Odo was frowning. "We're assuming that this being can simulate specific humanoids. That's something I've never quite been able to do."

"We can't take anything for granted, Constable."

"No, Sisko, of course we can't. But if that does turn out to be within his abilities, then after I catch him"— he sighed—"I hope he'll tell me how he does it."

* * *

After Bashir finished in Ops, he headed down to the infirmary. Nurse Latasa looked up from one of the medical computers questioningly, and Bashir said, "Preganglionic."

"Kiss me, you fool. But keep telling yourself, Doctor: it's only a password," she said, smiling. Then she pointed to a computer terminal. "This stopped working, Doctor."

"I'll get the chief on it when he has a chance," said Bashir. "But he's going to be somewhat tied up for a while. Is this one still operating?" He pointed to another computer terminal.

She nodded.

"All right, then," he said. "Copy the entire file we have on the med readings I took on the Edemian boy, Rasa. Also, load on all available information on panoria—symptoms, effects, everything."

Latasa's fingers tapped out a command. She slid an isolinear chip into a receptacle and waited a moment.

"Copy completed," the computer said primly.

She removed the isolinear chip deftly and handed it to Bashir. "Thank you, Nurse," he said.

"No problem, Doctor. May I ask what it's for?"

"Maybe," he told her, waving the chip, "we can pull something useful out of all the death that's going on around here. We may just be able to save a life."

He glanced around the infirmary. "It's quiet today," he said. "Where is everyone?"

She sighed. "Most of the Bajoran orderlies said they felt ill. I hear they're sealing themselves in their quarters until the crisis is over."

"Well, I appreciate your nerve, at least," said Bashir. "Don't worry, Nurse. We'll weather this storm."

"Whatever you say, Doctor," she replied.

Bashir flashed that famous smile of his once more and then walked out of the infirmary.

Latasa walked back to the broken medical computer, sat down in front of it, and punched an entry code onto it. There was still no response.

"Stupid piece of junk," she said and gave it a sharp rap on the side.

The computer struck back.

CHAPTER
15

"Now," SAID BASHIR, crouching behind the bar, out of sight, "you understand what you're supposed to do?"

Nog and Rom crouched with him, stared at him with open curiosity. "Yes, I understand," said Rom. "And I understand that you promised to put in a good word for Nog with Odo if we helped you out."

"What I don't understand is why you're doing this," said Nog.

"For my own reasons. That's all you have to know."

He peered over the bar and saw that things were just as he had seen them for the past couple of days.

The Edemians were in their little section of the Promenade. Matters had become somewhat boring, however. Stragglers were happening by, but very few of them. Most people were either hiding in their quarters or staying in small groups for mutual safety. No one was casually strolling.

Rasa was idly wandering about. His mother had wanted him to stay by their side, but Mas Marko had been firm. "You can't mollycoddle the boy, Azira," he had said. "Whatever life is left to him, he must use it to do K'olkr's work in whatever way he sees fit." And then he had added darkly, "Just keep an eye out for that Dr. Bashir person. He shows no respect for our ways, and I dislike his intentions."

Nevertheless, Azira kept a wary eye on Rasa, making sure that he didn't meander too far away.

Mas Marko was still calling out, "Come! Come, all within hearing! Share in the brilliance that is K'olkr!" And then he noticed one of those odd Ferengi individuals heading his way. Yes . . . definitely his way, straight toward him like an arrow. This he found to be fairly strange; the Ferengi didn't strike him, under any circumstances, as the religious type. Still, as Commander Sisko had put it, K'olkr moved in mysterious ways.

"The spirit of K'olkr has moved you to me, my son," said Mas Marko.

"Not likely," Rom said. "The spirit of Commander Sisko moved me. He wants to see you." He lowered his voice to a confidential tone. "I think he wants to update you on the shapeshifter business."

"Indeed." Marko nodded approvingly. "How good to see that he is following through. Hmmm. If he is indeed keeping to his promises, I . . . may actually have acted hastily."

Rom looked at him askance. "Hastily in what?"

"No matter," said Marko, waving it off. "What the Mas does, the Mas can undo. Del . . . you stay here."

"I think he wanted to see both of you," said Rom. But he wasn't the best when it came to improvising.

"He will content himself with me," Marko said firmly. "Del, make sure that Bashir does not come over here and harangue my mate, if you please."

"Yes, Mas Marko," said Del.

Mas Marko drew his robes around him and, looking every inch the imposing and intimidating religious leader of the Edemians, headed toward the turbolift that would take him to Ops.

Azira was suddenly nervous. Even though Del was with her, she still felt a sense of isolation. Deep Space Nine—already an alien environment for her—had become a strange and frightening place.

She was keeping her doubts and fears to herself because she knew this was not the sort of thing her husband would want to hear. But lately . . .

Lately . . .

It seemed to her that this place had somehow slipped past the notice of the almighty K'olkr.

Was such an oversight possible? Could the all-seeing eye of K'olkr have glossed over this . . . this floating pustule of a space station?

Perhaps Mas Marko and his followers had made a wrong turn and wandered into hell.

Yes, hell, she thought grimly. That was the word she'd heard bandied about recently. A place that a number of beings on Deep Space Nine believed in. A place where people who had transgressed were sent to suffer forever and ever unto eternity.

The Edemians didn't embrace the concept of hell. They believed in a realm called E'bon—a nether realm, to which those Edemians were sent who died while their confidence in the glory of K'olkr wavered. In E'bon they endured pain and punishment for their lack of faith, but only so that those poor tortured souls would truly repent their shortsightedness. They were kept in E'bon for an indeterminate period of time, and finally, their souls blackened and flayed, they would be sent back to begin a new incarnation, having been denied the right to move forward into the presence and glory of K'olkr.

It was hoped that, in their new mortal incarnation, they would carry with them, spiritually, the torment that they had been subjected to. Indeed, there was a theory that the most pious of Edemians were those who had undergone a stay in E'bon and were making up for it during their current stay on Edema. This simply went to prove that true glory could be attained by those who truly desired it.

Azira's mind wandered through the bleakest possibilities. Who truly knew what E'bon was like? Perhaps . . . perhaps the entire station was a fiction. Perhaps she and her party had actually been destroyed in space through some freak mishap. Perhaps they were dead and were now being subjected to a type of bizarre E'bonite torture. Dying one by one . . . dying by degrees . . .

She brushed off that possibility. It was absurd. As hideous as this reality was, it was indeed reality. No fanciful thoughts would change that. She was here, her husband was here, her son was—

Her son.

She looked around.

There was no sign of Rasa.

She felt the first dim rush of fear in her chest. She called his name, but heard no answer.

"Del," she said swiftly, "have you seen Rasa?"

"No, mistress," he replied politely. "I believe I saw him last in that direction." He pointed toward Quark's. "Shall I—"

"I'll look for him. You stay here, and if he returns, make certain that he stays put," Azira said. "This is not a good time for him to be wandering about this station unattended."

Del nodded in understanding, and Azira headed toward Quark's.

The entire place made her dark skin crawl. Then again, so did much of the station. Indeed, it seemed that any spiritual solace she derived came purely from looking at her son.

The son who would—in a year, maybe less—be joining K'olkr in the land of greatness. Basking in the presence of K'olkr . . .

It was not something she liked to think about. So she put it out of her mind as she approached Quark's establishment. Quark himself was standing behind the bar, idly cleaning a glass with a rag that looked dirtier than the glass had. He looked at her with curiosity. "May I help you?" he asked politely.

"I . . . I was wondering," she said, her hands fluttering in small patterns, "if . . . if by any chance you had seen my son anywhere about?"

"Your son?"

"We've been standing over there for several days now," and she pointed across the way.

"Ahhh!" said Quark, recognition seeming to dawn. "The religious folks. Yes, you've certainly been providing some entertaining diversion. Your son, eh? Now that you mention it . . . yes. Of course." He thudded his head with the base of his palm. "Forgetful, forgetful. He was with Nog."

"Nog?" The name didn't mean anything to her.

Quark nodded. "The son of one of my employees. As I recall, they went up there." He pointed up the steps that led to the holosuites.

"Thank you," she replied, and without hesitation went up the stairs.

Quark watched her go, but his expression changed. "All right, Bashir," he muttered. "We're even now. More than even. I don't know which aspect stings more: being outwitted by some wet-behind-the-ears Starfleet doctor or having to erase XXX-Three. Ahhh, well." He sighed, and then grinned, showing his pointed teeth. "There's always XXX-Five."

Azira, meantime, had gained the top of the stairs. The corridor ran a short distance. There was a damp, faintly musty smell that she found faintly repugnant. A row of doors lined the wall on the right-hand side.

She saw no one else around. "Rasa?" she called cautiously. When she didn't get an immediate answer, she called a bit louder, "Rasa!"

"Mother?"

It was his voice, all right . . . but it sounded very different than usual. It was weak, raspy. There was no strength to it. It sounded like sand blowing across a desert.

It was coming from the door in the middle. She went to it, but it wouldn't open. "Rasa!" she called, thumping on it. "What's wrong? What's happening in there? Let me in!" She turned and called out, "Mr. Quark! This door won't—"

But then it opened. Her head snapped around, and she peered in, trying to make out something in the blackness that filled the room.

"Mother . . . it hurts. . . ." It was Rasa's voice, unquestionably, but she couldn't see him.

Her heart was beating in triple time, and part of her wanted to run as fast and as far as she could. Something was deeply wrong here—wrong and twisted. She should run and get Security, get Del, get her husband . . . *someone.*

But that would mean abandoning her son to whatever in E'bon was going on in there. Alone, possibly to be claimed forever by whatever lurked in the darkness.

She mustered her courage, fighting to bring a measure of authority to her voice. "Rasa!" she called out. "Where are you? Come out here this minute!"

A spotlight shone down from the ceiling. A single light illuminating a single bed.

The bed was some feet away. She could hear faintly the slow, steady pulse of a monitoring device. The steady thump-thump-thump made her realize that it was measuring a heartbeat.

A memory came back to her—the first time that she had heard Rasa's heart. No, not heard . . . felt. When he was brought into the world, and so silent he had been . . . not a peep out of him. So quiet they had thought at first he was stillborn. But no. He had simply been quiet, from the very beginning, as if he was reluctant to bother anyone.

They had laid him down on her bare stomach, and she had felt it then. The rapid, frantic beating of his heart, thumping against his chest as if it might explode . . . much as her heart was doing at this very moment.

It made perfect sense that she would think of that moment just now, because the figure lying there in the bed, in the darkness . . . was her son.

But it wasn't.

Not entirely.

She walked forward on unsteady legs, not fully believing, not at all understanding. "Rasa . . . ?" she whispered.

The door slid shut behind her, but she paid it no mind. Her full attention was focused on the small boy who lay helpless in the bed.

And another light came on. A second spotlight, hitting a place on the other side of the bed. Standing there was Dr. Julian Bashir.

She recoiled from him, like a vampire shunning a crucifix. "What's happening here?" she hissed. "My . . . my husband told you to stay away!"

"I am staying away," said Bashir with a calm he did not feel. He had planned this with cold, efficient cunning, but now that it had come down to the crunch, his emotions were twisted into a tight knot in the pit of his stomach. "You came to me."

"It was a trick!" Azira stabbed an accusing finger at him, rolling back on her heels as she did so. "You . . . you tricked me into coming up here! Where's my son?"

"Rasa? Why . . . he's right here," said Bashir, and he swept his hand over the form on the bed, like a magician pulling a rabbit out of a hat.

* * *

Mas Marko stepped off the turbolift and was greeted with a less than patient look from Major Kira. "Mas Marko," she said, "I appreciate your concern, but we really cannot have station guests traipsing in and out of Ops."

"I understand your situation," said Mas Marko easily, "and I'd understand it even more, were it not for the fact that I am here at the request of your commander."

"What?" Her brows knit together, and she turned at her station and called up to Sisko. "Commander, did you ask to see Mas Marko?"

Sisko emerged from his office, looking puzzled. "No. Mas Marko, what gave you that idea?"

A warning bell was going off in Mas Marko's head. "A Ferengi," he said, "informed me that it was your desire that I come up here."

"Well . . . that explains it," said Sisko easily. "The Ferengi have a fairly underdeveloped sense of humor."

"Matches their sense of decency," muttered Kira who, fortunately for all concerned, had no idea just how accurate her statement was on a personal level.

"Whoever sent you here," Sisko said, "probably mistakenly believed that sending you on a wild-goose chase represented the height of wit. Which Ferengi did it?"

"I do not know, Commander," admitted Mas Marko. "Truth to tell, they all look alike to me."

"As we do to them, so I'm told," said Sisko. "I'm sorry you wasted your time."

"You needn't be. As long as I'm here—"

"Mas Marko . . ."

"You can tell me if you've decided to turn the shapeshifter over to the Edemians for justice."

"That's not going to happen," said Sisko firmly. "Again, this is a Bajoran station. And a Bajoran citizen is now on the list of victims. The Bajorans are a very spiritual people, but they will not tolerate murder. They want the killer, too, and since the crimes occurred on their station and under Federation jurisdiction, their wishes take precedence."

"That, Commander," said Mas Marko darkly, "is most unfortunate for you."

Something in his tone of voice made it quite clear that Sisko was going to have a problem on his hands. "Pardon me, Mas Marko, but that sounded to me like a threat."

Marko made no reply.

"I do not take kindly to threats," said Sisko. "Not as a Starfleet officer and certainly not as commander of this station."

Abruptly Dax looked up from her instruments. "Benjamin," she said, "sensors detect an incoming vessel. It has just come out of warp and is now approaching at one-half impulse."

Forgetting Mas Marko for the moment, Sisko came down to his Ops station. "Warn them off," he said. "Inform them they have no business here. The station is under quarantine, and the wormhole is still unpassable."

"They're not responding."

"On screen," said Sisko, taking a step forward and staring intently at the screen.

A ship appeared on the viewscreen. It was shaped somewhat like a starburst. It was bristling with weapons and looked as if it meant business.

"Mas Marko, please leave Ops," Sisko told him firmly. Without waiting to see the order carried out, he turned to Kira and said, "Have we got a make on that type of vessel?"

The answer came quickly and with confidence. It did not, however, come from Kira.

"It is an Edemian vessel of Holy War," Mas Marko

informed them calmly. "The ship *Zealous*, I believe. I summoned it."

Sisko turned and regarded Mas Marko as if he were some intriguing new specimen of insect, which at that moment had an equally intriguing flyswatter poised over it. *"You . . . summoned them?"*

"That's correct, Commander."

Sisko was fighting with everything he had to stay in control not only of the situation but of himself as well. "May I ask why?"

"You can ask," Mas Marko replied sedately. "But you already know the answer, as I'm quite certain you're aware. It is here to make sure that the wishes of the Mas Marko are carried out fully and completely."

Sisko gripped the underside of his console, his fist squeezing so tight that he almost dislocated a knuckle. "You . . . are *not* . . . in charge . . . of this station."

"Quite true," replied Mas Marko. "But I *am* in charge of that Holy War ship out there. And that ship, Commander, can blow Deep Space Nine to bits."

"You hypocrite," said Sisko with quiet fury. "You, who call yourself a holy man, would tell that vessel to open fire on us? Kill everyone on this station if your demands are not met? Destroy hundreds of innocent lives?"

"Commander." Mas Marko sounded faintly disappointed. "Of course not. I would never order the *Zealous* to fire upon you. However . . . I might indeed order it to take target practice on a point directly behind this station. I would not hurt you for all the world, Commander, but if Deep Space Nine is in the way of where my vessel happens to shoot . . . well, what is to be done? It would be tragic, yes. But these things happen. It would mean the death of me and mine, but K'olkr will welcome us into his embrace. You, unbelievers that you are, will not be quite so fortunate, I fear."

Sisko said nothing.

"You must understand, Commander. You say the people here are innocent. To me they are blind fools, unaware of the greatness that is K'ol—"

Sisko tapped his comm badge. "Security to Ops, immediately."

Mas Marko was filled with curiosity. "Now, why would you need a security team, Commander? Are you feeling insecure, perhaps?"

Two security guards appeared on the turbolift. Sisko pointed at Mas Marko and said, "Take him to a holding cell and leave him there. Check him over and make damned sure he doesn't have any communications devices on him."

When they took Mas Marko firmly by either arm, he seemed for the first time to lose his temper. "Just what do you think you're doing, Commander?"

"Your fanaticism is second to none, Mas, but your timing leaves a great deal to be desired," Sisko said. "If you seriously think I'm going to leave you running around unhampered so that you can communicate with your ship at leisure and have them blast us to molecules, then you're laboring under a misapprehension."

"This is an outrage!" thundered Mas Marko. "I am the voice of the living K'olkr!"

"Fine," said Sisko flatly. "If K'olkr wants to hash it out with me, have him swing by and we'll chat. In the meantime, you can stew." He gestured for the guards to take Mas Marko out of Ops.

He did not go quietly. "Sisko!" he shouted. "This is an insult! You may not treat a Grand Mas of the Edemians in this fashion! This is an ill-advised course, Sisko! Continuing on this path will lead you to—"

Sisko never heard where it would lead him, because Mas Marko's voice was cut off by the departing turbolift.

"They're still refusing to respond to our hails.

They've cut all forward motion," Kira said, looking up from her instruments. "They're just sitting there watching us."

"Let them watch," said Sisko. "Monitor their emissions. If their shields come up, or if they in any way indicate that they are powering up their weapons, then we take defensive action. Unless that happens, they can stare at us until pigs fly. And find out which of the Ferengi sent Mas Marko up here. Something's going on here that we're not aware of, and I want to know what it is."

"I deeply regret the aggravation I may have caused you and yours in recent days," said Bashir. "So . . . this is my way of making it up to you."

Hesitantly, drawn by her curiosity in spite of herself, Azira approached the bed slowly and gazed at it in unremitting horror.

"Not too long into the future," continued Bashir, fighting to keep his voice steady, fighting to maintain the detachment that was so important now, "you will have to say farewell to your son. I imagine you'll want to be strong for him. You'll want to be a source of comfort and confidence instead of—oh, I don't know—coming apart. In order to make that moment easier for you, I've created this simulation. It's quite accurate, I assure you. My medical records are precise, and panoria in its final stages is thoroughly documented. This, Azira, is what you have to look forward to."

Rasa was covered up to his neck by a blanket. His once-glowing eyes were so dim that it was practically impossible to discern any light at all. Furthermore, they had sunk into his head almost to the point of disappearing altogether. His skin had become shrunken and parched, and his breathing was labored. He tried to lick his lips, but his tongue made a scratchy sound.

"His body is utterly unable to retain liquids of any

sort," said Bashir by way of explanation. He might have been discussing a textbook case in a classroom. Nothing about his demeanor betrayed the fact that the look on Azira's face was like a knife to his heart. He knew what he was putting the woman through. It gutted the young doctor. But he struggled to retain his clinical detachment. "All attempts to keep him hydrated would fail at this point in the disease's progression. Look."

He pulled the blanket down, and Azira choked off a shriek. The child was naked from the waist up. She could see the outline of his ribs against his chest; his desiccated skin was like sandpaper, and his fingers looked like claws.

"Mo . . . ther," he croaked. He managed to stretch out a hand, grasping at air like a dying bird. "Mother . . . can't see you . . ."

"Make it stop," whispered Azira, clutching her hands to her bosom. "This is . . . this is a holo trick. Where's my son?" Her voice rose in a shriek. *"Where's my son?"*

"Rasa is fine, madam," Bashir said evenly, and then added as an afterthought, "At least . . . at the moment. But some months from now," and apologetically he once more indicated the holocreation.

The dying child tried to sit up. He looked in the general direction of Azira's voice. "Mo . . . ther . . ." Each syllable was an effort. He sounded as if his tongue was swollen. "Hurts . . . so much. . . . Make it stop hurting. . . ."

Azira's body was shaking so violently that for a moment Bashir was afraid she might pass out. His heart went out to the woman, and in every way he felt like a total cad. But there was no turning back now. As if reciting a laundry list, he said, "His entire body is shutting down. High fever. Dehydration. Blindness. Failure of several major organs. His body is racked by pain . . . I'd say he hasn't got much longer."

"That thing is not my son!"

"Azira," said Bashir, somewhat scoldingly, "this is what he will look like. This is not conjecture or guesswork. *This is it.* If you do not intend to be at Rasa's bedside when he dies, then this is a pointless exercise. But if you do plan to see him off to the great beyond, then I suggest you take this opportunity to practice saying good-bye. I hardly think he'll want the last words he hears to be 'That thing is not my son.' "

"Mother," Rasa croaked. "Hurts . . . Everything hurts. Why isn't K'olkr . . . making it stop? Why is . . . everything hurting? Why does . . . he hate me . . . so much?"

Reflexively, Azira mumbled, "K'olkr . . . K'olkr doesn't hate us. He l . . . loves us. All"—she swallowed hard—"all things have a purpose, and . . . and . . ." She couldn't get anything else out.

"Hold me . . ." The boy reached for her.

She stepped back, unable to get near the holo, and now her voice was pleading, broken. "Please . . ." she said, trembling. "Please . . . make it stop. Make it . . ."

Rasa began to convulse, and Azira shrieked, her hand going to her mouth, trying to stifle the noise. From head to foot, the boy's shriveled body shook, his head pitching back. Bashir stepped in behind him and gently lowered him back down onto the bed. Rasa's hands continued to rake the air for a few moments more, and his breath rattled in his throat. His last word was unintelligible, although it might have been "Mother." It was impossible to be sure.

The glow vanished from his eyes, his soul departing with his final breath. His head lolled slightly, but his hands remained in the air. Gently Bashir lowered them, crossing them over his withered chest.

Azira was sobbing openly, her chest heaving with racking sobs. Bashir calmly pulled the blanket up over the child's head and then turned to her. He seemed slightly puzzled. "I don't understand," he said. "Your son would be going off to grace the presence of K'olkr at this moment. Shouldn't you be celebrating? And . . . you didn't really say good-bye, did you? Tell you what: we'll try it again. Computer, rerun program."

The table shimmered a moment, and then Rasa was alive again . . . but just barely.

"In real life, of course," said Bashir, "we only get one chance. If we miss it, then it's gone. But here . . . here you can practice for Rasa's death as often as you wish."

And in that same horrible, near-dead voice, Rasa said, "Mother . . . ?"

Azira stepped forward quickly, her hand moving faster than the eye could follow. She swung as hard as she could, smacking Bashir's face. The blow stung, but Bashir made no move to rub his cheek.

"The truth is hurting you, madam," said Bashir, "far more than your hand could possibly hurt me."

"You . . . sadistic bastard," snarled Azira. She turned to flee the holodeck.

Bashir wanted to grab her, to shake her. To yell at her, *You call yourself a mother? You would willingly subject your child to the ravages of this disease? Let me save him! Let me do what all my training would have me do! Don't make me stand idle and allow this to happen! In the name of humanity . . .*

But Azira wasn't human, and besides, hysteria would be of no use. Bellowing could be far more easily tuned out than calm words that carried truth with them. And Bashir, the picture of composure, said, "Sadistic? Me? Dear woman, *I'm* not the one who will allow this to happen. You are. I'm simply showing you the consequences."

She fled the holosuite, sobbing frantically.

The moment she was gone, Bashir's detached demeanor collapsed. The pain that he was feeling, the empathy for what the woman was going through, he now allowed to show.

"Computer . . . end program," he said tonelessly. The image vanished.

He had just done a terrible thing, he knew. It was the act of a desperate man. But he was indeed desperate. He had not yet developed the ability to detach himself from the death of a patient, or from the inability to act in his fullest capacity as a healer.

He dreaded the thought that, at some point in the future, the death of a patient he might have saved would bother him less than it did now. Because at the moment, the idea of that child dying when Bashir could have saved him was a great, gaping wound in his medical heart, and the parents' refusal to let him treat Rasa was salt on that wound.

The question was, quite simply . . . had the holodrama done any good?

Rasa was gaping in astonishment at the hand-held holovid that Nog was showing him. On it two naked Orion women were doing things with each other that Rasa had never imagined any two individuals doing— much less two women.

"Wow" was all he could manage to say.

Nog smirked. "They teach you much about that in religious school?"

Rasa shook his head.

And suddenly he heard his mother shouting, *"Rassaaaa!"* Her voice seemed to be echoing from everywhere within the Promenade.

The youths had been hiding inside one of Quark's larger storage cabinets. But now Rasa got to his feet so fast that he cracked his head against the top. "She sounds real upset," he said.

Nog made a rude noise, which was pretty much the only type that Ferengis made. "What, are you afraid of your mother?"

"Yes," Rasa said matter-of-factly.

"Oh. Okay, then." Nog kicked open the door, and Rasa emerged into the light. He turned and looked back at the Ferengi. "Could I . . . uh . . . that is . . . you don't have another one of those, do you?"

Nog shook his head. "Hard to come by," he grumbled. "Not for sale . . . unless, of course, the right price is mentioned. Then we could possibly make a deal."

"Sorry," said Rasa apologetically. "No money."

"Then no deal."

"All right, then. Thanks anyway. It's been . . . it's been interesting."

He turned away and scampered in the direction of the Edemian setup. Nog leaned back, activated the holoviewer once more, and swung the door shut for privacy.

Azira, meantime, was on the verge of total frenzy. "Raaasaaa!" she shouted again.

Del was trying to calm her, to no avail. "Please . . . he'll turn up."

"*Raaasaaaaaa!*" It was the voice of a woman screaming over a cliff, watching a loved one plummet to his death while she stood there helpless.

The screaming attracted a security guard, who said with concern, "Ma'am, what's happened? Calm down, and let me help you."

At that moment Rasa came into view. "Mother?" he called, sounding extremely confused by his mother's hysterics.

She ran to him, crossing the Promenade in an instant. She grabbed him and pressed him to her bosom, holding him so tight that he thought he was going to break.

"Mother!" he said in embarrassed confusion. "What's wrong?"

"Nothing," she murmured. "Nothing. It's all right, love. Nothing is wrong."

The security guard and Del exchanged looks. Del shrugged. "Women," he said in a low voice, by way of explanation. "Sometimes the least little thing will set them off."

The guard nodded. "Tell me about it," he said sympathetically.

And as Azira clutched her son like a life preserver, she saw Bashir emerging from the holosuites. Her gaze stayed fixed on him as he trotted down the stairs without even glancing her way—until he got to the very bottom, at which point he afforded her a brief glance.

He kept his face neutral, but his expression said it all: *Hold him while you can. You won't have the opportunity much longer.*

And then he walked away.

Bashir returned to the infirmary feeling desperately unclean.

Do no harm. The first rule of medicine kept rattling around inside his head. He had tortured that woman. Nothing less. He was not simply charged with maintaining the physical well-being of individuals; he had to attend to their mental well-being also. And he had just put Azira through a mental wringer.

He kept trying to tell himself that he had done the right thing, that he was attempting to save the life of a young boy. But the notion rang hollow, even to him. Azira and her husband had already decided how they would handle their child's illness. Their culture had shaped and molded that decision. He had done nothing less than subject the woman to a crisis of conscience, browbeaten her, undermined her faith—all out of his selfish desire to save someone who hadn't asked for his help.

In trying to spare Azira hurt further on down the line, he had subjected her to mental torment that was even crueler than what life held for her. Had he not inter-fered, she might have remained blissfully ignorant of what was to come. She might have been able to cherish the time she had left with her child.

But now, thanks to Bashir, she would constantly picture what Rasa was going to become. Bashir hadn't deceived her; the depiction was accurate. But now it was going to dominate every waking moment she spent with the boy. She would never be able to look at Rasa again without seeing the ghastly sack of bones that he would become.

In the name of trying to save a life, Bashir had destroyed the little remaining happiness that Azira's son might have provided her.

And the hell of it was . . . he would do it again, in a heartbeat.

"Nurse," he called tiredly, feeling a hundred years old. His voice echoed in the infirmary. "Nurse Latasa," he said again.

Nothing.

The first faint buzz of alarm penetrated Bashir's general depression. "Nurse?" Now there was guarded concern in his voice.

Slowly he moved through the infirmary. Everything around him seemed to loom larger, more threatening. He thought of calling Security, but he was loath to sound a false alarm when they were facing such prob-lems already.

"Nurse?"

And then he remembered, and he almost laughed as he said, "Oh, right. How could I forget? Preganglionic," he called out.

He rounded a corner and jumped back as if he'd been electrified.

Nurse Latasa's bloodied body was smeared across the wall. Her head, with a permanently shocked expression on it, had been meticulously placed atop a computer terminal.

Just above her head, dried blood clung to the wall. A large "#4" had been smeared through it . . . and something else, as well. Four words etched on the wall above her head, also in blood. And the words were "Kiss me, you fool."

CHAPTER
16

"MILES?"

O'Brien put down the hydrospanner and crawled out of the circuit junction. His face and hands were smeared with dirt and perspiration. He stared bleary-eyed at Keiko's concerned face.

"What is it?" The raspiness of his voice surprised him, although it shouldn't have. He had been staying in communication with his people, talking constantly, cross-checking relays and the timing of everything that was being done.

Keiko was standing there, looking a little intimidated by the two security guards posted on either side of the hallway, keeping a watchful eye out. She held a small cup out to him. "Rice tea?" she said.

Genuinely touched, he thanked her and took the cup. He sipped the tea, and the warmth down his throat helped lift his spirits.

"You've been working so hard, and I just . . . I wanted to do something for you." She glanced around. "It seems there are security teams everywhere these days."

He nodded. "Odo has got them stretched to the limit.

Apparently I'm one of the key figures they want to guard."

"You're one of the key targets, you mean," she said.

Again he nodded, this time a bit more reluctantly. "Yeah," he allowed. "That's one way of looking at it." Then he paused and said, "Keiko . . . remember when Molly was born?"

The switch in subjects confused her. "What? Uh . . . yes, of course. I *was* there, after all."

"And where were you, precisely?"

The guards, looking suspicious, glanced at each other and then at Keiko.

Her face was the picture of confusion. "What?" And then she understood. She laughed a bit sadly. "Oh. Of course. I was in Ten-Forward, Miles. And Worf delivered Molly." Dropping her voice to approximate Worf's deep timbre, she said, 'You may now give birth.'"

"Ah, I knew it was really you all the time," he said, taking another sip of tea. And the guards relaxed somewhat. "Now remember . . . when you're in our quarters, you keep that phaser I gave you handy. And make sure it stays fully charged at all times."

"Yes, Miles. And you be careful."

"Of course." Then he lowered his voice so that the guards could not hear. "You know, up in Ops, we were discussing the possibility of evacuating people. And I said . . ."

She looked at him questioningly. "You said what?"

"I said that I wouldn't run under any circumstances and that you wouldn't want to leave if it meant leaving me behind. Was I . . ." He hesitated. "Was I wrong to tell them that? Would you want to leave, given the opportunity?"

"Leave?" She made a gesture that seemed to encompass the entire space station. "And give up all this? Don't be silly."

She kissed him briskly and headed back down the hallway. And as she left, O'Brien heard Odo's voice, with its usual fusion of amusement and contempt. "Things improving on the homefront, Chief O'Brien?"

O'Brien looked up, but before he could respond, the security guards tensed. Odo, however, said briskly, "Gamma zed alpha."

The guards promptly responded, "Alpha omicron delta."

"Passwords?" asked O'Brien.

"No, O'Brien, we're studying for a quiz on the Greek alphabet," replied Odo sarcastically.

"Here." O'Brien pushed the remaining rice tea at Odo. "This might put you in a better mood."

"I wouldn't count on it."

"Don't worry. I won't." He started to climb back up into the juncture point, then stopped and looked at Odo. "Tell me something. That card trick I did . . . I was certain I was holding up the card you picked."

"You were," said Odo.

O'Brien gaped. "But . . . but you said it wasn't—"

"No. You said, 'Is this your card?' It wasn't. It was *your* card. It was *your* deck. It wouldn't have been appropriate for me to claim that it was mine when I didn't own it."

O'Brien moaned. "And here I've been going crazy trying to figure out what I did wrong! I was going to go back to working on my sleight of hand."

"Face it, O'Brien. Magic isn't your forte."

"But I really want to entertain Molly at her party." He looked hopefully at Odo. "You know, Odo, with your abilities, I bet Molly would love it if you'd consider—"

"I don't do children's parties, O'Brien," Odo said. "I'm not that wild about human children."

"Or human adults," said O'Brien.

"Yes, well, that goes without saying."

Odo's comm badge beeped, and he tapped it. "Yes?"

"Bashir to Security." The doctor sounded haunted, horrified. "Odo . . . there's—"

He didn't even have to complete the statement. "Where are you, Doctor?" Odo said quickly.

"Infirmary."

"On my way." Odo turned quickly to O'Brien and said, "You may want to hurry with that, Chief. Matters do not seem to be improving."

Azira stood outside her husband's cell, clutching her son's hand as if afraid that he might vanish into thin air.

"Do you believe this outrage, my wife?" Mas Marko appeared not to know whether to be angry or amused. "Do you see what they have done?"

"You . . ." She paused.

"Yes?"

"Well, they probably felt they had no choice once the Holy War vessel appeared."

"That may very well have been my undoing," said Mas Marko. "The rightness of my act seemed so clear to me that it did not occur to me that they would take retaliatory action. How pathetic I must look. You are fortunate, my wife, that they have not imprisoned you as well."

"I have taken no action against them," she said. "If they do not perceive me as a threat, they will not punish me."

"Then do nothing to alter your status, Azira," said Mas Marko firmly. "I shall be free presently, I have no doubt. The *Zealous* will try to make contact if it does not hear from me soon. When they are unable to reach me, they will demand answers from Commander Sisko. I suspect the commander of the *Zealous* will not be pleased with the answers he gets, at which point Sisko will be faced with a decision: either he can release me or he can experience the terminal ordeal of having his station blown asunder. I think the choice will be fairly obvious, don't you?"

"As you say." She nodded deferentially.

"And you, Rasa," said Mas Marko. "How are you feeling?"

"Fine, Father."

"Good. Good lad." He looked up at Azira. "You know, I think the boy is starting to look healthier. By K'olkr, I swear it's so. Don't you think?"

"As you say." Again she spoke in that distant, even neutral fashion.

"Well, then." He clapped his hands briskly. "Carry on spreading the word of K'olkr. I shall join you before too long, I assure you."

"Marko . . ." She seemed hesitant, and then she drew herself up straight. "I just want you to know . . . I love you, and I have nothing but respect for you. Whatever happens, that will never change."

She was standing just on the other side of the forcefield. He regarded her with curiosity and rose to face her. "It goes without saying, Azira, that I feel the same way about you."

"I know. I know it does. Nevertheless, some things that go without saying should be said anyway."

She turned away from him and walked off down the corridor, leaving him thoughtful and just a bit uneasy.

Odo stared in quiet fury at the remains of Nurse Latasa and the message on the wall.

Kira was there as well, having been sent by Sisko to oversee matters and report back. She watched Odo's reaction carefully as the security chief stalked the area, clearly hoping against hope that somehow, some way, the shapeshifter might reveal itself.

It did not, of course. The odds were excellent that it was nowhere around.

Bashir was seated, looking dazed and nauseated. "Just . . . just a little while ago I saw Latasa." His voice sounded ragged. "Why her? Why not me? I was the one who interfered with him earlier. Why?"

"This is just one more confirmation that there's no rhyme or reason to these killings," said Kira. "The metamorph doesn't care that you interfered. He kills whoever he feels like killing."

"Yes," Odo said testily. "Yes, remind me of that, Major. Remind me that he does *whatever the hell he wants!*" And he slammed his fist into the bloodied wall.

Kira and the security guards stared at Odo in shock —partly because of their surprise at his totally unexpected, uncharacteristic outburst, and partly because his fist had flattened on impact, giving him what looked like an anvil at the end of his wrist.

Odo stared at it for a moment as if it belonged to someone else entirely. Then, after a moment's concentration, the fingers grew out and extended once more. He wiggled them experimentally. "You saw nothing, Doctor?" he asked, sounding rather conversational.

"Oh, I saw plenty, Mr. Odo," said Bashir grimly. "I saw the nonfunctioning medical computer, the one that's gone now. The original one turned up in a storage closet. The shapeshifter was hiding here—right here, disguised as the med computer."

"Sweep the room," said Odo quickly. "Make sure it's not still . . . *he's* not still here."

Kira saw the pained expression on his face at the slip. Odo said nothing further, but now merely stood with his arms folded, waiting for his men to give him the response that he knew, instinctively, would come— namely that they were alone there in the infirmary.

"Nothing, sir," Meyer said at length. "Nothing alive here that shouldn't be alive."

Odo was about to ask Bashir to perform an autopsy but quickly thought better of it. It was unlikely that an autopsy would tell them anything they didn't already know, and besides, Bashir hardly looked in shape to start going over the young woman to determine at what point precisely, during her last agonizing moments, she had died. That could wait.

He communicated as much to Kira, and quickly she agreed. "We'll have the body put in stasis," she said, "and have maintenance come in and clean up the . . . the remains." She felt sickened. "Gods, this is a nightmare. Just a nightmare."

"I wish it were," said Odo. "Then I'd hold out a hope of waking up."

Still flexing his fist, he walked out of the infirmary.

"This is an outrage!"

Sisko was gazing at the angry face of Mencar, the Edemian commander of the *Zealous*. The ship had finally contacted them, presumably, Sisko figured, because they had not heard from their fearless leader. Security had checked Mas Marko quite thoroughly and had indeed uncovered a communications device on him. To play it safe they had inspected the other Edemians as well but found nothing. That didn't surprise Sisko at all; it was typical of an individual like Marko to maintain himself as the sole source of communication with the home troops.

This is not my first outrage of the day, and it probably won't be my last, thought Sisko. Out loud he said, "I am sorry you are outraged. You are, however, in Bajoran space. Your presence is not welcome, and you would be well advised to leave."

"And you," said Mencar, "would be well advised to let us communicate with our Mas immediately."

"Your Mas," said Sisko, "is otherwise occupied. It is

in your best interest to take no actions that could jeopardize his welfare."

"Are you threatening us, Commander?"

"We are not the ones who are trespassing and loaded down with weaponry," Sisko reminded him. "We're simply a space station, Mencar. We're not in a position to force you to leave. We can, however, keep your Mas under wraps until you are prepared to discuss matters in a civilized manner."

"Lobb was of my family," said Mencar angrily. "We were first cousins. We grew up together. He was the youngest member of the family, and the joy he took in the simplest of things was a constant source of pleasure to us."

"I grieve for your loss," Sisko said formally.

"We want his killer! He must face Edemian justice!"

"Mencar, we are wasting your time and mine. When we have something to report, you will be among the first to know. Until then kindly let us do our jobs. Sisko out." The screen went blank even as Mencar was opening his mouth to continue the conversation.

"It would seem that we have a problem," said Dax.

"I'll put it on my list."

Dax suddenly looked up from her sensor array. "Benjamin," she said warningly, "we're picking up another arrival. It's . . ." She paused. "Oh, dear. It's a Cardassian warship. At three eight one mark four."

"On screen," said Sisko, sighing heavily. "Let's see it."

The viewscreen shifted, and sure enough, there was a Cardassian ship, big as life. Bigger, in fact. The vessel looked large enough to blast Deep Space Nine to pieces just by having everyone on board sneeze in the station's direction.

"They're hailing us, sir."

"This is Commander Sisko. How may we be of

service?" he asked, trying to sound casual. He wanted to give the impression that fully armed Cardassian ships dropped by all the time.

An image appeared on the viewscreen. It was a very familiar image—of someone Sisko had spoken with not all that long before.

"Greetings, Sisko," said Gul Dukat. "It's been far too long since we've gotten together."

"Ah. I see," Sisko replied. "This would be a simple social call, then. Quite a formidable ship to come calling in."

Gul Dukat looked around as if noticing the ship for the first time. "Yes," he said with a tinge of pride. "It is rather formidable, isn't it? This is the *Ravage,* pride of the second order. Enough firepower to knock a class-G star out of position." He smiled pleasantly.

"A pleasant exaggeration," said Sisko.

"Let us all hope so. You have other company as well, I see, besides the various ships that presently festoon the docking ring."

"If you are referring to the Edemian ship *Zealous,* yes."

"And their concerns are . . . ?"

"Theirs."

"Ah." Gul Dukat nodded. "Very well. And our concerns are ours. It has been some time since we spoke, Commander. Gotto is long dead, but his spirit is screaming for vengeance."

"We are working on finding his killer," said Sisko. "If you wish, you can come here and we can discuss the investigation."

"Oh . . . I do not think so, Commander," Dukat said easily. "I have no personal desire to be added to your list of deceased Cardassians. Nor, should difficulties arise, do I wish to be a guest of Deep Space Nine, as Mas Marko and the other Edemians are.

That could conceivably hamper the *Ravage* in doing its duty."

"You tapped into Edemian ship's transmissions," said Sisko.

"Quite so." Then the Cardassian's voice hardened ever so slightly. "We want Gotto's murderer."

"So do we," Sisko assured him. "And we will find him. We're in the process of . . ."

Dukat held up a hand and made a dismissive wave. "Do not bother to cite chapter and verse for me, Commander. Perhaps you find the details interesting, but I assure you that I do not. No . . . we Cardassians are interested only in the bottom line. The when, as in when you will capture him. And the how, as in how do you plan to deliver him to us?"

"We can't put a timetable on our operations," said Sisko.

"Well, now, that's the difference between us, Commander. I can. Specifically . . . if we don't have the murderer here, in our hands, within six hours . . . we will come over there in force. In *large* force. We will take over the operation and, if necessary, the entire station. It was ours, you know. You're there merely at our sufferance."

"I don't exactly read it the same way. Nor do I advise you to attempt a hostile boarding."

"Why not?" Gul Dukat looked rather puzzled by Sisko's statement. "You have . . . what? Fifty Starfleet personnel there? Sixty at most? Twice that number of Bajorans, perhaps? Commander, we have enough Cardassians on this vessel to send in two of our people for every one of yours and still keep the *Ravage* fully armed. I do not suggest you cross us in this matter. You and I have had *such* an enjoyable relationship thus far, Commander. I would hate to see it come to an end. Particularly a bloody end."

He smiled once more in a manner that gave Sisko chills, and then the picture disappeared.

There was silence in Ops for a moment.

"Benjamin . . . would you like me to say I committed the murders?" asked Dax.

He looked at Dax mirthlessly. "I'll keep that in mind as a last resort, old man. Thank you."

CHAPTER
17

Odo sat brooding in his office and didn't look up when Kira entered. She stood in the doorway until he finally said, "Kai."

"Opaka," she replied, and sat down. "You know, if this keeps up for much longer, I'm going to blow out some brain cells trying to keep all these passwords and cross codes correct." She paused, studying him. "You feel even worse than you did the other day, don't you?" she said.

"Did you hear what I said earlier?" Odo demanded. "I called him 'it.' How am I supposed to take umbrage at anyone who considers me some sort of outlandish freak when I call another of my kind 'it.'"

"You think he's one of you . . . whatever you are?" she asked.

"Ohhhh . . . I don't know." He rubbed his eyes. "Part of me doesn't want to believe it. I'd like to deny the possibility of being related in any way to that . . . that psychopath. And yet part of me would love to believe it . . . so that after all these years I could finally hold out some hope of learning about my background, as I've always wanted."

He lowered his hands and saw that Kira was staring at him. "What?"

"Your . . . uh," and she tapped her own forehead as indicator.

He reached up and felt his brow. There were imprints in it, left by his fingers. He frowned and it smoothed out. "Better?"

"Odo," she said wonderingly, "I haven't seen you lose control like that before. Are you sure you're all right?"

"Of course I'm not all right," he said testily. "You know I have to return every eighteen hours to my natural form. Well . . . I've been cutting my rest periods short lately. Every moment I'm lying in my pail, I'm wondering what he's up to. Where he is. What he's doing. Who else on my station is dying. Who else I'm failing because I haven't been able to capture him. Don't you see, Major?" He leaned forward, tapping the desk for emphasis and trying to make sure that he didn't mush up his hand again. "This is a security matter. I'm head of security. That makes it my responsibility. And every person who dies because I failed to apprehend the felon is another life on my head."

"No, Odo," she said flatly. "You can't take all that on yourself."

"I can, and I do. I'm sorry if that upsets you, Major, but that's the way I am. Damn. If only I could blame Quark for this somehow."

"Pardon?" The abrupt change in subject threw her for a moment.

"Quark. It's always so safe to begin and end an investigation with Quark. Nine times out of ten, when problems arise on this station, he's involved somehow."

"Not this time," said Kira confidently. "Murder isn't exactly up his alley. Besides, he barely squeaked out of being victim number four himself."

"Yes. I suppose he—"

Odo's comm badge beeped, and he tapped it. "Odo here."

"Constable," came Sisko's voice, sounding older and heavier by the moment. "Tell me you have something."

"What I have, Sisko, is four corpses and a pile of frustrations."

"And what I have," said Sisko, "is a warship making its presence known and my life more complicated. The Cardassians want results."

"Distract them, Sisko," said Odo sharply. "Put their minds on something else. Send Chief O'Brien out to perform some sleight of . . . hand. . . ."

His voice trailed off, and his eyes went wide.

"Constable?" came Sisko's voice.

No answer. Odo appeared to be looking inward.

"Odo?" prompted Kira.

"Constable?" There was some concern now in Sisko's voice.

"Sisko," Odo said slowly, "I have a thought. It's a bizarre thought. An unlikely thought. But a thought nonetheless. I'll let you know when I've got something. Oh . . . and check with O'Brien. Find out how long it will be before he finishes the relays. If things work out, I don't want our unwanted guest to slip away again."

"You sound as if you might be on to something, Constable."

"I just might be, Sisko. I just might at that."

Julian Bashir desperately wanted to get drunk.

Unfortunately—or perhaps fortunately—he couldn't bring himself to leave the infirmary. He just sat there, staring at the spot that had been routinely occupied by Nurse Latasa.

He felt that everything was slipping away from him. As if he might lose his grip on the sort of life that he wanted to lead. One in which he was a healer with an intrepid and friendly staff aiding him. Where people came to him, asking for help and he gave it freely, pleased to have the opportunity to help others.

Not this. Not this . . . this *situation.* This deplorable state of affairs, with death all around him, filling his soul like rotting meat assaulting his nostrils. One of his nurses dead. Others dead. A boy dying, and he was powerless to . . .

"Dr. Bashir."

He turned and saw Azira standing in the doorway. He was so wrapped up in his own thoughts and inner turmoil that he hadn't even heard the door open. "Yes?"

She was holding Rasa cradled in her arms. She didn't seem particularly strained by the effort: either the boy was lighter than he appeared, which was possible, or she was stronger than she looked—and considering that Bashir's face was still sore where she'd slapped him, he wasn't about to rule that out.

Rasa was asleep. Bashir could hear the raspiness in his chest. It wasn't quite as bad as it had been in the holodeck representation, but it wasn't exactly comforting.

"He sleeps very soundly," said Azira. "He always has. He . . ." And she looked up at Bashir. "Help him, Doctor. I'm . . . I'm not ready for him to sleep forever."

Not quite believing it, Bashir took a step forward. "Are you sure?"

She laughed bitterly. *"Now* you are asking me if I'm sure? No, Doctor. No, I'm not sure. I'm not sure of anything. And I'm not going to risk throwing my child's life away on that uncertainty. Do whatever you can."

She held the boy out to Bashir, who took him quickly. "What I can do," he said confidently, "is save his life."

"Then do it," she said.

"Have you consulted with your husb—"

"Do it, damn you!"

Her change in attitude was so rapid that it caught

Bashir off guard. But he was only momentarily taken aback. Then he simply nodded and said, "All right. This way, then."

He carried Rasa to a diagnostic table and laid him down. The medical sensors immediately snapped on, and Bashir promptly saw the same dismal readings he'd seen the other day. Now, however, it filled him only with a sense of challenge. "I took the liberty of synthesizing the medication required to combat the panoria," he told her. "It's called tricyclidine."

She studied him. "You were that certain that I would bring him to you."

"No. Not at all. I was, however, that hopeful. Now . . . I want to replenish his fluids. Get him stabilized. And while I'm working on that, I'll be introducing the tricyclidine into his system."

"The effects will be immediate?"

"This is hardly a miracle drug. He will feel somewhat more spry within the next forty-eight hours. But you mustn't let him overexert himself. Once we have him safely on the road to recovery, I can give you enough tricyclidine so that—if you ever are fortunate enough to leave this place—you can take it with you. It's easily administered, but must be done every day for the next twenty-one days. That's playing it safe. By that point, the disease will be completely out of his system."

"Are you sure?"

"Yes." He smiled for what seemed the first time in ages. "Yes . . . quite sure. I'm afraid that K'olkr will have to satisfy himself with sharing your joy over your son's survival rather than acquiring the boy directly himself."

"Yes." She ran a hand gently over Rasa's face. "Yes . . . I imagine that he will."

And then there came a horrified gasp from behind them.

Del had entered, and on his face was an expression of

utter horror and disgust. He might have walked into the infirmary and discovered Azira and Bashir coupling on a med table and not had a reaction more extreme than he was having right then.

"I . . . I thought I saw you come in here," he whispered to Azira. "But I . . . I can't believe—"

"Go away, Del," she said. She sounded very tired but very determined.

"You . . . you're mad!"

She turned on him, seething. "If you mean insane, no. But if you mean angry, yes! Yes, I'm angry! I'm angry at K'olkr for inflicting this disease on a child who has never hurt anyone! I'm angry at the beliefs that have held us back from treating my son so that he might live a long and productive life! I'm angry at myself for delaying as long as I have!" And, surprisingly, she turned toward Bashir. "And I'm angry at you, Doctor, for showing me a future I did not want to see! If you'd left me blissfully ignorant, then perhaps I could have held on to the beliefs that I've embraced all my life! But I can't live with the thought of my beautiful, beautiful little boy being reduced to that shell of life. I'm angry at *the entire damned universe!* But you started this, Doctor, and you will finish it. And you, Del, will get out. Now!"

"I will not!" snarled Del. "I will not turn away from the will of K'olkr! I will not ignore the light! I will prevent you from doing this. And I will save you from yourself and your own folly!"

He charged at Rasa, trying to grab the boy and yank him off the bed. Azira intervened, getting between the two and shoving Del back. Del lunged forward once more, and Azira threw her arms around him, trying to keep him in place. The Edemians struggled, hand to hand, and Del slammed Azira up against the bed, almost knocking Rasa clear off it.

Then there was an unexpected sound . . . that of a spray hypo hissing.

Del looked down in surprise to see a hypo pressed against his arm. It was being wielded by Bashir, and it had just been emptied directly into his system.

"Pleasant dreams," said Bashir calmly.

Del pushed Azira aside and tried to come at Bashir. He did not, however, get very far. Specifically, he took two steps before his consciousness fled, and instead of attacking Bashir, he managed only to stumble forward and sag into Bashir's waiting arms.

"Enthusiastic sort, isn't he?" said Bashir. Without further comment, he swung Del up and over onto another med table. "He should sleep for a few hours and be somewhat more reasonable when he wakes up."

"When he wakes up," Azira said with cold certainty, "he will go straight to my husband and tell him what has happened."

"Not a problem. Because we can also go your husband. And whereas Del is going to have a lot of religious fervor to spout, we, on the other hand, are going to be able to show Mas Marko his son—healthier than he has been in quite some time, the sparkle back in his eye, the spring back in his step." Bashir was feeling positively buoyant at the thought. "Rather than condemn what you've done, I have a suspicion that Mas Marko will offer up a prayer of thanks to K'olkr for bringing you people here, where Rasa could be treated and saved."

"You think so?"

"Yes." Bashir had slid the stabilizing unit into place over the boy and had activated the treatment. Already the lad's vital signs were leveling off. Bashir introduced a tricyclidine system into the unit, and it began to filter into Rasa's system. Satisfied that all the readings were normal, he looked back at Azira and said, "Why? Don't you?"

"Ah. You are finally asking my opinion," she said, her voice tinged with bitterness, "rather than simply inflicting your opinion on me, assaulting my beliefs, or passing judgment on our theology."

"Azira, I did no such—"

She put up a hand, stopping him in mid-sentence. "Doctor," she said firmly, "it would be a waste of time for me to tell you my opinion, because whatever happens is what will happen. I have made my decisions and must live with them, just as every sentient being must do. And what I think of the decision beyond that is of no relevance at all."

And she did not say another word as Bashir labored to save her son's life.

CHAPTER
18

GUL DUKAT of the Cardassian ship *Ravage* hailed Deep Space Nine once more. He maintained his air of decorum and pleasantry, but only just.

"Well, Commander?" prompted Dukat. "What news?"

"Your deadline has not arrived, Gul Dukat," replied Sisko. "Or are you going back on your word?"

"It has not arrived, true. But it does loom closer. I thought I would remind you of that."

"As you know full well, Gul, we have chronometers on board the station. They are keeping us apprised of the time very nicely, thank you."

"That is good to know. Oh, and Commander . . . I *do* hope you won't do anything to upset the delicate status quo."

"Such as?"

"Such as raising your shields, taking offensive action, allowing any ships to depart—that sort of thing."

"We would not raise shields unless we were attacked, Gul Dukat," Sisko said. "Nor would we take offensive action unless we were similarly provoked. As for departures . . . many of the difficulties we've encountered have resulted from my determination to make certain that everyone stays put."

"Then we understand each other."

"Thoroughly. Oh . . . and do tell that Edemian ship to keep its distance from us. Religious fanatics are always tiresome, and I have little patience with them."

Abruptly Dax announced, "Another hail . . . from the *Zealous.*"

"You can tell them yourself, Gul. Considering that you both showed up here waving your weapons around, I'm not particularly inclined to be generous toward either of you. I'll attend to my affairs, and you may feel free to do the same for yours," said Sisko unhurriedly. "Sisko out." And Gul Dukat's image had barely blinked off the screen before Sisko said, "All right, let's have the other one."

Mencar materialized on the viewscreen. He didn't seem to be in any better a frame of mind than earlier. "Commander! We have not yet heard from the Mas."

"That may very well be because we're holding him incommunicado," Sisko said.

"We are awaiting his instructions!"

"Well, then, it's to my advantage to keep the two of you from conversing with each other, isn't it?"

"This is—"

"An outrage. Yes, so I've been told," said Sisko.

Mencar paused a moment, as if figuring out the best way to approach the situation. "Commander," he said slowly, "just because I wish to receive my instructions from the Mas does not mean I am incapable of taking action on my own. Furthermore, the presence of the Cardassian ship does not sit well with me. Not well at all."

"We're not ecstatic about the situation either. If you would like to tell the Cardassians to leave, you are welcome to try. I doubt they'll listen to you with any greater attentiveness than they will to us."

Mencar frowned. "Do not," he said, "do anything to change the status quo until this matter is settled."

"You know, Mencar," said Sisko, his temper flaring, "I am getting somewhat tired of having everyone waving guns at me and telling me what I should and should not do. Now, here's what I'm telling you to do: get the hell off my subspace channel and permit me to attend to more important things! Sisko out." And he snapped off the channel.

"Were you absent from the Academy on the day they taught diplomacy, Benjamin?"

"Be quiet, old man," said Sisko tiredly. The strain of watching his back every waking moment—and of not having a lot of sleeping moments, for that matter—was beginning to take its toll.

The turbolift rose up into Ops at that moment, and a dog-tired Miles O'Brien stepped off. His normally curly hair was matted down with sweat. His uniform was filthy, covered with dirt and scoring from the several occasions when junctures had flared during cross-routing and singed his clothes. One had apparently come even closer: Sisko noted that half of one of O'Brien's eyebrows had been burned off.

"Chief . . . ?" Sisko was almost afraid to ask.

O'Brien nodded gamely. "'Sdone," he said. He headed over to the engineering station. In the crook of his elbow he was carrying a black box with a very old-style lever switch fitted into the top. Upon seeing Sisko's look, O'Brien told him, "We have to make do with what's available."

"By all means," said Sisko.

O'Brien placed the box atop the engineering console and within moments had it wired into his main circuit board. He scanned it, checked the readings, and was apparently satisfied with what he saw. "All right," he said. "Either this is going to work or . . ."

"Or what?" Sisko asked, somehow suspecting he wasn't going to like the answer he got.

"Or else it'll blow out every system on the station," O'Brien informed him.

"So it's all or nothing."

"That's about right."

"That's good to hear, Chief. If, God forbid, we want to contemplate a fallback position, knowing that we haven't got one will help me to save time down the road."

O'Brien looked at him bleary-eyed. "You want a fallback position, sir? I can think of one, if you'd like."

Sisko glanced at the viewscreen, on which the images of the Cardassian and Edemian ships were floating ominously.

"Somehow," said Sisko, "I don't think we're really going to have a lot of time."

Glav hadn't seen Quark for a while. He was starting to get apprehensive. He wandered along the Promenade, looking to see where Quark might have stashed himself. But there was no sign of him.

There was, in fact, no sign of anyone.

The absence of a crowd was starting to make Glav extremely nervous . . . and then he saw Rom ambling out of a storage closet, carrying a bowl of seenash for nibbling. He put it out on the countertop, and Glav headed over to him. Rom looked up questioningly.

"Where's Quark?" asked Glav.

"What? You haven't heard?"

"Heard what?" Then his eyes widened. "Did . . . the creature . . . ?"

"Oh, no! No, nothing like that." Rom grinned and gestured around the casino. "Welcome to Rom's."

Glav gaped openly. *What?*

"Yup. Quark sold it to me barely an hour ago for a song, and getting off DS Nine for good."

Glav couldn't believe it. "How . . . how much did you pay?"

"I told you. A song. I write songs on the side, and Quark has always liked them. So I traded one, along with all rights to it, in return for the casino. Quark thinks it could be a big hit. Listen." And in a badly off-key voice, Rom proceeded to yowl, "Oh, baby, oh, baby, now, you may think it's queer! You say you want to travel to the Big Dipper, but I got your Big Dipper right here! Oh . . ."

"That's very impressive!" Glav shouted over the caterwauling.

"You think so?" asked Rom. "There are eighteen more verses."

"Listen . . . listen to me," said Glav. "I don't understand. *Why* is Quark leaving? For that matter . . . how?"

"Oh . . . he said he decided that there's no future for this place. I think he worked out some sort of deal with a ship that's out there right now. He's in his quarters packing. In fact, he may be gone already. If not, maybe another five, ten minutes at most." He sighed. "Won't be the same without him."

"No . . . no, of course it won't," said Glav. "I . . . must go to see him off. If you'll excuse me . . ."

And he bolted from Rom's—formerly Quark's—as fast as his bowed legs would carry him.

Rasa opened his eyes.

Then he yawned rather loudly and tried to stretch . . . only to find himself encumbered by the medical unit.

Through his bleary eyes he was able to make out a familiar face smiling down at him. "Mother . . . ?" he asked.

"Yes, darling." She bent over and kissed him on the forehead. "How are you feeling?"

"A little achy," he said. "But . . . not like before. I

229

feel better than I did before." He seemed genuinely surprised by the realization. "Mother . . . am I getting better?"

She nodded. "Yes. Dr. Bashir is making you better. He's going to give us medicine, and before you know it, you'll be just like you used to be. You'll be my boy again."

Rasa leaned his head back and closed his eyes. His breathing was far more regular, and Bashir studied his vital signs with satisfaction.

Over on the other examination bed, Del snored peacefully.

Glav ran half the circle of the habitat ring before reaching Quark's quarters. Behind him, on a tether, he was pulling a wheeled suitcase, which rolled along briskly.

Arriving at Quark's quarters, he found the door locked. Disdaining the chime, he began to pound on the door. *"Quarrrkkk!"* he shouted. "You son of a space cow! Let me in! Let me—"

The door hissed open.

The light in the room was dim—dimmer than Glav was accustomed to. He thought he saw someone moving about, and he called out, "Quark! What's going on?"

He could make out Quark's dim outline as the Ferengi moved around in the quarters. There were suitcases out. Quark was clearly in the midst of packing. Now, though, he stopped, his back to Glav, as if he'd been caught looting someone's home. He sighed heavily and said, "What do you want, Glav?"

Glav pulled the suitcase in after him, and the doors hissed shut. "What do I *want?* Quark, I thought we were partners! I thought we were business associates! I thought—"

"No," said Quark softly, shaking his head, more subdued than usual. "No . . . that's what *I* thought, because that's what you wanted me to think. I figured it out, Glav. I figured it all out."

"Figured what out?" Glav laughed uncertainly. "What are you talking about? First you sell your bar; then you arrange safe passage out of here . . . without thinking to extend it to me. And now you speak in riddles."

He took a step forward, but Quark spun away, keeping his arms in front of his face and cowering in the corner in the traditional Ferengi cringe.

"Quark! What in hell has gotten into you?"

"It was you," said Quark, his voice low and intense, still cringing. "You're behind it. You're behind it all."

"Behind what all?" Glav didn't sound quite so indignant anymore. Actually he sounded more curious than anything.

"You didn't want to break Ferengi law, Glav—the law which says that if a deal is fairly and lawfully made, then seeking revenge—especially unprofitable revenge —is illegal. But you wanted me dead anyway. . . . Even after you had made your fortune, you still wanted my head.

"And then you encountered the shapeshifter. He was not a crazed creature, though, no. He was a cool, thoughtful assassin for hire. And he seemed the perfect agent to do your dirty work for you, because you were too much of a coward to do it yourself. And you also wanted to make absolutely sure that no evidence would point to you."

"This is an intriguing fairy tale, Quark," said Glav. "Please . . . go on."

"So you hit on a plan. You brought the shapeshifter aboard DS-Nine with you, disguised as something. He then went on a killing spree, murdering innocent people. But those crimes were a smoke screen for the real target: me. And you . . . you would be in the clear, because after all, you appeared to be in as much danger as anyone else. Because the killings seemed to be the random acts of a serial killer rather than the careful scheme of an assassin. Kill a few people, kill me, kill a couple more . . . and then disappear. No one would think to investigate a homicide individually when it was just one of a string. . . . You even kept me busy with your nonsense about a plan to buy this station."

Glav was silent for a long time.

Still cringing, Quark started to scamper backwards, bumping up against the wall. In the dim light he was a difficult target, but he was still accessible. "Glav, please . . . I'm begging you. Let me go. I . . . I won't tell anyone!"

"Unfortunately, Quark," said Glav, "it's not that simple."

His suitcase melted down. It became a mass of red and then re-formed, acquiring the surface and texture of a four-limbed being.

Meta now had two arms, two legs, and a head, but he had hardened his body into a solid red mass with only vaguely human features. Here he had no reason to ape human appearance. Here was going to be only blood and screaming and death.

He advanced on Quark, who let out a loud, terrified shriek. His begging and pleading did not register on the shapeshifter.

"A pity, Quark," Glav told him. "For a while there I was actually starting to like you, but you have to understand . . . it's just business."

The metamorph took two quick steps forward, his arms became two deadly spikes, and without hesitation, without mercy, he slammed them into the upper torso of the screeching Quark. He ripped his vicious weapons in opposite directions, like a twentieth-century doctor

232

with a rib spreader, and tore Quark apart from crotch to sternum.

Quark stumbled back, his arms pinwheeling from his shoulders, his ruined body thrashing about helplessly. And then, soundlessly, the Ferengi crashed to the floor.

Glav laughed triumphantly.

CHAPTER
19

BUT NOT FOR LONG.

Because Quark's chest started to re-form.

The shattered mass pulled itself together, making odd slurping sounds. Quark staggered to his feet, turning to face the metamorph, who only had time to gape in flat-footed astonishment before Quark struck out with a fist that had the force and shape of a sledgehammer.

Meta was hurled off his feet, thrown through the air, and slammed against the wall.

"Lights," said Quark's voice, except now it sounded firm, full of confidence and a hint—no, more than a hint . . . a very large dose—of arrogance.

The lights came up.

Quark's body finished reassembling itself. But now, in the full light, Glav saw to his horror that although the head had the general outline of Quark's—the large ears, the vague shape—the face itself was not Quark's.

The face was Odo's.

"Surprise," he said.

The two shapeshifters faced each other, Glav in the middle.

"Kill him!" shrieked Glav, pointing at Odo. "Kill him! What am I paying you for? Kill—"

The metamorph moved with lightning speed, his right arm honed to razor sharpness. It sliced through the air and through Glav's neck without slowing down. The Ferengi's mouth was still moving because he had not fully realized that he was dead. Then his head tumbled off his shoulders, and seconds later his body was on the floor to keep it company.

Odo was stunned, but only for a moment. "You killed Glav because your plan was ruined."

"No," said Meta calmly. "I intended to kill him all along. I never liked him. But I found his greed and his hunger for revenge very entertaining. I like to be entertained." He looked at Odo curiously. "You promise to be the most entertaining of all."

Odo took a step toward him. Meta tilted his red head slightly, as if trying to get a better look at the security chief. "So . . . what do we do now?"

"Who are you?" demanded Odo.

Meta chuckled low in his throat. "Don't you know?"

"No. I don't."

"Ahh," said Meta softly. "Now it becomes clear. You have no clue as to who you yourself are. Amnesia of some sort?"

Odo made no reply.

"And you perceive me," continued Meta, "as perhaps a link to your unknown past. But you're not sure. I may be like you . . . but then again . . . I may not."

"No. No, you're nothing like me," said Odo firmly. "I believe in justice. Nothing is more important to me. Respect for justice permeates every fiber of my being. So much so that I believe it's important to all my people."

"My," said Meta. "What an egocentric being you are. What is your name, egocentric being?"

"Odo."

"I see. It sounds like 'Oh no,' but spoken with a bad headcold."

"I'm aware of that," said Odo drily. "And you are . . . ?"

Meta shrugged. "Names are a handicap. You carry yours with you, and you feel the need to carry along the baggage of preconceived notions as well. For myself, I prefer my freedom."

"Freedom is not an option for you," Odo told him.

"Hmmm." He glanced toward the door. "Am I correct in assuming," he said, "that you have security guards—and others, perhaps—waiting outside that door?"

"That is correct," said Odo. "Escape is not possible."

"Indeed. Won't it be stimulating to find out," said Meta. He actually looked pleased. "Oh, and don't concern yourself that I'll do something dreary such as . . . transform myself into a duplicate of you. My assumption is that if you were clever enough to figure out what was happening around here, then you were certainly cautious enough to prepare some sort of coded identity-confirmation system."

"That's quite correct," said Odo.

"All right, then. That being the case . . . let us go out and greet your security guards."

As if he had all the time in the world, Meta strolled out the doors, with Odo directly behind him.

They stepped into the corridor. Meta looked right and left, slowly and amusedly.

At either end of the corridor, forcefields were in place. Standing just beyond the forcefields were security squads. With the squad on the right side was Commander Benjamin Sisko, armed with a phaser, as were all the security guards.

"So I am blocked into this corridor," said Meta, not sounding especially worried. "Sealed in at both ends."

"You will proceed to your left," said Odo firmly.

"Each screen will be deactivated for you to pass through, while at the same time the next forcefield will be activated. Once you've passed a forcefield, it will be reactivated. At no time will more than one section of corridor be available to you. There will be nowhere for you to run."

"Very clever," said Meta. "Tell me, Odo . . . did you have an easier time dealing with me when you thought I was simply some berserk, crazed monster? A bizarre aberration of your species . . . presuming we are of the same kind. Or do you prefer me this way—intelligent, articulate . . . even pleasant, if you get to know me and I don't kill you."

"I prefer you," said Odo, "in a forcefield holding facility. Now move."

Meta did not move. Instead he regarded the security squads thoughtfully. "They are all on the other side of the forcefields. Keeping them out of my reach, are you? Very wise, Odo. You know how easily I can kill them, and so you keep them out of the immediate zone of danger. That's very considerate. *Very* considerate. You're setting the ground rules in that respect, aren't you? It's just you and me within the forcefield area. And that's the way it should be. You and me."

"I told you," Odo repeated angrily, "to move."

Still Meta did not budge. His voice took on a singsong tone. "The game with Quark is over. That was just a means of killing time during the infinitely boring and unchallenging span that is my life . . . and, for that matter, your life, too. It's all a game, really, isn't it? We just chose to play on different sides."

"You don't choose the sides," Odo said sharply. "The sides choose you."

"No matter. It's time to move on to a truly challenging game. You and me, Odo. You and me. The main event."

Odo stepped toward him, stopping less than a foot

away. "I'm giving you one last warning," he virtually snarled in Meta's face. "Start moving or I'll knock you out and carry you there myself."

Meta's red face, which now had an almost crystalline look in its hardness, smiled. "I'll tell you what, Odo. I'll tell you all about yourself. Your race. Your roots. How to discipline and improve your obviously untrained morphing ability. Everything you've always wanted to know—if you will do one simple thing."

"I don't make bargains with murderers."

"This isn't a bargain. This is a challenge. All you have to do . . . is catch me."

And with that, Meta went liquid and vaulted toward the ceiling.

Sisko's comm badge was already on line; he'd established a link with Ops the moment Meta and Odo emerged from the cabin. And he shouted, *"Now, Chief!"*

The air in the duct crackled with energy, just as Meta was seeping into it. The shapeshifter writhed as energy coruscated throughout his form. With a loud, ugly plop, the creature fell to the floor not three paces away from Odo.

Odo took a step toward him . . . and that proved to be a mistake.

Meta's gelatinous form lunged forward, wrapping itself around Odo's legs. It yanked them together, and Odo started to fall backwards.

Even as he fell, Odo morphed, turning into an unrecognizable mass. The men of Deep Space Nine gaped in astonishment as the two creatures, now completely lacking any humanoid form, came together. They bubbled and seethed like lava, and it was impossible to tell who was winning, who was losing, or even, for that matter, who was where and what.

The forcefields were starting to flicker. "Keep the fields in place!" shouted Sisko.

O'Brien's voice shot back through the comm badge. "We're overloading the junction circuits with both the air vents and the fields going!"

"Shut down the air vents! Maintain the fields . . . and prepare to reinstate the vent charge at my order!"

Oozing about on the floor was the most outlandish sight that Sisko had ever beheld. Every moment or so he thought he saw something—the shape of an arm here, the vague outline of a leg there. The two masses were struggling against each other, and it was still impossible to tell how the battle was being fought, much less how it was going.

Suddenly the two masses separated violently, practically exploding in opposite directions. One of them crashed into a forcefield, and it crackled violently, the field energy sizzling through the amorphous being. It sagged forward and started to pull itself together . . . and Sisko saw that it was Odo.

The other shapeshifter re-formed itself faster than Odo, and just as Odo came together, the shapeshifter with a roar charged forward. Spikes lanced out from all over his body, and he lunged at Odo, trying to drive him back into the force screen once more.

Odo wheeled about—literally. His feet had shifted into wheels, and he sped backwards, gaining distance and a moment to compose himself.

Meta leapt forward. In midair his lower half morphed, and suddenly he was one-half humanoid, one-half coiled spring. He hit the floor and sprang forward—again literally. He crashed into Odo, the spikes lancing through Odo's body.

He had Odo pinned against the wall, his hands at Odo's throat.

Odo's throat disappeared along with his head, sinking down into his shoulders, leaving the metamorph grasping at nothing.

"Down here."

Meta looked down.

Odo's head was now projecting from under his arm.

And as Meta looked down in surprise, Odo grew another arm from his chest and slammed his fist into Meta, sending him reeling.

"This is crazy!" one of the guards muttered to Sisko. "They can't hurt each other, sir . . . can they?"

"They can wear each other out," replied Sisko tersely. "Morphing is a strain. The trick is to make whatever shifts are least strenuous but most effective. My guess is, whoever is left standing wins."

Meta's right arm was suddenly shifting again, and a huge double-edged battle-ax was projecting from just above his right shoulder. He swung it at Odo, slicing right through his middle, and Odo's form rippled just fast enough to get out of its way. In the meantime his own arm was changing, and when Meta swung the ax around again, it clanged loudly against the shield that Odo had created out of himself.

The deflected blow glanced off the shield . . . and crashed against the wall, rupturing a plate.

There was now a gaping hole in the wall.

That was enough for Meta, and he sprang through it, becoming a narrow column of gelatinous matter.

O'Brien had, of course, not prepared for that. It had taken him long enough just to booby trap the air vents. Hot-wiring the walls as well had not been an option. It turned out to be a costly compromise, for within the blink of an eye Meta was gone.

"Oh, no, you don't!" shouted Odo. *"Not this time!"* And as fast as Meta had gone through the opening, so too did Odo.

"They're in the walls!" shouted Sisko. "Ops, can we track them!"

"Negative! Repeat: negative! We have no sensor devices in the walls!" Kira said over the comm unit, and then added, her anger directed primarily toward herself, "Who the hell installs a security sensor net inside of walls and ceilings, anyway?"

"Presuming we all live through this," shot back Sisko, "we will."

In her quarters, Keiko O'Brien heard something inside the walls.

Molly was safely tucked away for her nap, and Keiko was working up the next day's lesson plans . . . and trying to remember what it was like back in the days when she hadn't spent every waking moment afraid for her own life and the life of her child.

Now she leaned forward, puzzled. Yes . . . something was definitely thumping around in there. It could be vermin, of course. She had shuddered when she'd seen mice scurrying through the hallways. But this noise seemed too loud to be rodents.

Perhaps it was coming from the pipes and conduits that carried energy through the station. The realization that something was thudding around behind the wall, and perhaps leaking energy, made Keiko uneasy.

She walked over to the wall comm unit and said, "Keiko to Chief O'Brien. Miles?"

O'Brien sounded extremely harried. "Keiko . . . can this possibly wait?"

"I . . . suppose so. It just sounds as if there's something inside the wall here. But if it's nothing dangerous, then it's all right."

It seemed to take a moment for what she was saying to register—a pause that she chalked up to Miles's fatigue from the pace at which he'd been pushing himself lately. "In the wall . . ." he said. But when he spoke again, it was with more alarm than she'd ever heard from him. "Keiko! *Get out of there!* Now! *Hurry!*"

The near-panic in his voice was more than enough to stir Keiko to action. She headed toward the room where Molly was soundly napping.

And at that moment the wall in front of her bulged outward crazily, metal shrieking in protest. Keiko gasped, trying to get past, but there wasn't room. She was cut off from her daughter.

The wall ripped open like a burst bubble, and two beings tumbled out.

One was barely recognizable as Odo. The other was barely recognizable as human.

They were pounding on each other furiously, as if trying to tear each other apart. Meta spun and hurled Odo into the far wall. Then he tore off a large section of the bulkhead that had been damaged and ran flush into Odo. Odo had no time at all to react before being smashed flat against the opposite bulkhead. He started to ooze under the metal that was imprisoning him, but the effort was sluggish and he was clearly tired.

Meta, fully reconstituted now, turned toward Keiko, who was backing up against her desk. He grinned lopsidedly.

"Hello," he said. "Nice station you got here."

He reeled toward her then, an animal snarl ripping from his throat, or what served as his throat.

And Keiko snatched the phaser up off the desk, swung it around faster than she would have thought possible, and fired.

If he'd been at peak energy levels, Meta could have morphed around the beam. But he wasn't, and he didn't. It hit him dead on, hurling him against the locked doors of the quarters. He went liquid and seeped out through the crack between the doors, vanishing.

Keiko spun and shrieked, bringing the phaser up as she saw something moving behind her. Another mass, but this coalesced into the familiar form of Odo. He put up a hand, trying to speak. Clearly he was exhausted . . . but he was also determined.

Keiko quickly went to the door and punched in the sequence to unlock it. Odo staggered forward, and Keiko extended the phaser to him. "Here, take this."

Odo shook his head. "Sorry . . . never use them," he said, sounding out of breath.

He stumbled out into the hallway, looking right and left.

No sign of the metamorph.

No sign anywhere.

Odo had lost him.

He sagged against the wall, trying to clear his mind. But there was no clearing, because black fury seared through him, shaking him. And he shouted in a voice that reverberated throughout the entire area . . . perhaps through the entire habitat ring, *"Coward! The game isn't over, coward! You keep running from me, coward! What are you afraid of? Eh? Afraid you're not as good as you* think *you are!"*

As he heaved himself away from the wall, he heard a faint suction-type sound, like something sticky being peeled off a flat surface.

He held up his hands and looked at them in horror.

His skin was running.

It was dribbling down in rivulets, and the phenomenon wasn't restricted to his hands. His chest, his legs . . . He put his hands up to his face, and yes, it was happening there, too; his face was beginning to slide apart. His entire body was melting like a candle.

The strain of the past several days—the lack of rest, the rapid morphing—was starting to catch up with him. The only thing holding him together was sheer willpower, and even that would eventually succumb to exhaustion. If he didn't catch the shapeshifter soon, all the determination in the world wouldn't prevent him from dissolving into a helpless puddle, unable to move until his body was sufficiently rested.

But that time was not yet. Not yet.

He focused his concentration, calling on reserves of energy, refusing to accept any weakness forced on him by the demands of his body. The demands of his *mind* were of foremost concern to him. And his mind would not, *would not,* allow the morph to get away again, free to kill at whim.

He pulled himself together, his body firming into its customary humanoid shape. He flexed his hands, satisfied to see that they were whole once more.

"Cowaaarrrrrddd!" he shouted once more, praying that the shapeshifter was somewhere within earshot.

Abruptly his communicator beeped. It was Kira, talking excitedly.

"We've got him tracked, Odo!" she practically shouted. "The security grid wasn't effective when he was imitating humanoids or oozing through air vents, but now—"

"Where, Major? Where is he!"

"Two sectors away from you! Corridor eighteen-A."

"Computer!" snapped Odo. "Seal off corridor eighteen-A!"

"Confirmed," the computer said serenely.

Ahead of him, he heard the forcefield flare up. The morph was clearly slamming himself against it, and Odo could hear a crackling as the field fought to restrain him.

Suddenly the lights overhead flickered, and there was the sound of something shorting out, the smell of something burning.

In Ops, O'Brien slammed a hand against a console.

"We've lost the security grid on habitat level fifteen, corridors eighteen to twenty-four," he snarled. "The circuit junctures didn't hold! It's backlashing through the entire power grid! Compensators aren't holding! Goddamn jerry-rigged Cardassian technology!"

"What kind of pressure could the metamorph have put on the forcefield that managed to—" And then, on the screen, Kira saw it—or, at least, barely managed to see it, because the screen was flickering out. "Odo!" she shouted. "Move! He's heading your way!"

Odo heard it, even felt it, before he saw it. But when he did, his jaw dropped in amazement.

The floor rumbled beneath his feet, and then with the speed and power of a berserk bulldozer, Meta rolled into view.

He had transformed himself into a giant boulder, rolling straight toward Odo.

And somehow, from amid the rumbling, came the words, *"Coward, am I?"*

Odo started to run.

He didn't want to morph again; he was afraid he wouldn't be able to pull himself back together. Even the strain of sustaining his ordinary humanoid form— the body he was most practiced at and, consequently, the easiest to maintain—was starting to wear on him.

He ran, staggered, stumbled, picked himself up, and ran again. He felt his body start to dissolve once more. His feet stuck to the floor, making a strange ripping noise like Velcro with every step.

The boulder was gaining on him. In his imaginings— or maybe it was real—the rumbling sounded like laughter.

Anger seared through him, and he allowed the anger to take him, to drive him. He leapt into the air . . . and morphed.

The boulder rolled toward him, but Odo wasn't there anymore. Instead, a high-powered drill, spinning furiously, was there to meet it.

The drill whirred, emitting a shrill scream, and

slammed into the boulder, penetrating it, tunneling into it, coring it out.

The boulder roared in protest and collapsed. The drill clattered to the floor.

Both shapeshifters re-formed, facing each other.

"You're under arrest," said Odo again.

Meta hit him.

Nothing fancy.

He just hit him.

With an anvil on the end of his arm.

It smashed into Odo's chest. Odo staggered back, a large anvil-shaped dent in his body. He dodged as Meta came at him again, and now his arms and legs extended, split, split again. . . .

Odo was completely gone. He had become a mass of tentacles, writhing and twisting, with no identifiable central mass. The tentacles lashed out, each one razor-sharp, slicing through Meta wherever he turned. Meta shrieked under the assault and ducked back, trying to find someplace where he would be safe from those vicious slithering arms.

Meta opened his mouth wide . . . wider. His body began to shrink, while his jaws continued to grow. Huge fangs sprouted, a tongue lashed out furiously, and within seconds he was nothing but one giant mouth.

It slammed shut on the multiple tentacles, trying to catch as many as it could, and began crunching.

The tentacles punched through the back of the mouth, and then the two morphs began to lose control of their shapes. Once more they were running together, dissolving. . . .

The pounding of running feet alerted them to the fact that security squads were heading their way. Suddenly Meta tore away, hurtling through the air in a stream of protoplasm. He pulled himself into a perfect sphere and rolled away.

Odo drew himself together, the fire of his anger

overwhelming, at least temporarily, the exhaustion that threatened to engulf him.

But then he started to succumb, and he was falling . . . except that Meyer and Boyajian were there, holding him up. "Are you all right, sir?" asked Meyer.

"Terrific," said Odo with bravado. "Never better. I'm just getting warmed up. Now follow me, but stay behind me! I'll engage the enemy. You stand back and wait for an opening! Understood?"

They nodded in unison.

"All right! Let's go!"

Meta had had enough, and more than enough.

Suddenly this game had lost its amusement value.

He had resumed his humanoid form because it was easier for him to get his bearings in that manner. But it was slower, and he was starting to feel the strain from the rapid shifts. But he was not as tired as Odo, he reasoned, and allowed himself a smirk of superiority. Nevertheless . . .

And then he saw what he wanted to see—a sign just ahead of him, with an arrow pointing off to one side: RUNABOUT AIRLOCKS AND SERVICING BAY.

Immediately he bolted in that direction, pleased that things were so clearly marked. And there he found them, just as the sign had promised: three airlocks, each leading to a runabout—one of the small ships that Starfleet provided for the convenience of the station's personnel.

Well, now the ship was going to serve at his convenience.

He saw quickly, in studying the control settings, that the runabouts were locked into place with mooring clamps. This, however, was not a problem.

He went to the wall on his left, lifted up the paneling, and reached in toward the massive lever that kept the runabout locked in place. He raised it, slid it down, and locked it into the open position. He went to the opposite wall and did the same. Then, for good measure, he used some small bit of his remaining energy to transform his hand into a spear once more. He slammed the blade into the grid that controlled the mooring clamps. Sparks flew and alarms sounded, but this was of no consequence to him. All that mattered was that no one up in Ops would try to slide the mooring locks back into place.

He went to the wall and punched the button that rolled the airlock door open. He stepped through it.

And then, from behind him, he heard Odo's outraged shout.

"Coward!" bellowed the security chief once more.

Meta had allowed that challenge to draw him back before. This time, though, the urge to depart the area superseded any desire to stay and exchange blows with Odo. So he gave a cheerful wave as the airlock rolled closed, shutting him off.

Odo, unable to stop his charge in time, slammed up against the airlock door, taking the impact with his shoulder. "Odo to Ops!" he called. "The shapeshifter is stealing a runabout!"

"He's blown out the command overrides," Kira's angry voice came back. "Let him go! We can always pull him back with the tractor beams."

"Let him *go?* Like hell!" snapped Odo. "I'm not giving him any chance to pull some last-minute stunt!"

"Odo, *wait!"*

But Odo was past listening. The airlock was sealed off, but the gaping conduits in the walls where the mooring clamps led through beckoned to him. Odo pulled his strength together and leapt into the conduits, morphing as he went. Within seconds he was gone . . . and a serpent had lashed itself around the mooring clamps. It moved with phenomenal speed, its body rippling, hurling it forward down the conduits, toward the service bay.

Meta was inside the runabout, firing it up. He made a very fast systems check, glancing around the interior with satisfaction. Yes, indeed, he could travel a fairly healthy distance in this vessel. Leave Odo forever wondering. Yes . . . yes, he liked that option a great deal.

Ideally the service elevator would raise the runabout to the surface of the habitat ring, but that wasn't absolutely necessary. Meta disengaged the airlock and hit the upward thrusters. The runabout began to lift.

Meta was glancing at the equipment board when he was startled by a loud noise, as if something had hit the front of the runabout with the sound and impact of a small meteorite. He looked up.

His mouth spread into a grin.

Odo had flattened himself against the front bay window of the runabout. His arms and upper torso had sprouted suction pads, and he was holding on, pounding furiously.

"Sorry," said Meta. "I don't pick up hitchhikers. Enjoy the ride while you can, though."

And with that, the runabout lifted out of the service bay, swung around, and fled Deep Space Nine . . . with the frustrated chief of security still pounding on the outside.

CHAPTER
20

"Gul!" SHOUTED THE weapons officer on board the *Ravage*. "They've launched a runabout!"

"Now, I know I told them not to do that," said Gul Dukat, sounding hurt. "Shields up. Phaser at three-quarter strength. Fire."

Sisko made it back to Ops just in time to hear Dax call out, "They've raised their shields! Power to their forward phasers!"

Sisko and Kira said at the same time, "Raise shields!" Kira glanced at the commander and promptly deferred to him as Sisko said, "Get me Gul Dukat on the—"

The *Ravage* cut loose, hammering the just-raised shields of Deep Space Nine. The station shook under the pounding, but Sisko knew immediately that something wasn't right. "That wasn't full strength," he muttered.

"No, Commander," Dax informed him. "Their phasers were only at three-quarter strength."

"Warning shots," said Kira.

"Get that runabout back here!" snapped Sisko. "Now!"

"Tractor beams activated!" said O'Brien.

The tractor beams lashed out, snaring the runabout. The small craft struggled in the grip of the beams, fighting to put distance between itself and the station.

And Odo, exposed to the vacuum of space, held on for dear life.

Mencar, commander of the Edemian Holy War vessel *Zealous,* saw the Cardassian ship fire upon the station. A most volatile and holy wrath seized him.

"Those Cardassian slime!" he snarled. "How dare they intercede in the holy business of the followers of K'olkr! Tactical! Target the Cardassian ship!"

"Disruptors on line!"

"Fire!"

The disruptors of the *Zealous* lashed out, striking the Cardassian ship square across the starboard shields.

Gul Dukat was astounded when the bridge trembled around him from the impact. "The nerve of them! This is a Galor-class warship of the Cardassian second order! Who in the seven hells do they think they're mucking with? Sentor, return fire, full strength!"

The *Ravage* ripped at the *Zealous,* hammering its forward shields. The *Zealous* fell back a short distance as the Edemian tactical officer rerouted power to shore up the main deflectors. The *Zealous* would have been sorely pressed to defend itself at that moment, but fortunately for the Edemians, Gul Dukat was abruptly distracted by something else.

"Gul Dukat!" declared Sentor at Tactical. "The station has caught the runabout and is trying to pull it in. But . . . sir, I think you should see this!"

"Full magnification," said Dukat, puzzled at Sentor's tone of voice.

The runabout appeared on their screens, and Dukat's eyes went wide.

Security Chief Odo was clinging to the front of the runabout. Oblivious, it seemed, of the fact that he was in space, Odo was pounding on the exterior of the runabout with single-minded determination.

"Is he out of his *mind*?" said Dukat incredulously. "What could possess Odo to . . ." And then the light dawned. "Of course," he whispered and then, louder, *"Of course!* The murderer must be piloting the runabout! Trying to get away! That's got to be it! Only Odo would be *that* obsessive!"

"Orders, sir?"

"Sentor," Dukat said with relish, "bring phasers to bear on the runabout. Prepare to fire." He added as an afterthought, "Sorry, Odo, but I'm sure that you, of all people, would understand the things that must be done in the name of justice."

"The Cardassians are no longer firing on the station, sir," Dax said. And then in alarm she said, "Benjamin! They're locking on the runabout!"

There was no more time, no more options. "Chief," said Sisko firmly. "Full phasers in short bursts. Distract them. And . . . fire!"

"Firing phasers, sir," said O'Brien.

Phaser blasts danced along the shields of the *Ravage,* shaking up the war vessel and angering Gul Dukat. "Sisko, you idiot! I would have left you alone! It's Gotto's murderer I want!"

And then the *Ravage* shook again, but the blasts had not come from the station.

"Edemian vessel at two one one mark nine!" warned the tactical officer.

Gul Dukat wasn't sure where to look first. The Edemian vessel was clearly the more immediate threat, but he could not, under any circumstance, let the attack from the station go unanswered. "Bring us about at a heading of four one eight mark six," ordered Dukat. "Lock photon torpedoes on the Edemians, and return phaser fire on Deep Space Nine! And try to hit that damned runabout while you're at it! Torpedoes and phasers, fire!"

The Cardassian war vessel fired in all directions, erupting like a star gone nova.

The runabout, a small target, was still twisting and writhing in the grip of the tractors. Consequently, and slightly miraculously, the phaser blasts missed the vessel.

They did, however, strike Deep Space Nine. And since it had previously been a Cardassian station, the war vessel knew exactly where to strike in order to cause the greatest damage.

"Damage to the inertial damping field!" O'Brien bellowed over the ruckus in Ops as DS9 was being pummeled by the *Ravage*. "Damage to the subprocessor modules! Shields at thirty percent and dropping!"

In the infirmary, debris started to fall from the ceiling. Bashir threw himself over the unmoving form of Rasa to shield him. Azira shrieked, convinced that the wrath of K'olkr was going to bring death and destruction to them all.

Del, still asleep, rolled off the med table. He hit the floor and continued snoring.

In Ops, Dax delivered the worst news of the afternoon. "We've lost cohesive power on the tractors! The runabout is breaking loose!"

* * *

And indeed it was.

Meta howled in triumph as the runabout shook loose the station's tractor beams and lunged toward safety.

But then safety was suddenly blocked by the looming image of the Cardassian war vessel.

Meta banked the runabout hard around, angling away—and there, right in its path, was the staggering but still functional Edemian holy war vessel *Zealous.*

Odo hung on, helpless, furious at the situation he'd gotten himself into. He had let his opponent lure him into a situation that was in no way advantageous to Odo. Grimly he thought that next time, he . . .

Next time?

What in hell made him think there was going to be a next time?

Meta's hands flew over the navigational systems. The runabout went hard about, dropping in a cloverleaf maneuver, and gracefully steering through the obstacles, scampering toward safety.

And then Odo realized where the runabout was heading. Indeed, he realized it before Meta did, because the metamorph was less familiar with this area of space than Odo was.

But Odo knew, beyond any question, that if the runabout did not change its course, it would hurtle into the heart of the Bajoran wormhole in less than thirty seconds.

And then he saw it—the muzzle of the microtorpedo launcher, one of the runabout's few armaments.

It was a dangerous move, but he saw no alternative. Odo oozed up the side of the runabout, heading for the muzzle. He caught the briefest glimpse of the metamorph's puzzled expression, and then he got to the muzzle. In a flash, driven by desperation, he was inside, making his way through the inner workings of the ship. He stretched his mass to its utmost, barely molecules in thickness.

He seeped into the cabin, then pulled himself together as fast as he could. The metamorph heard him and turned to face him, a look of amusement on his features.

Odo reached for him, drawing his fist back, ready to overpower him and commandeer the vessel . . .

And then the world exploded around them.

"The runabout's been hit!" shouted Dax.

Indeed it had. A stray disruptor bolt from the Edemian ship had struck the small vessel broadside, rupturing the hull. The atmosphere of the ship rushed out as the vacuum of space pushed in, and within seconds the runabout blew apart.

"Sensor sweep!" ordered Sisko, remaining as cool as possible under the circumstances. "If there's any hope—"

"Got 'em!" crowed Dax. "Reading two life-forms."

And then Deep Space Nine shook once more.

"The two ships are firing at each other!" said Kira. "We're getting the stray shots!"

"We can't beam Odo and the morph aboard while we have shields up!"

"That won't be a consideration much longer, Lieutenant," O'Brien informed Dax. "Shields at twenty percent and still dropping. And as soon as we don't have shields—"

"Get me the Edemians and the Cardassians on subspace! Now! And get me full magnification on Odo and the morph!"

The viewscreen shifted, and there, indeed, was the chief of security. His body was flowing, shifting, the pressures of space threatening to rip it apart . . .

And still he was battling. Battling with the morph, who was undergoing the same stress. Not conceding anything, even the likelihood of imminent death, the two shapeshifters were outside the wreckage of the runabout, intertwined, hammering at each other, struggling with everything they had and more than they had.

Insanely, Sisko thought, *the Constable is the most single-minded individual I have ever met.*

"Get me both ships!" he shouted again. And then, before the order was even acknowledged, he had them on line. "This is Sisko!" he snarled. "I am ordering both of you idiots to stop firing at this station and at each other immediately! Do you hear me? Unless we can safely drop our shields to operate the transporters, someone is going to die! And if that happens, Starfleet and I are going to hold you both personally responsible. And I can assure both of you, with utter certainty, that if there is one thing in this galaxy that you do *not* want, it's *to have me angry at you!"*

The shapeshifters hurtled through space. As per the laws of physics, bodies in motion tended to stay in motion unless acted upon by another force.

And then another force started to act upon them. The force known as the Bajoran wormhole.

Odo and Meta started to pick up speed. Odo knew what was happening, but Meta did not—not at first. His attention was fully focused on Odo. A hand sprouted from his chest and swept toward Odo, clawing him.

Odo tried to shout at him that this was insane, that this was the wrong move, but there was no air for his voice to carry through. He lost his grip, and Meta kicked away from him, putting some distance between himself and Odo.

Clearly Meta's plan was to float in space, hope to be picked up by a passing ship . . . something. He was a survivor. He knew things that Odo did not, tricks that Odo had not learned. The vacuum of space held no terrors for him.

He saw Odo spiraling away from him, and he grinned to himself.

And then he became aware of space starting to distort around him.

He looked around, twisting in confusion as dim alarms sounded in his mind. Something was not right, most definitely not right. He felt odd, light-headed. Suddenly nothing seemed natural, and the depths of space no longer seemed quite so fear-free.

And then it was all around him.

It roared into existence, its mouth yawning around him—an incredible array of colors, and sound that was not sound . . . sound that could not be heard but could be *felt*, howling through him, pounding him, assaulting every molecule of his form.

The Bajoran wormhole drew him in. Even under the best of circumstances it would have been nearly impossible for Meta to survive a trip through the wormhole unprotected. Still, it might have been vaguely, remotely possible.

Under the best of circumstances.

These, however, were the worst of circumstances.

This was the Bajoran wormhole while it was undergoing subspace compression, the galactic phonomenon that had shredded a Borg ship without difficulty.

One unprotected shapeshifter was no challenge at all.

Meta twisted around, besieged inside and out. He twisted around, caught a last glimpse of Odo in the distance, and stretched out his hand. . . .

Odo saw it.

As the metamorph was sucked down into the maw of the wormhole, Odo saw the renegade reach for him. They were too far apart, and besides, Odo was hardly in a position to help anyone. In a few moments he, too, would be yanked into the wormhole to meet a dismal and terminal fate.

Still, just for a moment he saw, or sensed, the panic in the metamorph. Meta knew what was about to happen, would have done anything to avoid the hideous destiny that was his. And in that extremity, he sought aid from the one being who was like him.

And Odo would have done anything at that moment to save him.

Unfortunately there was nothing to be done.

Meta descended into the swirling pit of the Bajoran wormhole. He screamed into the airlessness of space, not out of pain but out of awareness of what was happening.

His body was ripped apart, atom by atom, scattering in a million directions at once. He felt himself being disassembled, being scattered all along the inner walls of the howling god that was the wormhole. He fought against it, but he had no chance in hell, because he *was* in hell, splintered like shards of glass.

Images—of all those he had killed, of the life that he had led, of the waste and self-satisfaction and murderous enjoyment that had constituted his existence—flashed before him, and suddenly he wanted to take it all back, all of it. Please, anything. Just make it stop. Give him back his life. . . .

And when he realized the futility of that wish, as he felt the last of himself being torn apart, his consciousness clinging to him, he begged the great howling god that if he couldn't have his life back, then at least end it now. *End it.* . . .

But it didn't end.

His consciousness did not flee, could not. Every molecule of his body was independently aware. Ripped apart, scattered all along the interspatial conduit of the wormhole, every bit of him was aware that he had lost his body, lost his existence, and was waiting for it to end, in the name of God, waiting for consciousness to vanish and oblivion to claim him.

It didn't happen.

It never happened.

His awareness of nonexistence, of being everywhere and nowhere at the same time, was embedded throughout the wormhole. He tore through the space-time continuum, assaulted by images, assaulted by *himself.* And moments later, his molecules blew into the Gamma Quadrant, and he would never, given a million million lifetimes, be able to pull himself together. A cosmic Humpty Dumpty.

He would remain forever on the cusp of death, suffering, screaming in a voice that only he could hear. Or maybe he could not hear it, but it was nowhere and everywhere, and the voice kept saying, *Let it end. Let it end. . . .*

And it never would.

The wormhole beckoned to Odo.

It roared into existence around him as he passed the outer perimeter, and a thought passed through his mind, one searing and infuriating awareness: *Dammit! Who's going to keep an eye on Quark?*

And then he felt something surround him. At first, he assumed it to be an effect of the wormhole. But no . . . this felt familiar somehow, and since his personal experience with falling into wormholes was, naturally, limited, he concluded that this was something that must have happened to him before.

Then the wormhole disappeared, as did the depths of space.

He felt something hard beneath him, and the familiar smell of stale air—because O'Brien *still* hadn't gotten the damned air filters to work properly. He squinted against the light, and then the faces of Kira and Sisko were in his field of vision, smiling at him.

"Welcome back, Constable," said Sisko.

Odo nodded . . . but only once.

Then his head slid down into his chest. He had been leaning on his arms, but now his elbows dissolved, his biceps and triceps merging.

His feet were swallowed by his legs, which in turn blended with his hips . . . and before the astonished eyes of everyone in Ops, Odo became a very large puddle of red goo.

Sisko and Kira stepped back, treading carefully so as not to get any of Odo on their boots. They looked at each other questioningly, and then with a shrug Sisko tapped his comm unit.

"Sisko to Maintenance," he said calmly. "We need a cleanup in Ops. Please bring a mop . . . and a fairly large pail."

"I am impressed, Commander," said Gul Dukat. "Such forcefulness in your tone. Such anger. Such . . . What is the word?"

"Arrogance?" suggested Mencar.

Both commanders were on the DS9 viewscreen, conferenced together by Sisko. Sisko, the picture of calm, had his hands behind his back.

"Yes! Exactly so," said Gul Dukat. "In many ways, Commander, you would make a creditable Cardassian."

"I'll take that as a compliment," Sisko said. He heard O'Brien mutter, "I wouldn't," but he let it pass. "It was necessary to get your attention, gentlemen, since both of you were fighting over an entity whose fate was being attended to outside the confines of this station."

"Indeed, the matter did become rather moot rather quickly," agreed Dukat. "And it would have been a pity to sacrifice Odo on the altar of the Edemians' stubbornness."

"*Our—*" Mencar bristled.

Sisko spoke quickly before matters could escalate again. "Fortunately it has been attended to. It is not the way I would have liked it, gentlemen."

"Nor we," said Mencar.

"Nor I," concurred Dukat. "Then again, I suppose we must settle for justice—justice handed down, perhaps, by someone greater than ourselves."

"K'olkr," Mencar said reverently. He didn't notice Gul Dukat rolling his eyes upward, but continued, "Which reminds us . . . Mas Marko—"

"Is being released from his . . . enforced accommodations even as we speak," said Sisko. "He will be able to leave at his convenience. My science officer informs me"—and he glanced once more at Dax, who nodded confirmation—"that the wormhole has settled down. The subspace compression has reversed itself. If Mas Marko wishes to continue his mission, he may do so."

"Perhaps," said Dukat slowly, "the wormhole was hungry . . . and its appetite has been sated."

"I tend to be more pragmatic in these matters, Gul," Sisko said.

"As do we all," Dukat replied. "Is Odo all right, by the way?"

"Last I saw him, he was looking rather pail," said Sisko, ignoring the low moans this prompted from his crew.

"Well, tell him we salute his courage," said Dukat.

"As do we," put in Mencar. "He has acted in the name of K'olkr . . . as do all things."

"I'll tell him. Sisko out."

They both blinked out, and Sisko turned to see that Kira was standing almost toe to toe with him.

"Commander," she said in a low voice, "I must protest."

He raised an eyebrow. "Really?"

"I believe that you are taking unseemly delight in Odo's exhaustion, which has led to his current . . .

difficult state," she told him stiffly. "It's not appropriate, it's not respectful, and it's not fair."

"I will admit to some degree of amusement," allowed Sisko. "The constable, for all his good points, has made his impatience with the Federation in general, and with me in particular, fairly evident. Still . . . I apologize, Major. If you find it upsetting, I will not make such disrespectful comments about the constable again."

"Thank you, sir," said Kira. "We should count ourselves fortunate that he wasn't killed."

"Yes," Sisko agreed solemnly. "I would have hated to see him kick the bucket."

CHAPTER
21

MAS MARKO stood in the infirmary, looking at the life readings on his son. Marko's face was unreadable, and Bashir took that as a good sign. Obviously, it meant that he had not dismissed the rightness of the doctor's actions out of hand. Azira stood nearby, her arms folded, not saying a word.

"As you can see," Bashir said, "the life signs have stabilized and, in several instances, are higher than they were before. Clearly, with the medication I've given him so far, and with the continued administration of the tricyclidine, Rasa will live a full and healthy life." When Marko said nothing, Bashir added helpfully, "K'olkr could not possibly object to that."

Marko fixed him with a passionless gaze. "I see, Doctor. So you have now added theology to your fields of expertise."

"Look, I'm sorry," said Bashir, "but I just don't see how saving Rasa's life so that he can continue to do your god's work can be a bad thing."

"That is the problem, isn't it, Doctor? For you see, the work of K'olkr is performed on all levels—among the living and beyond that simple state, unto eternity.

By your interference, you have disrupted whatever plans K'olkr had for my son. Rasa is forever tainted. Whatever effectiveness he might have had in this incarnation . . . is gone."

"Don't you think you're being a bit extreme about this?" asked Bashir.

But Mas Marko was not listening to him. He had turned toward Azira. "You," he said softly. "You . . . let this happen. Wanted it to happen. How *could* you?"

She couldn't look into his glowing eyes. "Marko, we have been a part of each other's life for as long as I can remember. We were joined, promised to each other, when we were just beyond infancy. I remember you when you were Rasa's age. He looks so much like you did. And you spoke to me back then of the things you were going to do—your dreams, your hopes, the accomplishments that were so important to you. And I've watched you, taken pride in you, as you achieved your goals, one by one. Every time I looked at Rasa, I saw so much of you in him. And I"—her voice trembled—"I love you too much, loved both of you too much, to allow Rasa's life to end before he could accomplish any of his own goals. It . . . wouldn't have been fair." Now she looked at him. "I didn't care what K'olkr's plan was. No plan of his—no matter how divine, no matter how inspired—could have made his death fair. Could have made it right."

"And who are you," said Marko, "to question his plan? He is K'olkr! And you must answer to him!"

"I am Azira," she replied evenly. "And I answer to myself."

There was a long moment of silence.

"The *Zealous* is waiting for me," he said after a time. "I am told by Commander Sisko that the subspace compression has subsided. I will return to Edema, gather together new followers, and make the pilgrimage. And as for you . . ."

He drew himself up and then walked around her in a slow circle. He muttered a string of words that Bashir did not understand. Azira closed her eyes, obviously in pain, but she did not allow a sound to escape her lips.

"Wh-what's happening?" demanded Bashir. "I don't understand."

Mas Marko finished walking in the circle and then turned to face Bashir. "It is the consequence of your actions, Doctor. You tempted Azira off the holy path, and she succumbed to your enticements. The wife of a Mas must be held to the strictest standard, as must his offspring. Azira and Rasa are tainted. Forever tainted. No forgiveness on my part—even if I had forgiveness to give—could expunge this sin from them."

Bashir looked from Marko to Azira and back again. "Wait . . . What are you saying? This is—"

"They will never be welcome into the arms of K'olkr, for the son's path has been altered and the mother has lost faith. She has elevated herself above K'olkr, and that cannot be. . . . Azira, I have spoken the words and walked the path that you cannot follow. We are forever divorced. Furthermore, you are forever excommunicated. If you walk the soil of Edema, you will be shunned by all followers of the word of K'olkr. Some of them can be . . . violent," he added reluctantly. "I do not approve of their methods, but neither will I deter them."

Bashir's anger erupted. "You heartless bastard!" he shouted. "This woman saved your son's life! And this is how you thank her? By cutting her off from you? From the life and world she knows? You can't do this!"

Marko whirled on Bashir, faster than his size would have had Bashir believe possible. For just a moment his solemn voice seemed to crack. "You know nothing of what I can and can't do, Doctor! Do you think this *pleases* me? Do you think I *wish* to do this? My people do not believe in remarriage; I shall spend the rest of my days alone. Do you truly believe I find that prospect desirable? *Do you?*"

He drew his robes tighter around him, as if trying to draw protection and strength from them. "You did what you felt you had to do, Doctor. And my wife—apologies, I meant to say my former wife—did as she felt that she had to do. And now . . . I do what I must do."

Bashir looked to Azira. "This is . . . You can't . . ." But he could think of nothing further to say.

Mas Marko walked slowly toward the door. Despite his great height, he seemed very small and vulnerable at that moment. He paused at the door as it opened and then said softly—so softly that Bashir had to strain to hear him—"May K'olkr watch over you, Azira. You and Rasa both."

"If he wishes," replied Azira.

And then he was gone.

"Doctor," said Azira after a moment, "if you would be so kind as to arrange for us to have passage to . . ." She thought about it and then shrugged. "To anywhere, really. Perhaps to Bajor. That would not be a lengthy trip, and I understand Bajorans are a fairly religious people. Maybe their god will embrace us, even though our own has turned his back on us."

"I . . . I'm sorry, Azira," said Bashir, knowing that "I'm sorry" didn't even begin to cover it. "I . . . I mean, had I known—"

"If you had known, you'd have what?" Her voice was full of scorn. "You'd have behaved differently? Spare me, Doctor. You were fixated on one thing and one thing only: saving a life. Even if I had warned you of what would happen, it wouldn't have mattered to you. You forced me to choose between my son's life and my own life—the life I knew with my people and my husband. And if you were put into the exact same position, there is every likelihood that you would do the exact same thing again. Wouldn't you?"

"Very possibly," he admitted. It galled him to confess that, because even when he had been doing it—when he'd been subjecting Azira to the holoscenario from hell—he had felt a measure of guilt. All that, however, had been washed away by the pure excitement and triumph of saving the boy's life, of looking death in the eye and saying, "Not this time. Not this life. Not yet." And so again he said, "Very possibly, yes. But I had no idea of the consequences when I took those actions. The only thing of significance to me was that your son would live. You, on the other hand, were perfectly aware. If *you* had it to do over again, would *you* take the same action?"

She gazed at the sleeping child on the medical bed. The child who had cost her everything—her mate, her religion, her planet, her friends . . . everything.

"I wish I knew," she said faintly. "I wish to K' . . . I wish to God I knew."

The door hissed open, and Sisko was standing there. He was scowling.

"Doctor," he said. "I've had a chat with Del."

"Yes?"

"And now . . . I'd like to have a chat with you. A long chat."

"Yes," Bashir said softly. "I rather thought you would."

CHAPTER
22

BENJAMIN SISKO walked into his quarters, flexing his arms and feeling a lot stiffer and a lot older. "Jake?" he called.

His son came to him from the next room. Sisko smiled, because Jake was wearing a helmet. "Is it safe?" he asked warily.

"Of course it's safe," said Sisko. He stretched out on the couch. "The Cardassians left hours ago, along with the Edemians. If any two races ever deserved each other, it's them."

"And the morph guy?"

"Gone. I doubt we'll be seeing him again."

"It's too bad he and Odo couldn't have been friends or something. It's kind of sad for Odo, I guess."

This, of course, had already occurred to Sisko. "Yes . . . I guess it is," he said carefully.

Jake shifted uncomfortably where he was standing, and Sisko looked at him questioningly. "Something wrong?"

"Well, I . . . I don't know how to say this, really. . . ."

"Ohhh, boy," said Sisko. He sat up and braced

himself. "Okay. What happened now? Did you and Nog—"

"Huh? Oh . . . no. No, nothing like that. I just . . . Well, I just wanted to say thanks. I mean about, you know . . . saving my life and junk."

"Oh. And junk." Sisko nodded. "I see."

"Yeah. I mean, I was thinking about the other day. About how you said you'd try to keep me safe. And you did. You saved my butt."

Again Sisko nodded. "Does that make you feel any better about being out here?"

Jake considered it a moment.

"No."

"Ah. Well . . . give it time. These things *always* take time. Just do your best. No one can ask more of you than for you to do your best."

"So . . ." Jake moved over toward him and sat on the armrest of the couch. "So if, for example . . . let's just say that I was . . . oh . . . failing math, but I told you I was doing my best. Would that make it okay?"

"If that was the absolute best effort that you could give . . . then, of course, I would have to be satisfied with it. And after all, Albert Einstein failed math."

"Yes, sir." Jake smiled.

"On the other hand," continued Sisko, "you ain't Einstein. And if you flunk math, I'll kick that butt of yours—the one I just saved—all around the habitat ring. Got it?"

"Yes, sir."

"Good. Glad we had this talk, son."

Odo sat at Quark's, at a table with Dax and Bashir. Quark was at that moment bringing over a large carafe of ale, and saying loudly, "Another free drink for my great good friend, Odo, who risked his life to save me!"

Odo looked at him disdainfully. "I was doing my job, Quark. That's all. Furthermore, in case you have forgotten . . . if you hadn't done dirt to Glav early in your misbegotten career, this calamity wouldn't have been visited on the station in the first place."

"A minor detail!" said Quark.

"I also noticed when we set up the trap, that you made sure to keep yourself as far away as possible."

"Only because I so admire your skills as a security officer," said Quark. "I would have been in the way. But if you insist that you were only doing your job . . . then, fine. If there's one thing I like, it's having the score be even. Isn't that right, Doctor?"

Bashir nodded glumly.

"Good." And Quark sauntered off.

"Doctor . . . is everything all right?" asked Dax.

"Oh. Yes. Everything is fine. I . . . saved a life," said Bashir after a moment.

"Good for you!" said Dax. "Who?"

"The little Edemian boy . . . Rasa."

"Well, that's excellent, Julian," Dax told him. "You must be very happy. I mean, saving lives is what doctors do, isn't it?"

"Yes," he said tonelessly. "Yes, it is. Uh . . . if you'll excuse me." And he got up from the table and walked away.

Dax watched him, concerned. "That's strange. Usually he can't take his eyes off me. Now he barely notices I'm here. Funny. His infatuation seemed so silly to me before . . . but now I find I'm a little bothered by his sudden indifference. Isn't that funny?"

"Hilarious," said Odo. He was frowning at Quark, who was back behind the bar. *"One* of those damned Ferengi pulled a fast one the other day. He sent Mas Marko to Ops for no reason that I can discern. I'll have to worm it out of one of them."

"Odo . . ." Dax looked at him in surprise. "Don't you ever take a break? There's a world outside of law enforcement, you know. Do you . . . do you wish to discuss the shapeshifter? The encounter must have been very difficult for you."

Odo looked at her questioningly. "Why should I want to discuss that? It's a dead issue. He's gone. Questions remain unanswered, but there are always unanswered questions lying about. No use fretting about it." He rose. "If you'll excuse me, Lieutenant, I have a prior obligation I must attend to. I'm not looking forward to it, but it's an obligation nevertheless."

"Odo, are you *sure* you're all right with . . ."

But he didn't stay around to hear the question . . . or answer it.

Molly O'Brien, three years old that very day, her face covered with birthday cake, stepped out of her quarters and gasped. She clapped her hands together in pure delight. Behind her, the children who were her guests, including Dina, squealed with excitement when they saw what was waiting.

The dappled pony stood in the corridor, tail swishing from side to side. O'Brien stood beside it, adjusting the saddle. "He's just for today, Molly," he said. "But today is a very special day, so it's all right. So who's first? Could it be . . . the birthday girl?"

Molly laughed, running to her father. Keiko came up behind her, trying to wipe her face clean with a napkin, but Molly squirmed so much that Keiko wasn't entirely successful. It didn't matter. Nothing mattered except that this was the happiest Molly had been in ages.

"Okay. Let's go." And O'Brien began to walk alongside the pony, Molly perched atop the saddle and looking very proud.

"I have to admit," said O'Brien, apparently talking to Molly, "this is better than my magic tricks would have been. I guess my sleight of hand wasn't particularly good . . . although, you know, pumpkin, it did serve a valuable purpose. Because thinking about misdirection

—about getting people to look at one thing so that they won't look elsewhere—that got Mr. Odo thinking. You remember Mr. Odo, the nice security chief? He started thinking about misdirection, and one thing led to another . . . and it made him realize how someone was fooling him into looking at one thing when really he should have been looking elsewhere. Wasn't that smart of Mr. Odo, sweetheart? And because he did, a bad man won't be hurting people anymore. Isn't that nice?"

"Yes, Daddy," said Molly happily. She wasn't really paying the least bit of attention. She was too busy waving at passersby as the pony patiently carried her around the habitat ring.

"And because I was helpful to him," continued O'Brien, "Odo felt that he owed me. He thinks it's very important for everything to be just and right and fair and all that. And since I helped him, he felt he had to help me. And also because your mommy helped him with a well-timed phaser shot. Isn't that wonderful, Molly, that he is so honest and moral that he felt he had to pay us back?"

"Oh, yes, Daddy." Molly stroked the pony's thick neck. "I want to name him Fluffy. Can I?"

"Suuure," said O'Brien. "Remember, it's just for today . . . but Fluffy sounds fine to me. Does it sound fine to you, Fluffy?"

And Fluffy muttered, "So help me, O'Brien, if you *ever* tell *any*one . . . es*pecially* Quark—"

"Not a word from me, Fluffy," said O'Brien. "And, hey . . . just to show my appreciation . . . would you like a sugar cube?"

Fluffy snorted disdainfully.

"No?" O'Brien shrugged and popped the cube into his own mouth. "More for me, then."

And Fluffy clip-clopped on his way.

ENTER A NEW GALAXY OF ADVENTURE
WITH THESE EXCITING

STAR TREK ® AND **STAR TREK**
THE NEXT GENERATION ™

TRADE PAPERBACKS FROM POCKET BOOKS:

THE STAR TREK COMPENDIUM by Alan Asherman.
The one must-have reference book for all STAR TREK fans, this book
includes rare photos, behind the scenes production information, and a
show-by-show guide to the original television series.

THE STAR TREK INTERVIEW BOOK by Alan Asherman.
A fascinating collection of interviews with the creators and stars of the
original STAR TREK and the STAR TREK films.

**MR. SCOTT'S GUIDE TO THE ENTERPRISE by Shane
Johnson.** An exciting deck-by-deck look at the inside of the incredible
U.S.S. *Enterprise*™, this book features dozens of blueprints, sketches
and photographs.

THE WORLDS OF THE FEDERATION by Shane Johnson.
A detailed look at the alien worlds seen in the original STAR TREK
television series, the STAR TREK films, and STAR TREK: THE NEXT
GENERATION — with a full-color insert of STAR TREK's most exotic
alien creatures!

**STAR TREK: THE NEXT GENERATION TECHNICAL
MANUAL by Rick Sternbach and Michael Okuda.** The long-
awaited book that provides a never before seen look inside the U.S.S.
Enterprise 1701-D and examines the principles behind STAR TREK:
THE NEXT GENERATION's awesome technology — from phasers to
warp drive to the holodeck.

THE KLINGON DICTIONARY by Mark Okrand. Finally, a
comprehensive sourcebook for Klingon language and syntax—includes a
pronunciation guide, grammatical rules, and phrase translations. The
only one of its kind!

All Available from Pocket Books

POCKET
B O O K S

555-01